Unfortunately f̶...
core of the Terran...would shrug off a jet of
white-hot gas that vaporized metallic armor.

Unfortunately for the Republicans, Albrecht
Waldstejn had allowed for that when he made his
plans.

"Guns, *now!*" Communicator Foyle was shouting
as Sergeant-Gunner Jensen reached out of his trench
and crimped the grenade fuze. No Republican
saw the motion, an arm thrusting full length, then
withdrawing beneath the sheet which had covered
it until then.

The five further seconds which Jensen waited
were as long as any block of time he could
remember. He held his shoulder weapon tightly
by its grip and barrel shroud. Jensen was not very
good with the individual weapon, not like he was
with the splendid automatic cannon he had
abandoned. At this range, it would serve very
well, though, if no stray round or ricochet—

The grenade went off ninety centimeters from
Jensen's head. Then the world exploded.

THE FORLORN HOPE

DAVID DRAKE

A JIM BAEN PRESENTATION

TOM DOHERTY ASSOCIATES

THE FORLORN HOPE

This is a work of fiction. All the characters and events portrayed in this book are fictional, and any resemblance to real people or incidents is purely coincidental.

A TOR Book

Published by:

Tom Doherty Associates, Inc.
8-10 West 36th Street
New York, New York 10018

First TOR printing, January 1984

ISBN: 812-53-610-X

Can. Ed. 812-53-611-8

Cover art by Alan Gutierrez

Printed in the United States of America

Distributed by:

Pinnacle Books, Inc.
1430 Broadway
New York, New York 10018

DEDICATION
to Susan Allison
considered as a person and as an editor

Forlorn hope ... 1: In early use, a picked body of men, detached to the front to begin the attack. . . .
b. *transf.* and *fig*, chiefly of persons in a desperate condition.
c. *pl.* The men comprising such a body; hence, reckless bravos.
d. A perilous or desperate enterprise. . . .
OXFORD ENGLISH DICTIONARY

CHAPTER ONE

The starship came out of its envelope just long enough to unload the first rack of bombs. It flashed yellow, then it was gone—hypersonic and untouchable by anything not also in a star-drive envelope. The ship's hull, heated by its microsecond exposure to atmospheric friction, left a lambent after-image above Smiricky #4.

The flash meant nothing to Lieutenant Albrecht Waldstejn, Supply Officer of the 522nd Garrison Battalion. Above the western end of the valley where the flash had appeared, the sky now danced with sparks that grew as they tumbled closer. The sonic boom had not arrived. The bomb clusters which shed velocity and their ablative shells in balls of fire were only an unexpected light phenomenon to the young Federal officer.

His companion, Colonel Guido Fasolini, had seen

thirty years of war on almost as many planets.
Bombing from a starship was a difficult technique
to master, but the mercenary colonel had seen it
before. He did not deny his senses by insisting that
the Republicans here on Cecach could not possibly
be doing it also. In the long run, that meant that
Fasolini had probably hired his Company on with
the wrong side again.

In the short run, it meant that he had about
fifteen seconds to get his ass under cover.

"Come on!" Fasolini roared to his companion.
Waldstejn was still staring in bemusement at the
sky. The younger man turned to see the mercenary
sprinting for the nearest shelter as fast as his
stumpy legs could carry him. There would be time
to get the details later, Waldstejn thought as he
ran after the Colonel.

They were at the lip of the shelter when the first
shock hurled them in.

It was the sonic boom rather than the stick of
bombs hitting. The over-pressure of a three-kilo-
tonne starship at Mach 5 was colossal. It flattened
everyone in the compound who had not already
ducked. Dust shuddered and rose among the dry
grasses of the valley. The pall spread in a broad
wake to mark the spacer's track on the ground
beneath.

"Are they shelling us?" Lieutenant Waldstejn
demanded. "They can't be—that's from the west!"

Colonel Fasolini snorted. "When you've lived as
long as I have," he said, "you'll learn your own
artillery's just as dangerous as the other bastard's.
But that was a spacer, and it's bombing us."

The two men were a contrast in more than age.
Waldstejn was well above standard height, but he

was willow thin. His brown hair was cropped short enough that the blond roots were visible, and he was inordinately proud of the narrow moustache which was within a hair's margin of being the width of his upper lip. Waldstejn's uniform was crisply new; he was Supply Officer, after all. He wore the garment with the brown-beige-gray pattern out, as being more suitable for the present surroundings than the brown-green-black camouflage to which it could be reversed. In his belt were holstered a two-way radio and a small pistol which he had never fired.

Waldstejn could have posed for a recruiting poster. Guido Fasolini, on the other hand, looked as grim as a gun barrel, even in his present rear-echelon billet. In the dim light seeping through the beryllium-filament roof, the mercenary's uniform looked muddy black. Under the direct sun it had been the same ragged mixture of buff and gray as the dust and dry vegetation of the immediate landscape. On a glacier, the fabric would have the hue of dirty ice. It would never look sharp, and it would never call attention to the man or woman who wore it.

Fasolini himself was stocky. Middle age had brought him a paunch on which only the harshest campaigning could make inroads. But the Colonel did not—could not—look soft. His hair was black and greasy. It spilled from beneath his armored cap. His radio was built into the fibers of that helmet, leaving his crossbelt free for its load of grenades and a pistol-stocked launcher which no one could mistake as being only for show. Fasolini was clean-shaven, but his whiskers were a black shadow against the swarthy skin of his jaw.

The siren above the 522nd's Headquarters began to howl. There was a brief blat of sound as well from a klaxon on the *Katyn Forest*, the starship which was loading pigs of copper at the far east end of the large compound. The warning signals froze the civilians in the mining and smelting operations above ground. They also did more harm than good to the inexperienced garrison battalion. What frightened the mercenaries, however, and caused *them* to bury their faces deeper in the floor of their shelters was a simpler sound. Barely audible over the siren were the pop-pop-pops of clusters bursting to rain tens of thousands of bomblets across the target area.

"For what we are about to receive," Colonel Fasolini muttered, "Lord make us thankful."

"What do you—" began Albrecht Waldstejn. Then the anti-personnel bombs began to go off in a crackling rush that swept down the valley like a crown fire.

"Yeah, coming along just fine," said Churchie Dwyer. He squinted at the bed of coals with a brew-master's eye. The gangling mercenary patted the reactor vessel. It was a proprietary gesture like that of a sailor introducing a floozie to his companions.

Dwyer and Del Hoybrin were using a huge 500-liter fuel tank from an ore-hauler. Probably the tank had been dismounted years before when the broadcast power grid was extended to the mining complex in the valley over the ridge. The tank was rusty and still had a varnish of fuel additives, but that would not make a hell of a lot of difference to the quality of the final product. The mash itself had been culled from what was available which would ferment. When it came time to distill the result into high-proof slash, it would be cooled in a radiator scrapped from a lithium refrigeration system.

They were going to get rich from this one, they were. All those miners without access even to the weak beer issued to the garrison battalion—beautiful.

"Should I put on some more wood, Churchie?" the other mercenary asked. Del Hoybrin was built on the same cylindrical lines as the fuel tank. Alongside Churchie, he looked almost as big as the tank as well. For that matter, he did not seem a great deal smarter than the vessel.

"Del, Del, don't be in such a hurry," Dwyer chided. He patted the ground beside him. "Sit back and relax, my friend. All we're doing now is keeping the little darling warm so our beer ferments. Think of her as a beautiful woman. You wouldn't expect to go up to a beautiful woman and—" Churchie gestured at the billet of brush-wood his companion held—"just stick your log in, would you?"

Del frowned. "I don't know what you mean, Churchie," he said. He tossed the wood back on the tangle he had cut the day before.

Both men leaned back with their legs splayed, staring at the shimmer of coals in the long trench. Cecach brush would barely sustain combustion. It was perfect for a slow fire. "Sure, this is the life," Dwyer murmured. "And when we get back to a liberty port with what we've made from this gig. . . ."

Their post was on the ridge line, three hundred

meters away and just out of sight behind the swell of the hill. The main purpose of the garrison was to keep the civilian contract workers at their posts despite rumors and Republican propaganda. The vast Smiricky Complex provided a significant proportion of the Federal government's foreign exchange. The authorities in Praha could not permit its workers to stream away as had the agricultural laborers of the nearby latifundia.

There was, however, the threat of a quick thrust by Rube infiltrators or spacer-inserted commandos. It was against that possibility that the indigenous garrison had been stiffened by what was, despite Fasolini's self-conferred colonelcy, a mercenary company of about fifty effectives. The 522nd had neither the training nor the political reliability to be steady under attack. The two laser cannon were the only battalion weapons which could be depended on to stop even light armor at a distance. Nobody really expected the 522nd to stand and volley hand-launched anti-tank rockets at point-blank range.

"Should we be getting back, Churchie?" Del asked nervously.

Dwyer started. He had been visualizing himself and—thus far—five women. Despite his revery, the gangling mercenary's hand snatched up his gun when his companion spoke. A moment later, after his eyes had scanned the horizon and his brain had sorted the words for content, Churchie set the heavy weapon back down. "Lover," he said in irritation, "I sure wish you wouldn't do that."

The bigger man blinked. His own gun was slung. Its weight was too insignificant to him to call itself to his attention, even when he was resting.

Del was the only man in the Company who fired bursts of full-charge loads as a matter of course. He blinked in surprise when observers asked him if he didn't mind the recoil.

Churchie sighed. "Look," he said patiently, "if they want us, they'll call us, right?" He tapped his beryllium cap where it covered his right ear.

Del stared. His left hand began as if of its own volition to scratch his ribs beneath a bandolier.

"And if just maybe Hummel comes out to check in person—and why the hell would she?" Churchie continued, "why, we're out making a dangerous reconnaissance through our own minefields, right? Doing our job with a smile." He smirked, broadly enough to prove that dentists of Hister made bridges from stainless steel. "What we *know* is, that she's not going to crawl out to get us when she doesn't even know there's a path through the mines."

"If you say so, Churchie," the big man said after further consideration. He stared up the slope behind them. Del had done most of the heavy work involved in the project, digging the trench and manhandling the fuel tank into position. Churchie alone had chosen the path through the belt of air-sown mines that ringed the ridge, though. "I just . . . ," Del said. "Well, aren't we a long way from the shelter if somebody attacks?"

"Attacks!" his companion repeated incredulously. "Attacks?" He waved his long, dirty fingers in an arc across the horizon of brush, grass, and silence. "Do you see an attack? Do you see anything? You've been listening to the radio, haven't you?" Dwyer pointed accusingly at Del's chest. "Seven years in this business and you don't know that what *any* government says is a lie? Look, when there's going to be an attack, *I'll* tell—"

High overhead to the west, they caught the flash of the starship starting its bombing run.

Del Hoybrin was dumb as a post, but he was experienced and his reflexes had kept him alive before. The big man jumped up, heading for their shelter, and Churchie Dwyer tackled him before those reflexes could get his friend killed.

Del came down on his face with a thump and a squawk. "Not there!" Churchie screamed, "here!" He began to slap madly at the coals with the butt of his gun. Some of them scattered into the brush. The rest stirred into bright orange life.

"Huh?" said Del.

The big man might just have been able to bound three hundred meters uphill in the time available, Churchie knew. What Del could not have done, no way in hell, was to run full-tilt up the crooked path without stumbling into a mine. That left one choice, a bad one, but better than no shelter at all when the shrapnel sleeted in. Furiously, Churchie Dwyer tried to brush the coals out of the trench. After a moment, Del began to help. He was used to doing things which he did not understand.

They were veterans. They ignored the sonic boom, ignored also the siren that panicked the indigenous troops in the compound. When the clusters began to separate in the sky overhead, however, Del paused and looked at his companion. "Churchie?" he said.

Dwyer reversed his gun again and jerked its charging handle with his left hand. The stabilized plastic stock was now mottled with gray blisters. It was hot enough to singe cloth. Churchie spaced five fast shots down the length of the makeshift reactor. Mash and half-fermented beer sprayed from each entrance and exit hole, sizzling on the coals beneath.

Fasolini's troopers carried cone-bore weapons. They squeezed down their projectiles at pressures which only barrels of synthetic diamond, grown as a single molecular unit, could withstand. At the muzzle, an osmium needle was expelled at over three thousand meters per second. The fluorocarbon sabot which had acted as a gas check in the bore was gaseous itself by the time it spurted out behind the needle. The weapons were specialized; but it benefitted mercenary soldiers, like whores, to be able to provide specialized services for their customers. The gun was meant to bust armor and brick walls. It opened the fuel tank like one of Jack the Ripper's girlfriends.

Churchie flung the weapon aside. "Come on!" he shrieked at his companion. He rolled into the trench. Del blinked, then obeyed.

The edge of the cloud of bomblets swept over the brew vessel in its fury. The two mercenaries were already screaming.

Sergeant-Gunner Roland Jensen clacked down the loading gate of the automatic cannon which was both his duty and his darling. "There, Herzenberg," he said to the plump trainee, "*that's* how you insert a fresh can. Now, I want you to line up five more cans for continuous feeding."

Trooper Tilly Herzenberg looked doubtful, but there was nothing in the section leader's blond arrogance to suggest that he was not serious. Putting her back in it, she slid a second drum of ammunition across the base plate to align with the drum Jensen had just loaded. Cooper, Pavlovich, and Guiterez, the veteran crewmen, watched and stuck knives in the dirt.

The automatic cannon was the only crew-served weapon in Fasolini's Company. It was the apotheosis of the shoulder weapons which most of the troopers carried. What the individual guns could do to light armor, Jensen's cannon could do to most tanks.

The cannon had a single barrel which was a trifle over three meters long. The bore at the muzzle was seven millimeters. Through it blasted a five-hundred gram osmium pencil which had with its sabot a diameter of twenty millimeters when it was slammed into the breech.

The relationship of projectile to recoil impulse was a constant before an ape man threw a rock and fell backwards off his branch. Nothing armorers have done in succeeding ages has changed that relationship in the least. The diamond bore and modern propellants made it possible to push the cannon shot to literally astronomical velocities, but the base and receiver had to be massive to slow the recoil to the point its pounding did not shatter the gun. The cannon mount had its own treads and motor. It served as well to draw a caisson of ammunition. Sergeant Jensen drove from the little saddle forward; and the rest of the crew hoofed it or found their own transport on a move.

Guiterez jumped up. "Sarge," he said, "what was that in the sky?"

Cooper and Pavlovich had been on Sedalia when Imperial spacers had free run above them. They dived for the shelter. Guiterez recognized an answer even when it was not verbal. He threw himself in with his buddies.

Roland Jensen glanced up at the thin, icteric track the starship had drawn across the heavens. His eyes were as pale as the sky. "Right, Herzenberg," he said in a mild voice, "I'll take over now. I want you to raise the muzzle to 45°." Ammo drums weighed sixty kilos loaded; Jensen slid one of them into position with either hand. "Use the gauge like I showed you."

"S-sarge," the trainee said, looking at the shelter opening. When she had enlisted three months before on Beauty, she was unaware that Fasolini had already contracted with the Federalists on Cecach, thirty-seven light years from her home. In fact, the Company had enrolled her—without any particular qualification of strength or skill—solely to make up the contract Table of Organization in a hurry.

She dropped into the gunner's seat and punched the gun live. Then she heeled up the rocker switch to elevate the muzzle as directed.

Sergeant Jensen was snapping the feed lips of each ammunition drum into the female connector of the drum ahead of it. Rigging them this way increased the chance of malfunction, but neither he nor any of his crew were going to pop up to feed a fresh can in normal fashion.

"Sarge, I'm ready," said the trainee in a voice raised two octaves by the sonic boom a moment before.

Jensen locked the last can in place and leaped to the gun. Leaning across Herzenberg to get a sight line, he rotated the cannon mount 10° to the right to eyeball it in line with the track down which the

starship had disappeared. The gun had electronic
sights that would spike a gnat at a kilometer, but
at this instant there was neither time nor a hard
target for them.

With his right hand, Jensen threw the Continuous Fire toggle. His left hand grasped Trooper
Herzenberg by the collar, and he lunged for the
shelter. The muzzle blasts of the cannon were so
loud that the rain of bombs was a flickering white
light, not a sound, to the cowering gun crew.

Warned by the flash, Trooper Iris Powers grabbed
her boots and jumped into her shelter. Lieutenant
Hussein ben Mehdi was right behind her.

The shelters were half-cylinders, each grown from
a single crystal of beryllium. The shelters would
not stop a shell or even a bullet at any normal
range, but they were generally proof against the
tiny splinters spraying from overhead bursts. That
was the threat against which foot-soldiers since
the Napoleonic Wars had been least able to protect themselves.

Shelters were light, but they did not fold up like
the canvas tents for which they substituted. The
rigid bulk of thirty curved plates, three meters
long by two across, required as much transport as
the Company's ammunition did. Like self-camouflaging uniforms and a considerable allowance for
target practice during stand-downs, the expense
and administrative hassle of the shelters was simply a matter of plant maintenance. Fasolini's plant
was not hardware but the Company itself, the
trained, effective troops who could command top
dollar and could be expected to survive for another lucrative contract.

Turning the curved roof of a shelter into real living quarters required considerable effort. The ground had to be ditched out at least deep enough that its occupants could lie flat below the shrapnel of nearby ground bursts. In addition, those who failed to raise coamings around their shelters could expect to be swimming the next time it rained. At Smiricky #4, most of the troopers had paid civilian miners to dig them in. Powers and Sergeant Hummel had chosen to do the job themselves. The walls of their dug-out were as deep and plumb as those of Colonel Fasolini's Operations Center.

That did not make the shelter spacious, a fact which suited ben Mehdi very well indeed at the moment. The Lieutenant was of middle height with a wrestler's build and a smooth, dark complexion. He was the only other 'officer' in Fasolini's Company, but he was not really the Colonel's second in command. His rank was due neither to his military prowess nor to his administrative ability. Fasolini had an accountant's brain under his coarse exterior, but that exterior itself could be a handicap in negotiations. The Colonel used ben Mehdi, his 'Executive Officer', as a suave front in conference rooms where polish and a raised eyebrow were worth more money than all the bluster in the world.

Hussein ben Mehdi had no general distaste for garrison duty, but Smiricky #4 was three hundred kilometers from even a decent brothel. The Lieutenant was bored, and the attack seemed to have been arranged precisely to help with the project by which he hoped to improve his time. He moved fast enough to be inside Powers' shelter when the

sonic boom rattled it, but he was careful not to
brush dirt on his uniform either.

"Oh!" said Trooper Powers. She had just taken
off her left sock. Her toe-nails were varnished a
deep scarlet. In confusion, the blonde trooper
twisted the bare foot under her and picked up one
of her boots.

"Any port in a storm, hey Powers?" said Lieutenant ben Mehdi with a warm smile. "Hope you
don't mind the intrusion." He reached out to grip
between his thumb and forefinger the boot which
Powers held. Ben Mehdi's fingers were long, their
nails perfectly shaped. There was enough strength
in them to pluck the boot away from someone
much huskier than the petite blonde who faced
him now.

The shelter roof was translucent. It filtered light
heavily toward the blue end of the spectrum. That
alien tinge heightened Powers' look of tension as
she huddled toward the corner of the dug-out. The
two bed-rolls, hers and Sergeant Hummel's, were
parallel with a narrow aisle between them. They
were on wooden frames which kept them off the
floor. The frames were low enough, however, that
the dug-out's occupants could sit up without risk-
ing their heads to shrapnel through the unprotected ends of the shelter. Hussein ben Mehdi leaned
forward as he sat on the bunk beside Powers. She
gasped as the Lieutenant dropped the boot he had
taken from her and hooked her right sock with an
index finger. "Lieutenant?" the Trooper said. His
left arm slid behind her shoulders despite her efforts to press herself tighter against the wall of the
dug-out.

The anti-personnel bombs lashed down like the

wind-driven edge of a hail storm. Each bomblet was about the size of a man's thumb, a tiny segment of a cylinder, more or less the same as the tens of thousands of others released from the same cluster. They armed on impact and detonated a half second later, generally when they had bounced a meter or two back into the air. They spread a sleet of tiny shrapnel which stripped trees and killed all unprotected animals in the target area. After an attack, hundreds of bomblets which had failed to go off the first time lay in the grass, ready to shatter the leg of anyone walking carelessly.

Inside the shelter, the flashes lighted the mussed bedrolls with savage brilliance. The crackling detonations merged into a single prolonged roar. One large fragment sailed through both plastic end-sheets with a buzz that vibrated on the back of ben Mehdi's neck rather than in his ears.

"They'll be making another couple passes, of course," the Lieutenant said as he reached for the zipper at the throat of Powers' tunic. The vicious crack of the automatic cannon a kilometer away was an irritation now that the bomblets were only occasional thumps delayed by a freak of chemistry. "It won't be safe for anyone to leave their shelters for, well, plenty of time," ben Mehdi went on. He brushed aside the hand Powers raised to block his. He began to unzip her. "You know," he said, "you're a very attractive woman, Iris."

The little blond whipped her left fist around at Hussein's face. The blade of her spring knife was no longer than a finger, but that would have taken it to the Lieutenant's brain if he had not been expecting the attack.

Ben Mehdi caught Powers' wrist with his right

hand while his left still clamped her other arm to her body. She tried to twist the knife to cut the sinews across the back of the officer's hand, but her weapon was a spike with no real edge. Hussein ben Mehdi increased the pressure of his grip until his thumb stood out in a pool of white skin on the woman's wrist. Then he gave a quick snap as if casting with a fly rod. The knife skittered out of her numb fingers.

"Now that's a friendly way to treat a guest, is it?" the Lieutenant said. His face still smiled, but his lips were drawn as hard as his teeth. "Now, Hummel's in the OC, so we're going to be alone till the All Clear sounds. And I *know* you like men, baby, because I *saw* you last night with one of the zoomies from the *Katyn Forest*. That's what light amplifiers are for, right? Now, I'm a man, and just to prove it—"

Ben Mehdi lowered Powers' hand toward his fly with the same ease with which he had disarmed her. The little blonde spit in his eye.

The bombing had both blown trash onto the shelter roof and studded the beryllium mesh with needles of glass shrapnel which conducted light. Within, the effect turned the blue ambience into mottled shadows and points as bright as jewels by contrast. Iris Powers' upturned face was bestial and hideous as a result. The Lieutenant's face, as he slapped the woman with the full strength of his open hand, was as horrible with no lighting to augment it.

Power's head bounced against the dug-out wall. She lolled back, stunned. Her eyes were glassy. The outline of long, strong fingers was already swelling up in red on her cheek. The light flickered again from the east as the starship rolled out for its second pass.

"I tell you, bitch!" the Lieutenant shouted. "I'm going to do you a favor. I'm going to show you just how good it can be with a man so you won't have to—"

The end flaps shook with the sonic boom and the entrance of Sergeant Johanna Hummel.

The Lieutenant jumped as if the non-com were one of the second stick of bombs herself. In some ways, he might have preferred that to what he got. Jo Hummel hit the floor feet first, but she let her momentum carry her onto the occupied bunk. The point of her left shoulder took ben Mehdi in the middle of the back. He slammed forward again, pinned against the earthen wall as easily as he had pinned Powers an instant before. The blonde trooper flopped sideways when the Lieutenant released her.

It sounded as if the sky were tearing apart. A sun-bright streak glared through the filter of the roof.

"Close quarters, Lieutenant," said Sergeant Hummel. She was wheezing with rage and the distance she had run, but her words were loud enough to be distinct even against the background. "*Fucking* close quarters, hey?"

Hummel was as tall as the Lieutenant, with the same blocky, powerful torso. She had felled men larger than herself with sucker punches, but in any simple test of strength, ben Mehdi could have bested her. They were both in excellent physical condition. However, all other things being equal, a male's greater percentage of muscle to total weight would have told.

All other things were not equal. Hummel's gun was socketed in the Lieutenant's right ear.

"Sergeant," snapped ben Mehdi, "watch what you're doing! I won't tell you twice!"

"Real cramped in here, ain't it?" Sergeant Hummel said. She twisted her weapon to force ben Mehdi's head back against the dirt. The steel barrel shroud had been dented. The corner of it tore a ragged gash in the officer's ear. His mouth, open to shout another order, instead passed a high-pitched whimper.

In a voice as close to gentle as the surrounding noise permitted, Sergeant Hummel said, "Bunny? Are you all right?"

Trooper Powers sat up again, levering herself with a hand on the back wall. Hussein ben Mehdi's weight still anchored her thigh to the bunk. She braced her free foot to tug herself away. The hand-print on her cheek was a flag.

Hummel made a sound at the back of her throat like millstones rubbing. She stood, gripping the unresisting lieutenant by the shoulder and raising him with her. She held her gun by the pistol grip, the butt cradled in the crook of her right elbow. Her index finger was on the trigger. The muzzle moved with ben Mehdi's head, anticipating each of the man's cautious attempts to duck away. Outside, the bombs were sailing in with calliope shrieks. This run, there were no high-altitude pops as clusters separated.

"What's the matter, Lieutenant?" Hummel rasped. "Worried maybe my gun's pointing a little close to you, what with all of us shoe-horned into this little dug-out? Don't you worry, *sir*. I've killed lots of people, but I never killed one when I didn't mean to." She spun ben Mehdi and gave him a hard shove.

The Lieutenant sagged against the dirt coaming. His breath made the end flap tremble. He turned his head fearfully. Hummel's gun was no longer touching his ear, but the tiny hole in its muzzle was aimed to take out his left pupil without touching the surrounding sclera.

The earth shuddered and a bomb went off with a muffled roar.

"Since the accommodations don't suit you, Lieutenant," the Sergeant said, "maybe you'd better leave, don't you think? You'd be best off at the Operations Center. And I think you ought to start now."

Three more bombs detonated. Two were below ground. The third hit something heavy and metallic. It rang like a bell even before the shattering explosion.

"Jo, *Allah!*" the Lieutenant pleaded. "Not *now*— not during incoming!"

Debris from the first bomb, pebbles and the heavier clods, pattered on the shelter roof. Hummel smiled and gripped the shroud of her weapon to emphasize rather than to steady it. "This stick's armor piercing," she said. "Just keep your head down and you'll be fine. Oh—and don't step on anything left over from the first pass, hey? But that's the sort of chance we gotta take when there's someplace we need to go."

Ben Mehdi tensed. Behind the Sergeant, Powers was pulling on her boots with apparently total concentration. The ground shook under the impact of more bombs.

"Your choice," said Hummel. Her index finger tightened.

Hussein ben Mehdi bolted from the dug-out, into the haze of dust and combustion gases. His ear had dripped a bright streak of blood onto his shoulder.

Sergeant Hummel waited only until she was sure that the Lieutenant would not burst back in behind the muzzle of his grenade launcher. Then she whirled, tossing the gun onto her own bunk to free both hands. She clasped Powers. The blonde woman began to sob in a mixture of relief and fury. "There, there, Bunny," the Sergeant said, stroking the other woman's silky hair. "There, there."

When the fusillade of fragmentation bombs sputtered away, Lieutenant Waldstejn rose and started to climb out of the shelter. Colonel Fasolini grabbed him by the ankle and pulled him back down. "What the hell's your hurry?" the mercenary asked. "We've got a long afternoon ahead of us. They aren't done, not by a long shot."

The Lieutenant settled back on his haunches uncertainly.

Albrecht Waldstejn had a commission as a result of the two years of law school he had completed before being conscripted. His posting as a supply officer of a garrison battalion resulted from negative attributes rather than a demonstrated genius for administration, however. Waldstejn's parents had been forceful enough in opposing Federal war policies that the couple was taken into preventative detention. Their deaths were almost certainly the transport accident the government claimed—but the government still thought it wise to put the son under military discipline. After the four-week curriculum to which officer training had been reduced, the young man had been shunted into a slot where he was unlikely to cause trouble.

Waldstejn's initial mistake with the 522nd was to reorganize the mess his predecessor had left. The young officer broke for fraud all three of his underlings, including the quartermaster sergeant who had run the section while previous supply officers drank themselves insensible.

That left Waldstejn with no non-commissioned officers, two privates dumped on his need because nobody else in the battalion wanted them, and the smouldering hatred of his commanding officer. Major Lichtenstein had been receiving his rake-off on goods sold illegally from the battalion stores in the past.

Waldstejn got along rather better with Colonel Fasolini. The mercenary leader had a tendency to look for the easiest way to get the job done, but at least his notion of what the job *was* had similarities to Waldstejn's conception. Major Lichtenstein commanded a battalion of screw-ups and criminals, with no promotion to be expected this side of the grave. Lichtenstein's priorities were not those of the government in Praha, and they were shared by most of the officers and men in his command.

"Why are you so sure the bomber won't be shot down?" Lieutenant Waldstejn asked. He craned his neck out of the shelter but kept Fasolini in the corner of his eye. The whole floor of the valley swirled like mist from a lake at sunrise. Bomblets which had been flung wide left ragged clots of dust up to the ridge lines and beyond. The explosions had started a few grass fires, now blurred in with the dust pall but sure soon to replace it. "Matter of fact, I'm surprised I don't hear the lasers firing by now."

Fasolini settled himself against a wall. The shelter was unassigned. It had been set up between the Colonel's Operations Center on the compound perimeter and the building of the Complex which housed the 522nd's HQ. The Colonel was a cautious man. He had provided for just the sort of eventuality which had occurred—an attack sudden enough to catch people between the headquarters. Hunching his shoulders to keep the X of his crossbelt from biting him, the mercenary said, "They aren't firing because they don't have a target. And the bomber won't be shot down because it's not a bomber, it's a starship. Only time they need to worry's when they're out of their hyperspace envelope to fire—" he snapped a thumb and finger for emphasis, loud as a pistol shot— "or when somebody goes after them in another spacer. *You* know how long it takes to get a starship programmed to operate this close to a planet. They must've spent weeks, and it'll be weeks before your side puts anything up to stop them." The older man frowned. "Not that I think they'll hang around *that* long," he concluded.

"But why here?" Waldstejn said, aloud but more to himself than to his companion. They were speaking in English, the tongue of convenience throughout the human universe. Fasolini had a smattering of a score of languages. He could ask for directions or a woman on most planets. Waldstejn, however, had only his native Czech and business-course English. A month as acting liaison with the mercenaries had sharpened his English into a fluency equalled only by the multi-lingual curses he had picked up in the same school.

"Why the hell's that gun firing?" the Colonel said, frowning toward the northeast corner of the compound. Waldstejn knew the automatic cannon was emplaced there, toward the most probable channel for armor but almost a kilometer away from the nearest mercenary position. The plan in Praha had been to seed pairs of mercenaries every four hundred meters or so along the perimeter. Fasolini had agreed to man observation posts on both ridge lines—the mercenaries' electronics were an order of magnitude better than Cecach manufactures. Further, Fasolini had agreed to put the cannon at least temporarily where it was most potentially useful. But after taking a good look at the 522nd Garrison Battalion, the Colonel had told Major Lichtenstein that he had no intention of putting his whole force out in packets which would be left with their asses swinging as soon as something popped. You cannot stiffen gelatine with B-Bs; and you could not keep cannon fodder from running just because there was one team still firing within earshot. Most of the Company was therefore bivouacked on a short segment of the northern perimeter.

That meant the cannon was far enough away that Lieutenant Waldstejn had forgotten it. The distance had also thickened the sharp muzzle blasts into something quite different from what he had heard—painfully—during a demonstration firing when the Company first arrived. Waldstejn's lips pursed in speculation.

Fasolini touched the wear-polished spot on his helmet that keyed the radio. He said, "Top to Guns.

What the *hell* do you think you're up to, Roland? Shut her down before our whole fee goes up the spout!''

The mercenary listened a moment. To Waldstejn, out of the net, the reply was only a tinny burr like that of a distant cicada. The gun continued to fire its eight shots a second, regular as a chronometer.

"Listen, I was on bloody Sedalia too," the Colonel shouted suddenly. "I don't *care* what you figured, I'm not having ammo *I* buy pissed down a—"

Waldstejn touched the older man on the shoulder. "I'll clear it, Guido," he said. "I'll get an acquisition request off today."

"Hold on!" Fasolini snapped. He took his fingertip from the communicator control. "What do you mean, you'll clear it?" he demanded. *"You* don't have authority to supply one of those mothers— there isn't a unit like it in the whole bloody Federal army."

"And by the time somebody in Military Accounts has figured that out," the local man said reasonably, "we'll both have long white beards. Look, the noise'll make a few of them—" he waved. The breeze carried a burden of faint moans, people too slow or too ignorant to get under cover before the bombs hit— "think they're in a battle, not an abattoir. Requests from independent commands have an automatic clearance up to fifteen thousand crowns—and believe me, the Major knows better than to flag a chit *I've* approved." The pride in Waldstejn's voice was as obvious as it was justified.

Fasolini squinted at the younger man. Instead of replying directly, the mercenary keyed his communicator again. "Top to Guns," he said. "All right, you've got clearance, Roland. But it's still a bloody waste." To Waldstejn alone he added, "Damned fool thinks they'll be programmed to whip-saw back and forth on the same track, so if he keeps enough crap in the air they'll fly right into—"

The sky flashed a yellow that went white and terrible in the same instant. Fasolini's mouth froze in shocked surmise. Both men leaped up to stare skyward, even though they knew the bombs were soon to follow.

Sergeants Breisach and Ondru were shrieking in the bare lobby of the warehouse where the wave of anti-personnel bombs had caught them. The sheet-metal roof was in scraps and tatters that writhed with by-products of the explosions. Sunlight poured through the dozen meter-diameter holes and the myriads of pinheads stabbed by fragments. The metal had stopped most of the glass-fiber shrapnel itself, but blast-melted droplets of the roof had sprayed down on the lobby.

The sergeants had timed their visit to be sure that the Supply Officer himself was absent. They had a proposal to which they had expected the two privates on duty would agree without argument. Instead, they had received flat refusals. Now neither of the non-coms was seriously injured, but the shower of molten iron had not improved tempers which opposition had already frayed.

Private Hodicky rose gingerly from behind the counter. He boosted himself to the top of it. Hodicky was only a meter fifty-six in height. He could not have seen the floor simply by craning his neck over the broad counter. A splash of metal the size

of a thumbnail crackled from a request form on
the counter. It left a brown discoloration on the
paper. "Are you guys all right?" the Private asked
nervously.

Behind Hodicky stood Jirik Quade—dark and
scowling and quite obviously regretful that both
sergeants were able to get to their feet under their
own power. Quade ran a hand through his hair,
trying to comb out the flecks shaken from the
walls and ceiling by the bombing.

The warehouse personnel had been protected by
the counter-top itself. In the lobby, Sergeant
Ondru's uniform looked as if he had been dragged
through barbed wire on his back, and the tear in
Breisach's scalp was no less bloody for being
superficial. Breisach's obscenities were uncontrolled
and unintelligible, but Ondru retained enough ra-
tionality to pick a scapegoat.

Ondru leaped to the counter. He was tall enough
to look Hodicky straight in the eye, even before he
gripped the Private by the collar and dragged him
forward.

"Now Sarge—" the little private cried, scrab-
bling at the back edge of the counter to avoid
being pulled onto the lobby floor. "Now Sarge, we
didn't—"

"You little bastard!" Ondru shrieked. "You kept
the gate closed so we couldn't get in under cover,
didn't you? Hoped we'd be killed! Well, you little
prick, *I'll* show you killed!"

Smiricky #4 was on permanent Yellow Alert.
Officers and non-coms were required by regula-
tions to go armed at all times. Ondru carried his
assault rifle in a patrol sling that cradled it muzzle-
forward at his waist. Like the Intruder patch he

had bought from a drunk in Praha, the sling was the affectation of a man who had not seen combat in the seven years of bitter war that had wracked Cecach. Now it put the grip of the rifle in place for the Sergeant's right hand. He raised the muzzle at the same time as his other hand dragged Hodicky's face down to meet the weapon.

Private Quade hit Ondru across the temple with the edge of a metal-covered receipt book.

Ondru dropped as if his legs had been sawed off at the knees. There was a pressure cut through his blond hair, as clean as anything a knife could have left. The book flew out of Quade's hand and flapped into a lobby wall. Hodicky lurched back when the Sergeant released him, but his companion had already started to vault the counter and finish the job. Quade's mouth was open but soundless, and his eyes held no expression at all.

"Mary and Joseph!" Hodicky cried. He grabbed Quade by the waistband and jerked him to a halt. "Q, boys," he said, "let's talk this over!"

Private Quade was no taller than Hodicky, but for an instant as he twisted he towered over his companion like the angel with the flaming sword. Then Quade's expression cleared. His hand, raised to strike though he had no weapon to fill it, lowered as Hodicky watched transfixed. "Jeez, Pavel," the black-haired man mumbled, "you know not to touch me when I get, get, you know. . . ."

Then the loudest noise in the warehouse was a click. Sergeant Breisach had recovered enough to draw back the charging handle of his own rifle. "You little faggots," the non-com said in a quavering voice. At his feet, Ondru moaned. The side of the fallen man's head was a sticky mat of blood. "I ought to shoot you both, but I'd rather see you hang. And you will, by God, don't think your prick of a lieutenant's going to save your asses this time."

Quade turned slowly. At this range, the light projectiles of the assault rifle would shred the plywood counter and the men behind it. The little man's eyes were going blank again. His muscles braced for an action which was quickly slipping out of conscious control.

"Sergeant, hell, what're you talking about?" Hodicky babbled brightly. His companion frightened him worse than the man with the gun did. Breisach might or might not be ready to kill; Quade was beyond doubt ready, though Hodicky hoped he alone of the spectators knew that. "We're partners, right, Sergeant Breisach? Just like you say—we slip you booze out of the stores and you boys split the profits with us after you move it. Sure, we're all friends here." Hodicky's right hand was resting on Quade's waistband again.

Sergeant Ondru had risen to his hands and knees. Breisach swallowed and took a step backward. His hands were relaxing minusculey on his pointing rifle. The Sergeant's body was beginning to quiver with the pain of his own injuries. His mind was not wholly able to absorb the return to the subject which he and Ondru had come to the warehouse to discuss.

"Say," Hodicky rattled on, "you boys'll need uniforms too, won't you? Q, go on back and get a—large-long and a large-medium, right, Sarge? Go on, Q, the boys won't want to wait."

Quade shook himself like a dog coming out of the water. "W-what did you say, Pavel?" he asked thickly.

"Go get a couple uniforms," Hodicky repeated in a low voice. "Large-long, large-medium. Quick, Q, it's what the Lieutenant would want."

Nodding, not really aware of what he was doing, the black-haired private walked through the door to the back. With a smile too stiff to be wholly engaging, Hodicky said, "Now, Sarge, maybe you could point that thing some other way? Don't want any accidents that'll screw up profits, do we?"

Briesach grunted, fumbling for the safety catch. Blood seeping from his shrapnel wound glued his collar to his neck. "If you bastards think you're going to try something cute when this is over—" he began. He did not finish the threat. The sonic boom of the follow-up run sent all of them, even the logy Ondru, scrambling for cover again.

From the sensor screens within the massive hull of the *Katyn Forest*, the shower of anti-personnel bombs was merely an intriguing spectacle. First Officer Vladimir Ortschugin spat into the bucket and watched the show. Idly, he reached for the stick of tobacco in a thigh pocket of his coveralls. The *Katyn Forest* was a freighter, not a warship, and her home planet, Novaya Swoboda, was quite neutral in the struggle taking place on Cecach. The starship was at Smiricky #4 to load cargo at double rates for the hazard allowance. Nothing that had happened thus far justified the bonus.

The bombs swept the broad valley like surf on a dun beach. Pin-prick flashes flattened nearby grass and lifted rings of dust from the soil. Then, while the after-image of the opening still clung to the brain, the main body of the cluster overran it in undulant glares of white light. The wave rushed past the buildings of the Complex and the bunkers set out five hundred meters in a perimeter. One miner stood in the open. He blinked at the sight until it washed over him and left him liquid and as formless as yesterday's sand castle.

Ortschugin watched unmoved, letting the sensors distance him and save his sanity.

The bridge was dancing with the bright chaos of the screens. The Power Room communicator shrilled, "Ortschugin! When are those idiots going to shut off the conveyor? Don't they know we can't secure the ship until they do?"

The First Officer raised his eyes to Thorn, the other crewman on the bridge, and then to heaven. "Excellency," he said, "I can't raise anyone in Central Warehousing. I'm sure they've gone to cover." The ones with common sense, at least. "Why don't we just—" relax would be the wrong word— "wait it out. The most these little bombs will do is scratch the finish of the hull. For that, it doesn't really matter whether the holds are closed or not."

The *Katyn Forest* was a hundred and fifty meter cigar. Her bridge and hyperdrive inverter were forward; her engines were astern. Most of the ship's length was given over to her holds amidships. Hold One, forward, already held several carboys of mercury, a by-product of the smelting process. The remaining cargo volume was being filled with copper ingots by the Complex's automated loading system. The conveyor belt was not in the least affected by the fact that Captain Kawalec and the crewmen stowing the copper under her direction had bolted into the Power Room. The great cargo doors could not be closed while the conveyor was hooked up; and the conveyor could not be disconnected so long as hundreds of tons of ingots continued to roll up it and spill into Hold Two.

Not, as Ortschugin had said, that it made any real difference to the freighter.

"The Front has collapsed, then," said Thorn, fingering his beard as he watched the screen. "I hope that doesn't mean we'll be overrun here."

"Ortschugin!" the Captain demanded. "See if you can get those cretins now that the bombing's stopped. I want to raise ship and get the hell out of here! Full holds be damned, I'm not paid to be shot at!"

"I'll try again, Excellency," Ortschugin replied. He carefully turned off his sending unit after he had spoken. "Don't get your bowels in an uproar, bitch," he muttered before he made another perfunctory call to Central on the land line. No one answered, of course.

The lower curve of the freighter's hull rested a meter and a half deep in the ground. Normally the *Katyn Forest* would have docked at a proper spaceport like the one at Praha. Copper would be carried from the smelter to the port on ground-effect trucks which hissed down the line of broadcast power pylons. Increased pressure on the Front thirty kilometers to the east had brought a modification. A starship would be landed directly at the mine and refinery complex to eliminate the slow process of transferring the cargo and to free scarce transport to carry materials to the Front.

From what the crew had seen when the *Katyn Forest* popped out of hyperspace on her landing run, the Federal side of the Front needed more help than it was likely to get.

Everyone else in the Smiricky compound had to

depend on government news. The Federal and Republican governments had in common with each other—and with most human governments over the millennia and light years—the fact that they lied as a matter of course when reality did not suit their purposes. A navigational template had been computer-generated on the screens of the *Katyn Forest* from data a week old. It showed disquieting contrasts from the present scene. North and south of Smiricky #4, the Front—limned on the darkness by shell bursts—had bulged inward through the net of Federal strongpoints. If the bulges became penetrations, as they were almost certain to do, it would be kitty bar the door to Praha itself.

The rumble of ingots being dumped amidships was joined by a series of slower, hull-shaking clangs. Kawalec was trying to clear the vessel's own cargo-shifting apparatus in order to straighten the recent jumble. Ortschugin frowned and touched the communicator. "Excellency," he said, "they'll probably make another pass. It might be best to keep yourself and the crew under cover until this has all blown over."

The response came on the Power Room line. Nadia Kawalec had not risked her *own* life among possible live ordnance. "Don't act stupider than you already are, Ortschugin," she snapped. "They're bombing here just to scatter the locals and keep them from blowing the place up. Well, *that* may work, but they're not going to catch us too!"

Why the hell not? the First Officer wondered silently. The copper would not be paid for until it was delivered on Novaya Swoboda. The Rubes would be just as glad of that golden egg as the

Federals had been. The *Katyn Forest* and her crew
had little to fear on that score.

He looked at the screens. The dazzling flash of
the starship blowing up chilled Ortschugin as it
would have chilled any spaceman who saw it.

The starship in fact destroyed itself. It had been
adapted to a job for which it was not intended in
the belief that its hyperspace envelope and its high
real-space velocity would be adequate protection.
Starships were not armored in the technical sense,
but their hulls were of braced steel a hand's breadth
thick. That was needed to withstand the torque of
hyperspace inversion. The momentary friction of
Mach 5 in an atmosphere made the attacking
vessel's nose glow, but it was intended that the
ship be back in her envelope before any structural
damage occurred.

A single osmium shot from Jensen's cannon met
the starship in the instant it dumped its second
stick of bombs. The projectile had started to tum-
ble as it ripped an exit hole through the top of the
spacer's hull amidships. During the instant of its
glowing passage, the round tore through the power
boards of the hyperspace inverter. At the speed of
a slow comet, with its cargo bay open to destroy
even the semblance of streamlining, the vessel tried
to plow through a planetary atmosphere. Its fragments burned white as they tumbled across the
sky.

The debris held Ortschugin transfixed for long
seconds. At last he glanced down at the glowing
tracks of the bombs which the spacer had released
before it dissolved. Cursing, incredulous, the First
Officer grabbed for the intercom again.

The *Katyn Forest* was in the war after all.

*   *   *

Churchie Dwyer did not bother to look around. He thrust himself out of the trench with his eyes still screwed shut against the pain. "All right, Del," he said in a squeaky voice. "We're all right." He turned, crouching on all fours, and slitted his lids enough to permit him to examine the brew vat.

Their side of the ridge had not been part of the intended target. It was well within the scatter range of the clusters, however. The air was sharp with residues of the explosives. The two bomblets which had gone off directly over the tank had opened ragged holes in the upper sheet steel.

None of the shrapnel had penetrated the bottom of the fuel tank. Del and Churchie were unmarked—by the bombs themselves.

The trench hissed and steamed with the half-cured mash still dripping onto the coals. The mercenaries' uniforms were of tough material, but not all the coals had been quenched when the men threw themselves down. Churchie could feel the cracking of fabric that had melted into the flesh of his shoulders and buttocks. His hands and scalp had not been exposed to the coals directly, but the steaming brew had parboiled all his bare skin.

The vat, the brew, and Churchie's dreams of wealth beyond a vault-blower's were ruined utterly.

Rising, the lanky soldier kicked the tank. It thumped, but it would not ring. Screaming with rage, he kicked it again.

"Churchie, I'm burned," said Del Hoybrin, and good *God* he was! The big man had crawled into the trench face down, as if it were not a fire-pit. He had saved his bollocks at hideous cost to his knees and elbows.

Dwyer drew his wrist knife. The nickel steel of its blade had been collapsed to crystals of four times their natural density. It was a day's work on a diamond sharpener to give it shaving edges, but it would hold those edges even if it were punched through body armor. Short-gripping the blade, Churchie began to separate the bigger man's flesh from his uniform. He worked with a surgeon's skill, oblivious to what had moments before been the ungodly pain of his own burns. Under his breath Dwyer muttered, "Shouldn't have sold our goddam wound cream to those hick miners who thought they could get high on it.... But don't worry, baby, we'll get you relieved and fixed up down the hill, just as soon as—" the sky flashed—"*got* the bastard!"

The starship's lengthy disintegration brightened the heavens and Churchie's stainless-steel smile. He watched with practiced eyes as the bomb load separated into eight fireballs on parallel trajectories. He sheathed his knife with the care its point demanded, then grabbed his companion by the arm. "Come on, Del," he said, "let's get the hell back to where we're supposed to be so we can call for a relief." He picked up both guns by their slings.

"Churchie, there's bombs," said Trooper Hoybrin. He pointed at the fireballs with an index finger as thick as a broom-handle. "Shouldn't we—you know?"

The gangling veteran clapped his friend on the shoulder. "Come on, sweetheart," he said. "The first load was for us, keep our heads down. These aren't clusters. I'd suspect those bastards in the buildings and the spacer are going to something to do besides laugh at us in a little bit!"

When it was too late, Vladimir Ortschugin realized the point that he had missed. The Republicans might have been willing to deal with the *Katyn Forest* on normal business terms if she had landed in their territory. Since she had not done so, however, it was well worth their time to see that the starship stayed on the ground until they captured it. The Smiricky Complex itself was not the target—it could not fly away from the onrushing Republican columns.

All eight armor-piercing bombs of the second stick were aimed at the grounded starship.

Ortschugin and Thorn could watch the missiles swell on the screens, but they could do nothing to stop them. The crewman had fumbled out a golden crucifix at the end of a rosary. Tobacco juice, unnoticed, was drooling from the corner of the First Officer's mouth.

The first bomb landed a hundred meters short. The earth quivered, then shot up in a steep, black geyser from the buried explosion. Almost simultaneously, one of the next trio hit the *Katyn Forest* astern. The vessel pitched like a canoe in the rapids. Both men on the bridge were thrown to the deck.

The impact of the bomb was followed by its slamming detonation within the Power Room. Dissonant vibrations made the thick hull slither. They drove the surviving crew to shrieks of pain. In Hold Two, a cargo grab whipped. The rotary teeth which had been hooking ingots into the feed pipe snatched a crewman's leg. She screamed, but the operator was unconscious and there was no one to prevent her from being hauled all the way up the twenty-five centimeter pipe.

No one else died in the hold. Captain Kawalec was alone in the Power Room when the bomb exploded on the main fusion unit.

On the ground, the *Katyn Forest* supplied its internal needs from the auxilliary power unit forward. The main bottle was cold when it fractured. That saved the ship and most of Smiricky #4. It would not have mattered one way or the other to the Captain, who must have been within touching distance of the bomb when its two-hundred kilo charge went off. The five survivors of the crew shed more tears for the main drive than they ever thought of doing for Her Excellency Nadia Kawalec, however.

Ortschugin rose to his feet. He wiped his face with the back of his hand. The instruments worked perfectly. The emergency tell-tales pulsing for the Power Room hull and the main fusion unit left no doubt as to what the damage had been. The bearded First Officer pushed the general address system. "Shut off all equipment and report," he croaked to the crew. "The bombing's over for now, you don't have to worry." After a moment he keyed the system again and added, "This is Ortschugin speaking, the Acting Captain."

CHAPTER TWO

The lobby and counter area of the warehouse were silent except for the scraping of the front door which Albrecht Waldstejn had unlocked to enter. Enclosed, the fumes of the explosives were more noticeable than they had been outside. The Lieutenant's stomach roiled, not only at the odor. There were splashes of blood on the lobby floor.

He stepped forward. "Hodicky!" he shouted. "Quade! Where the hell are you?"

Hodicky popped out of the main storeroom so abruptly that Waldstejn cursed despite his relief. "Private Quade all right too?" he asked in his next breath.

"Oh, yes sir," the little enlisted man said. "Q's up on the roof, checking the part we can't get to from below because of the racks. If it's all like this—" he waved at the lobby roof with its bright splotches of sky—"just the sheeting and not the beams, we'll have a quick fix done before dark."

Somebody finally shut off the siren at Headquarters. Waldstejn had not realized how irritating its distant throb had been until it ceased. "How do you plan to fix that?" the officer asked, duplicating Hodicky's upward wave. Maybe, he was thinking, they could set a fan in the front doorway blowing out to vent some of that damned sweetish stench.

"Well, sir," Private Hodicky said brightly, "the plastic sheeting for waterproofing the insides of dug-outs came in yesterday. We'll use it ourselves instead of issuing it. And I just checked stores. There's thirty liters of spray epoxy, that'll be plenty to tack the sheets down with." He frowned. "Now, we're not talking blast-proof, but a quick fix to keep out most of the rain—that we can have up while it's still daylight."

"Well, I'll be damned," Waldstejn said. He nodded his head in agreement. "Just the two of you, though? You don't need some more bodies?"

Hodicky snorted. "You think they're—" he thumbed in the general direction of Headquarters— "going to assign more men because *you* ask them, sir? No, Q and I'll handle things, don't you worry."

The Private glanced upward. The roof quivered thinly to the touch of boot soles. "Ah, sir," Hodicky said as he eyed the roof, "you wouldn't mind if a couple bottles of gin evaporated from the booze locker, would you?" Immediately within the main storehouse were two large steel cabinets. One held small arms and ammunition, the other held the battalion's medical supplies and the officers' liquor rations. Their hasp locks would open to

Waldstejn's thumbprint alone. "There was a lot of
stuff flying around a few minutes ago. Some it it
probably busted a bottle or two, don't you think?"
Hodicky hopefully met his superior's eyes.

"I think," said Lieutenant Waldstejn very carefully, "that if anything evaporates from that locker,
you will get the same three years in the glasshouse
that Quartermaster Stanlas got when I caught him."

The silence was broken only by the measured
pad of Quade's boots, coming nearer along the
ridge line. "However," the Supply Officer continued,
"I will very cheerfully withdraw two bottles of gin
from my own ration as a present for you and
Private Quade when you've finished with the roof."

"Mary, you scared me, sir!" Hodicky gasped
through his smile. "We'll get right on it." He turned
to dart back into the store room. But as the little
man did so, he paused and turned again. "Sir," he
said, "I ought to just keep my mouth shut, I know,
but. . . . Look, it's just as much against regs to
issue your own booze to enlisted men as it is to let
a couple bottles disappear. What's the deal?"

Waldstejn smiled, more at himself than at the
question. "Look, Hodicky," he said, "if you get
caught and my ass comes up on charges as a
result—fine. I trusted somebody I shouldn't have
and I got burned for it like I deserved. I never
swore to anybody I'd make sure enlisted men got
pissed on beer and officers on spirits. But my accounts are going to be straight because *I* say they
will, not for some damned regulation. Now, go fix
the roof while I take a look at what's happened
inside." He walked toward the counter's gate.

"It's like you said, Pavel," Private Quade called

from above. His head was silhouetted against one of the larger rips in the lobby ceiling.

"Come on down and help me carry," Hodicky shouted back. "We're in a hurry."

Hodicky waved the Lieutenant through into the stores area and followed him. In a low voice—though there was no one nearer than Quade, whose rapid footsteps were slanting toward the ladder at the back of the building—the Private said, "Ah, sir, I noticed lots more rat droppings than we'd thought when I was checking things out a moment ago. The shipment of warfarin hasn't come in—" it had, but Hodicky had checked the invoice himself—"and you know how they give Q the creeps. While you're in the locker, why don't you withdraw some digitalis from medical stores. I'll lace some flour with that and put it out for Q, you know. I don't like it when he gets upset."

The holes in the roof now lighted the warehouse more than the glow strips did. Waldstejn frowned at his subordinate in puzzlement. If Hodicky knew that digitalis was poisonous, then he did not have some wild-hare idea of using it to get high on. The officer sighed. "All right," he said, "but be careful. You two are the only staff I'll get from the Major, and I don't need you keeling over with heart attacks."

"Thank you, sir," the Private said. He began to walk briskly down the aisles toward the back door of the building.

"If this bombing means what I'm afraid it does," Waldstejn called after him, "I guess we're going to have worse problems than rats in a little bit."

Maybe you will, Pavel Hodicky thought as he

jogged between racks of boots and uniforms. For the Privates, though, a couple of rats named Breisach and Ondru were the number one problem. If Hodicky did not take care of it fast with spiked gin, Q was going to do it his own way. At the moment, Hodicky was still uncertain which result frightened him more.

CHAPTER THREE

The pounding on the door was audible over the gnat-swarm keen of the computer terminal. Private Quade wore a taut expression as he returned to Waldstejn from the front lobby. "I shouted through the door like you say," the Private explained. "He won't go away. You let me—" Quade drew a trembling breath— "and I'll get him to leave."

"No, wait here," the Lieutenant said. His desk beside the terminal was littered with computer tape and hand-written notes. It was a rush job and he was a long way from finishing it. Quade's condition, however, indicated that Waldstejn had better take care of the problem fast. In many ways, Jirik Quade was an ideal subordinate. He was dogged, and he would accomplish without complaint any task within his capacity. Quade seemed honest; he was as strong as men half again his

49

size; and his utter loyalty to Waldstejn, the first commanding officer who had treated him like a human being, was embarrassing.

Still, you do not ignore your guard dog when it starts to growl at children; and Waldstejn did not intend to ignore Private Quade when he started to shake with frustration and rage. The Major could wait for his figures.

The Supply Officer did not bother to close his tunic front, but he did snatch up the equipment belt which he had looped over a drawer pull. He carried it in his left hand. The weight of the radio and holstered pistol made it swing as he strode.

There was a rustle from the other end of the warehouse. Private Hodicky was scrambling out of his sleeping quarters at the back. This was Quade's night for late duty, but Hodicky could hear the knocking and shouts; and he could extrapolate an outcome as well as his Lieutenant could. Waldstejn decided to handle the problem himself anyway. His rank and his assurance that he was acting on instructions of the battalion commander might quiet someone determined to get supplies on the orders of some lower officer.

Besides, it would give Waldstejn a chance to unload some of the frustration which he owed properly to the Major's request.

The knocking, paced but determined, continued as the Lieutenant strode through the lobby. When the call from Headquarters came through, Waldstejn had ordered Quade to letter a sign for the front door: CLOSED BY ORDER OF BATTALION COMMANDER. NO REQUESTS ACCEPTED UNTIL FURTHER NOTICE. Now as Waldstejn threw open the door he shouted, "What's the matter with you?

Can't you read the bloody sign?" Then he blinked. Switching to English and a subdued tone, he said, "Oh, ah, Vladimir. Look, I've got another fifteen, thirty minutes work for my CO and there's nobody else here who can run the computer. I really can't even talk to you now."

"Ah, sir," said Private Hodicky from behind the counter. "I can handle the computer, if that's what you want. We had the same unit in my lyceum."

The little man had not intended to admit his competence with the system. As short-handed as the Supply Section was, he would probably wind up with his previous duties as well as work on the computer. For another thing, it was the lyceum computer which had gotten him sent down with six months active and a forced enlistment for the duration of the war. Hodicky had broken into the school office at night and used its terminal to transfer funds to his own bank account. The transaction had been flawless from a technical viewpoint; but the branch manager had known perfectly well that a seventeen year old slum kid should not have been able to withdraw thirty thousand crowns. Using common sense instead of what the terminal told him, the manager had called the police.

But Hodicky had not expected to be serving under an officer like Lieutenant Waldstejn, either. . . .

"I don't mind waiting," said Vladimir Ortschugin. He massaged the heel of the hand with which he had been pounding. "But I need to talk to you as soon as you're free, Albrecht."

"Sure," the Lieutenant said, "just a second." He had tossed a few glasses with the spaceman in company with the two mercenary officers. He could not have remembered Ortschugin's last name for a

free trip to Elysion III, however. Switching back to
Czech, Waldstejn exclaimed, "You can really work
that bitch, Hodicky?" The Private nodded. "Well,
you're one up on me," Waldstejn continued. "They're
in the middle of a staff meeting and somebody
decided they had to know everything about arms,
ammunition, and ration stocks. Not just *our* stores,
mind, but unit stocks as well. That means we've
got to run platoon and section accounts, issued
and expended, for the whole six months to get the
bottom line. You can really handle that?"

"Yes, *sir,*" the little man said. He turned and
trotted back toward Waldstejn's alcove.

"That's a silver lining I didn't expect," the tall
officer muttered in English. He led Ortschugin into
the counter area where there were a pair of tube-
frame chairs. They left the outer door open. After
struggling with the accounts for two hours, it would
be relaxing to handle the sort of oddball supply
requests that might come up at this time of night.

"I apologize," Ortschugin said. "I know you must
be busy, but—" he took a leather-covered flask out
of his breast pocket and uncapped it— "we know
now what we must have, and it is crucial that we
learn as soon as possible who we must see to get
it." He handed the flask to Waldstejn, shifting his
cud of tobacco to his right cheek in preparation for
the liquor's return. "We must have a truck power
receptor so that we can fly to Praha on broadcast
power."

Waldstejn choked on his sip of what seemed to
be industrial-strength ethanol. "What?" he said
through his coughing. It was not that the request
was wholly impossible, but it certainly had not
been anything the local man had expected.

The Spacer drank deeply from his own flask and belched. He stared gloomily upward before he resumed speaking. Several of the brighter stars were tremblingly visible through the plastic sheets. "Our powerplant is gone, kaput," the bearded man said at last. "Replacement and patching the hull, those are dockyard jobs. We *can* fly, using the APU to drive the landing thrusters—but minutes, you see, ten, twenty at most before the little bottle ruptures also under load and we make fireworks as pretty as those this morning, yes?" He swigged again, then remembered and offered the flask to Waldstejn—who waved it away. "So we are still sitting when your Republicans take over, yes?" Ortschugin concluded with a wave of his hand.

The Swobodan's flat certainty that the battalion would be overrun chilled Waldstejn. "That may be, I suppose," the local officer said carefully, "but—well, from what you said that night with Fasolini, that you just shuttled cargo, you didn't mess with politics. . . . I wouldn't think it would make much difference to you. The Rubes don't have much time for mercenaries, I'm told, but like you say, *you* just drive a truck."

Ortschugin did not at first answer. He began craning his neck, trying to look all around him without getting up from his chair. Waldstejn, guessing the ostensible reason for the other's pause, hooked a wastebasket from under the counter. The spaceman spat into it.

The delay had permitted Ortschugin to consider the blunt question at length. He found he had no better response to it than the truth. "You are right, of course. The problem is not—" he gestured with both hands and grimaced— "patriotism, it is

mechanics. We can use the broadcast power line
to fly to a dockyard—*if* we have a tuned receiver,
and *if* the dockyard is in Praha. Budweis has an
adequate dock, surely; but there is no pylon system to Budweis. We must leave now, and for Praha,
if the *Katyn Forest* is not to lie here until she rusts
away . . . and ourselves, perhaps, with her. I—"

The Swobodan paused again. He made no effort
this time to hide his embarrassment at how to
proceed. At last he blurted, "We—Pyaneta Lines—
can pay you. To save the vessel, they will pay well,
only name it. But there are troops guarding the
trucks still in camp, and the officer in charge will
not deal with me. You are our last hope."

Waldstejn stood and walked idly to the terminal
on the counter. He cut it on. "Diedrichson won't
deal with you?" he remarked. "Wonder what got
into him. It wasn't honesty, that I'm sure of." He
began tapping in a request, using one finger and
wondering how Hodicky was doing on the other
terminal. "Diedrichson and the Major are close as
that," the Supply Officer concluded, crossing his
left index and middle fingers and holding them
up. A massive silver ring winked on the middle
finger. A crucifix was cast onto the top in place of
a stone setting.

The local officer turned again to his visitor. "So,"
he said in a tone as precise as a headmaster's,
"because you couldn't bribe the fellow in charge of
the vehicles themselves, you decided to bribe the
Supply Officer. Right? Figured I'd be an easier
mark than Diedrichson because we'd had a few
drinks together? That *is* right, isn't it, Lieutenant
. . . you know, I've forgotten your last name?"

Ortschugin set the flask down with a thump on

a shelf beside him. He did not meet Waldstejn's eyes. "Albrecht," he said quietly, "I came to you because I know of nowhere else to go. I am no longer First Officer—" he raised his bearded face— "I am Captain. Her Excellency died in the attack."

The spaceman stood and his voice took on a fierce resonance. "The vessel, the four crewmen who remain, they are *my* responsibility. If I must steal to save them, if I must bribe—I *will* save them." He slammed his broad, pale hand down on the counter to punctuate his statement.

Lieutenant Waldstejn's icy distaste melted. He reached out and laid his hand on the back of the spaceman's, squeezing it. "Hell, I'm sorry, Vladimir," he said. "I'm just pissed because you're getting out of this hole and I probably won't." He drew a deep breath. "There's an antenna in stock; we're set up for some transport maintenance here, you were right. You can have it." Then, "Got anything left in your flask?"

Ortschugin bellowed with delight. He embraced the slighter man. "But of course you can come out with us," he said. "This base, this Smiricky Complex—in days it will be in Republican hands. Who will know?"

The tall Supply Officer snorted bitterly. "I don't think you give the Morale Section all the credit it deserves," he said. "They've saved the Rubes a lot of trouble by shooting people they decide are deserters."

"You are afraid of that?" the spaceman exclaimed. He stepped back and handed Waldstejn the liquor. "No problem. We'll hide you aboard and take you off-planet when we're repaired."

Waldstejn drank, choked, and gave Ortschugin a

wry smile. When he could speak again, he said,
"Seems to be my night for making speeches. Look,
Vladimir, I'm no hero . . . but I took this job, and I
guess I'll stick with everybody else." He shook his
head. "Hell, I don't know . . . ," he added, but he
did not make his subject clear.

Business-like again, the Lieutenant continued,
"I'm doing this for one simple reason, my friend. I
want your cargo to be shipped from Praha, not
Budweis. And I'm not giving you an antenna, I
don't have any authority to alienate government
property."

Ortschugin frowned, but he waited for the rest
of the explanation.

"I *do* have authority," the Supply Officer went
on with a grin, "to hire transport in an emergency.
I think we can justify the emergency—" he waved
at what was left of the roof above them— "and so
I'm hiring you to transport one power-beam antenna, surplus to local needs, back to Central Stores
in Praha. Now, get your crew here with a wagon.
I'd as soon it happened while it's still dark and the
folks who might ask questions are in Headquarters."

Ortschugin whooped again. He went out the door,
bawling snatches of a song which sounded bawdy
even in a language Waldstejn could not guess at.

Someone cleared his throat at the inner doorway.
The Lieutenant looked up. Both his subordinates
stood there. Hodicky held a long coil of twenty-
centimeter computer tape. "Oh," Albrecht Waldstejn said. "He'll be back—the crew of the freighter—
to pick up the truck power antenna in a few
minutes. Here, I'll okay it right now." He found a
request form and began to fill it out, checking the
unit number from the terminal display.

"We'll take care of it, sir," Hodicky said. "I've got the figures—" He waved the tape so that it rustled. "Want me to feed it to Headquarters?"

Waldstejn gave the request to Quade and took the tape. "Four bottles, Private," he said after a glance at the print-out. "And a morning off if I can swing it." He looked up. "No, I'll carry it over as hard copy. They didn't splice the land-lines cut by the bombs yet, just ran commo wire point to point. Their terminal isn't connected—" the young officer glanced around to see that no one outside was listening— "not that anybody there could be trusted to push the right button for a print-out anyway. Hold the fort, boys," he added as he walked out of the warehouse.

Waldstejn sobered as he walked toward the concrete Headquarters building. Dimly on the eastern horizon were the flickers and rumbling of others trying to hold forts in grim truth.

And failing.

"Ouch, you butcher!" cried Churchie Dwyer. "Did you learn to use that in a stockyard?"

"You'd bitch if they hanged you with a new rope," Bertinelli replied calmly. Bertinelli was a Corpsman. He carried a gun like everybody else, but he ranked with the sergeants for pay division. He was secure both in the light touch he knew he had and in the fact that nobody else in the Company could handle the medical tasks as well. "It's just like I told you, I learned in a morgue on Banares, putting accident victims back in shape for open cremation. Now, lie back—" he gestured with the debriding glove with which he was cleaning Dwyer's burns— "or I don't answer for what it's going to feel like."

"They sure are doing a lot of talking," said Del Hoybrin. Bertinelli had recleaned the big man's sores first. Now Del knelt with his triceps on the lip of the bunker, staring up at the transponder. The communications gear hung from a balloon tethered a hundred meters over the 522nd's radio shack. Through the night visor of his helmet, the minuscule heating of the transponder's circuits as it broadcast was a yellow glow. Satellite communications had died in showers of space junk at the beginning of the war, but there were other ways to boost tight-beam communications over useful distances.

"Well, you might at least give me something for the pain," Churchie grumbled. He lowered himself again onto the cot that doubled as an operating table.

"I'm *going* to give you something," Bertinelli said. "I'm going to give you a square meter less skin if you don't shut up and lie still." He touched the deep burn over Dwyer's right shoulder blade. The mesh of sensors and tiny hooks in the glove's pad began to purr. Under the control of a microprocessor in the wristlet, the glove was lifting off dead tissue to prepare the area for antiseptic and a covering of spray skin. In the same mild voice, the Corpsman added, "I can see the bombs starting fires and blowing the trash into your shelter. But I'm *damned* if I see why you thought you had to lie in it. And I'd like to know what you found to bathe in that had such a pong, too."

"Do you suppose we'll get paid again before we move, Churchie?" Del asked. "I'd like to—for the girls again, you know. Usually there aren't girls where we go." There was a troupe of prostitutes at Smiricky #4, intended for the contract miners but available to the garrison as well.

"Think we'll be pulling back soon, then?" Bertinelli asked with just a hint of tension. He lifted the glove and began to spray the debrided area.

"Sometimes," Del said in a neutral voice. "They're doing a lot of talking."

Churchie snorted. He continued to lie flat with his eyes closed. "Happen to notice which direction the transponder dish was pointed, baby?" he asked.

Del turned to his companions. The featureless visor was a stage beyond even the big man's usual moon-faced innocence. "East, Churchie," he said.

"Right, my dear," Churchie agreed. "And does that tell you anything?"

The Corpsman had stiffened, but after a moment he went on with his work in silence.

"No, Churchie," said Del.

"Right again, sweetheart," Churchie bantered with his eyes closed. "Well, it might mean that they're talking to the Federal commander at the Front, that's true . . . but they haven't any business doing that, we're not under Second Army control, we're handled by Central from Praha. . . . And Praha's west of here, unless they moved it since last night. So, and seeing how high they lifted that balloon before they started to jaw . . . I'd put pretty good money that our local friends have opened negotiations with the other side."

Bertinelli began to curse under his breath. He moved the glove to his patient's left shoulder.

Del resumed his observation of the transponder

balloon. "What does that mean, Churchie?" he
asked.

His friend snorted again. All the humor was gone
from his voice as he replied, "Wish to hell I knew,
darling. Wish to hell. What I'm afraid it means is
that Fasolini's Company is deep in shit."

The only light in the Operations Center was the
green glow of the phosphor screen. It emphasized
the wrinkled anger of Colonel Fasolini's face as he
said, "Gibberish! Goddam *gibberish!*"

Sookie Foyle snapped her fingers in frustration.
"Look, Colonel," she said, "I'm a Communicator,
not a magician. You get me a copy of the code pad
the indigs are using, and I'll let you know what
they've got to say. Otherwise it's garbage—" she
waved at the groups of meaningless letters which
continued to crawl across the screen—"and it's
going to stay garbage."

The three sergeants—Mboko, Hummel, and Jensen—stirred restively in the darkness. They were
the tacticians of the Company, but the present
situation was too amorphous for their skills to be
of any use. Lieutenant ben Mehdi bent forward
and said, "We don't have to read the transmis-
sions to know what they're saying, do we, Guido?
The only thing we don't know is the exact terms
the Major's holding out for—and that doesn't matter to us, because we ought to be making terms
with the Republicans for ourselves, right now, before it all hits the fan. Otherwise, we wind up
taking whatever we're offered."

There was silence again in the OC. The Communicator looked at Fasolini. The skin at the corners

of her eyes was tracked with sudden crow's feet. She did not speak.

"If it's the contract you're worried about," ben Mehdi went on, "the *force majeure* provision clearly—"

"*Shut up!*" the Colonel snapped. His subordinates froze. "Sorry, Hussein," Fasolini went on in a tired voice. He rubbed his face with his palms. "You see, I tried that before I called you in, bounced a signal to the Rube CinC, Yorck, on his internal push." The stocky man managed a smile and squeezed Foyle's shoulder. The Communicator beamed.

"They won't deal," Fasolini went on, "not on any terms we can take. They don't like mercs, they don't use them themselves ... and they like us even less than most."

"They wouldn't deal on *any* terms?" ben Mehdi pressed with a frown.

Colonel Fasolini looked up. After a moment, he said, "No terms we can take. They're real unhappy about their starship this morning." The only sound in the OC was the sigh of the fan in the communications terminal. "They know it was us that did it. They want the whole gun crew—" Fasolini neither raised his voice nor looked at Sergeant Jensen— "and every tenth man at random from the rest of the Company. The others they'll give passage off-planet without guns or equipment." He shrugged. "I told Yorck if he showed himself within a klick of the compound, I'd personally blow him a new asshole."

"*O*-kay," said Sergeant Hummel. She appeared to be looking at nothing in particular, certainly not the Sergeant-Gunner beside her. "Let's don't wait around. Two trucks'll hold the personnel, the equipment we ditch and put in a claim for it at Praha."

"Lichtenstein's got a guard on the trucks," objected Sergeant Mboko. The sheen of his smooth, black face stood out above the absorptive cloth of his uniform.

"So he's got a bloody guard!" Hummel snapped. "They're the least of our problems. We grease them quiet, load the trucks, and *bam!* we're out of the compound and heading west before the indigs know what hit them. They can't shut off the power, because the pylons are energized from both ends of the line."

"The *guards* may not be a problem," retorted Sergeant Mboko, "but the bunkers on the perimeter are. There's a straight line of sight right down the pylons for what—three kilometers? Every bunker's got anti-tank rockets. Do you really think even the indigs are going to miss straight no-deflection shots with wire-guided missiles?"

Sergeant Jensen cleared his throat and spoke for the first time since Fasolini had dropped his bombshell. "It was not the crew who shot down their ship, Colonel," said the big blond. "It was me alone. Perhaps if you offer me, General Yorck will—will be. . . ." Jensen's voice caught.

"Shut the hell up, Roland," Lieutenant ben Mehdi muttered.

"Well, all this may be a lot of fuss over nothing," said Colonel Fasolini. "It's just a matter of dealing with Lichtenstein when he gets the bottom line himself. And Lichtenstein will deal, no trouble there. I just thought you all had better know how the land lies in case we need to move fast."

The Colonel stood up. He was by a decade the oldest person in the shelter. Just now, as he shrugged his crossbelts out of the creases their weight drew over his collar bones, he felt his age. "Wish to all the saints that we knew how the *real* land lies," he said bleakly. "Waldstejn, their Supply Officer, he was complaining the other day that one of his convoys had managed to route itself to some old working thirty klicks from here. They had one truck go off when they were turning around and they just left it there. Now, if we could find *that* and get it on track again.... But we've got jack-shit for a bearing, and I don't see wandering around Cecach till the Rubes find time to round us up and shoot us. I guess we wait."

"Colonel," said Communicator Foyle. She pointed toward the terminal. "Distant input—must be Yorck."

Garbled characters were crawling across the bottom of the screen again, leaving phosphor ghosts of themselves as each line shifted up to make room for the next.

"Better get to my section," Sergeant Hummel said. She picked up her weapon, carrying it at the balance instead of slinging it.

"Yeah," said Colonel Fasolini. "Maybe we don't wait too long."

· The doors and curtains of the Headquarters building were closed, but the bombing had stripped the black-out shutters from one of the front windows. Waldstejn had not bothered to pick up night goggles when he left the warehouse. Enough light still shone through the curtains within to show him the squad on guard. There were two non-coms present,

Sergeants Breisach and Ondru, though presumably only one of them had the duty officially. They
had approached him with an offer shortly after he
took over as Supply Officer. Waldstejn was not
sure whether the pair of them were genuinely dim-
witted, or, more likely, that they were so crooked
that they made the rest of the 522nd look good.
Under that assumption, the Sergeants thought that
Waldstejn had cleaned house on his subordinates
in order to have all the graft for himself.

Albrecht Waldstejn had disabused them in a ti-
rade which he believed had impressed even that
pair.

At the moment, Sergeant Ondru was having a
loud argument with one of the Signals staff. Rather,
Ondru and his men were grinning as a signalman
shouted and waved the envelope he carried. "Sorry,"
the non-com said, "I've got orders not to pass
anybody. Major wouldn't like it. Now, maybe if
you'd give *me* this important message you're so
hot to deliver, I could decide if it's really important enough to disturb the brass."

"Why don't you start doing your job, Ondru,"
the tall officer said as he joined the group, "and
stop poking your nose into things that are none of
your business."

The infantry squad stiffened. One man even stood
up. Sullenly, Sergeant Ondru said, "I've got my
orders."

"I've got my orders, *sir!*" Waldstejn snapped back.

"I've got my orders sir," the non-com parroted.
He stepped aside. Either he had been told to pass
the Supply Officer, or he had decided not to make
an issue of it. At best, there were too many ways
that the young officer could make life unpleasant

for the soldiers who drew their supplies from him. At worst—well, nobody really thought that Waldstejn would be trying to crash a staff meeting to which he had not been summoned.

The signalman plucked at Lieutenant Waldstejn's sleeve. The officer recognized him by sight, but the only name he could think of was 'Porky', the pudgy man's nickname. "Sir," the signalman pleaded, prodding Waldstejn with the envelope he carried, "the land-line's out, somebody must've tripped over it, and I've *got* to get this message to Major Lichtenstein. Can . . . ?"

It did not sound like something a Supply Officer should be getting involved with. Waldstejn did not touch the envelope. "Put it on the air, then," he suggested. "Somebody in there surely has a working receiver."

Porky nodded like a man trying to duck his head out of a noose. "Lieutenant," he said, "they do, but the mercs have them too. I don't *dare* put this on the air in clear." He swallowed. Despite the rapt silence of the squad on guard, he added, "It's from the . . . it's from east of here."

Waldstejn took the envelope in the hand that held his own print-out. "All right," he said, "I'll deliver it to the Major."

His face was still as he opened the door into the building. Maybe it *was* something that a Supply Officer got involved in. At least, if the Supply Officer had friends among a group of mercenaries that might be set for a long fall.

"Look," Captain Tetour said abruptly, "what if they won't take any offer? We'd be better off fight-

ing than surrendering. You know the stories that
all Federal officers are executed in the field."

Brionca, the Operations Officer, sneezed out her
snuff and slapped the table for emphasis. "We've
been through that, dammit, we can't fight, the
armored regiment they'll send will plow us under.
What we need to think about is how we'll sweeten
the pot so they've *got* to deal."

"Well, I've been thinking some more about that,"
said Captain Strojnowski. He watched the point of
his stylus click on the table instead of looking
around at the others. Strojnowski's Third Company was perhaps closer to being a military unit
than was Tetour's First, and the Captain himself
had shown promise in line service before discrep-
ancies had shown up in his pay vouchers. "We've
been talking as if they'll just swarm down the
valley with tanks and troop carriers. But they won't
risk that against Fasolini's men; and besides, we've
got the two laser cannon—"

"Which gave us so much air defense," Brionca
thundered, "that they weren't even switched *on*
until after the ship had blown up. Want to bet
your life it'll be any better when it's tanks ripping
us apart?"

"Now wait a goddam minute," said Stoessel, the
young lieutenant in charge of the lasers. He had
been included in the council of war even though
he was not a member of the 522nd Garrison
Battalion. The guns were detached from Central to
Smiricky #4, but their chain of command still ran
directly to Praha. "You guys give me a target," the
lieutenant continued in a high voice, "and I'll hit
it. But there's no acquisition system in the universe that'll hit a starship that's in normal space

only a—" He broke off, suddenly aware of the disdain on all the faces watching him. "Not that I *want* to engage tanks," he concluded lamely. "I mean, they mount lasers too, and they're armored. . . ."

"Then don't worry about it until somebody tells you to," snapped Captain Khlesl, the Intelligence officer who cradled a handset between his shoulder and ear. He turned to the Battalion Commander on the chair beside him. "Major," he said, tapping the handset without taking it away from his ear, "I think the damned thing's broken again. Maybe we'd better send one of the guards over to Signals and see—"

Someone knocked on the door to the outer office. An officer swore. Major Lichtenstein himself began to rise from his seat with an expression of fury. His face smoothed into mere sourness when a voice, muffled by the door panel, announced, "Sir, Lieutenant Waldstejn with the figures you requested. Also a message from the Signals Section— they say the line's gone down again."

Captain Brionca was closest to the door. She pulled it open without any need to be asked. Smoke and warm air swirled from the meeting room. The draft from the outer office felt cooler because that within had been heated for hours by eight bodies. "Give me that," she said, reaching for the papers the Supply Officer held. Other staff officers were getting up.

"Sit down, Brionca," rumbled Major Lichtenstein. "Bring them here, Waldstejn."

The Lieutenant stepped briskly to the head of the table and attempted to salute his commanding officer. Lichtenstein ignored that and snatched the sheaf of papers from the other's hand. "Not this crap," he muttered as he slid aside the supply print-outs. His staff was tense. "Here we are, Mary love us," the Major went on in a caressing voice. He ripped open the envelope from Signals.

Major Wolfgang Lichtenstein was much of an age and build with Colonel Fasolini, his mercenary counterpart. Liquor had broken the veins of his face and brought him to the command of the 522nd. He had been drinking this night as well, but it was tension and not alcohol which had kept the Major in a state of nearly comatose silence during most of the staff meeting. His fingers trembled. He had to lay the sheet of message paper on the table to unfold it after he had teased it from the envelope.

"For *God's* sake, what is it?" blurted the artillery lieutenant.

"Mary and the blessed saints!" the Major wheezed. He slumped back in his chair as if relief had severed his spine. "They've made an offer we can live with. Mary, Mother of God!"

The Intelligence Officer snatched up the document before Captain Brionca could reach it from the other side. "Why," he said, "they'll accept the battalion as a unit and integrate it into their own forces! We've won! Officers may be reassigned, but no prison or executions!"

"Don't know that I want to be Rube cannon fodder either," someone muttered. He was answered at once by a waspish, "Have you looked at the choice?"

"But what's the catch?" Captain Tetour objected. "They know they've got our balls in a vise!"

"No catch," insisted Captain Khlesl, holding up

the message form. " 'No quarrel with fellow citizens of Cecach, only with the government of idolators in Praha.' " He slapped the paper down. "All we have to do is to turn over the Complex unharmed. And to disarm the mercenaries and turn them over too."

There was abrupt silence around the table. "What do you mean, no catch?" Strojnowski said sourly. "Fasolini may have ideas of his own about turning in his guns."

"Wait a minute," someone said in amazement. When the others turned, they saw the speaker was Albrecht Waldstejn. The Supply Officer had not left the room. "Why are we concerned about the terms the Rubes might offer? There's twenty-three ore haulers empty in the compound right now. They'll hold all the troops and most of the civilians—and if we move fast, we can be clear before they cut the pylon line."

"Get him the hell out of here," Captain Tetour said.

Lieutenant Dyk commanded the Second Company since the regular CO had been invalided out with bull-head clap. Dyk had not spoken during the meeting proper. Now, faced with a chance to score off Waldstejn, he said, "Because we've got orders from Praha to hold to the last man! If we retreat, Morale Section will have every one of us shot. Every officer for sure."

"Frantisak's right, though," Brionca said. "We can't just waltz over to the mercs and say, 'All right hand over—' "

"God *damn* it!" Waldstejn shouted. His hands were clenched. "If *we* can't go, we can put *them* on a truck before we surrender. That's *murder!*"

"You damned fool!" Dyk shouted back. "Those foreigners are the only thing between you and me and a firing squad!"

"Another word from him," said the Major as he lurched to his feet, "and they won't have to shoot him." A flush and the shadows of the overhead light hid the patterning of Lichtenstein's face. His right hand was fumbling at the flap of his pistol holster. The motion seemed almost undirected and the fingers never did touch the gun butt. "You're out of uniform, Lieutenant," he muttered. His hand fell away from the holster. Taking a deep breath, the Major shouted, "Guard! Guard!"

Lieutenant Stoessel sprang up to fetch someone, but his zeal was unnecessary. Sergeant Ondru rushed into the outer office with his slung rifle clattering on the door jamb. More formally, the non-com paced the three steps to the inner doorway and saluted. "Sir?" he said. Members of his squad were peering through the open doors.

"Have three men take Waldstejn here to his quarters," the battalion commander said, gesturing with a heavy thumb. "Tie him to a goddam chair and make sure he stays in it."

The Supply officer turned and slammed a fist into the wall. He did not speak.

"If you're real lucky, Lieutenant," Lichtenstein snarled at the younger man's back, "I'll have you untied when all this is over."

Waldstejn walked past the Sergeant. He shrugged his arm away from the hand with which Ondru would have gripped his upper arm.

"He doesn't talk to anybody!" the Major shouted. Everyone else in the office was silent, watching. "He tries any crap, *shoot* him!"

Sergeant Ondru carefully closed the building's outer door behind him. "Breisach, you take over here for me," he told his startled companion. "Doubek, Janko, come on—we're going to escort our prisoner here to his quarters." He prodded Waldstejn between the shoulder blades with a stiff finger.

"And make sure your night goggles are on," the Sergeant added. "We just might get a chance to shoot an escapee." He prodded the Lieutenant again. This time he used the muzzle of his rifle.

"Halt!" cried the first of the guards to see him.

Colonel Fasolini flipped up the visor of his helmet. "It's me, Fasolini," he said in Czech. "Your CO just sent for me."

"You're alone, then?" Sergeant Breisach demanded. "We were told there was two of you." The whole squad was on its feet and tense.

There was reason enough to be tense, the squat mercenary knew; but perhaps these local troops were reacting only to the morning's raid. "No, I'm alone," Fasolini said. "I make the decisions for the Company by myself." He entered the building at the Sergeant's assenting nod.

Fasolini stood out like a wrestler in a law office among the battalion staff. His helmet and the grim burden of his crossbelts made him utterly alien. Chairs scraped as Federal officers rose to greet the mercenary. "Glad you were so quick, Colonel," said Captain Khlesl. The little Intelligence Officer had been chosen to make the presentation. Now he reached across the table to shake the mercenary's hand. "Do sit down. A drink?"

The Colonel seated himself in the chair left va-

cant for him. Captain Strojnowski across the table
would not meet his eyes. "No drink," the Colonel
said. "Maybe later."

"Right," agreed Khlesl, "right." He smiled, continuing to stand. "You see, Colonel," he continued,
"the strategic situation has deteriorated very
sharply in the past twenty hours. The—I'll call
them the enemy—has broken through—"

"I know what the Rubes've done," Colonel Fasolini
said bluntly. "At the moment, I'm more concerned
about what you propose to do about it. I assure
you, me and my boys'll agree to any reasonable
suggestion."

Major Lichtenstein belched, then looked around
as if he suspected someone else of making the
sound. The room was silent.

"Well," Captain Khlesl said, "yes. The truth of it
is, Colonel, that the plan we have decided to imple-
ment is surrender. We have some reason to believe
that General Yorck will be quite generous in his
terms . . . though of course we'll have to disarm all
the troops in the compound first. We—we here are
as good patriots as any on Cecach, but with Republican armored columns certain to encircle us within
another day at most, well. . . . There's no point in
causing needless slaughter, is there?"

"After all," put in Captain Tetour, "the garrison
was put here to keep the civilians in order and to
keep the Rubes from making some sort of raid on
it. Well, we've done that. But they've got tanks
from *Terra!*"

"Sure, I can see that," the mercenary agreed
with a smile that slashed, then slumped back to
stark reality. "Thing is, we've got a notion that
General Yorck may not be quite so generous to

mercs as he might be to . . . brothers and sisters of the Cecach soil. Eh?" He smiled again, a reflex and not a real plea. Captain Khlesl's grin had stiffened into a bright rictus.

"Now, I wouldn't be surprised if some of you people kept off-planet bank accounts," Fasolini continued. "Doesn't mean you're not patriotic, it's just common sense, spreading the risk." He gestured with both hands, palms down, fingers splayed. "The rest, you can get an account easy enough. Now, what I'm offering is a pre-accepted order on my agents on Valunta to transfer—" his eyes counted— "thirty-one thousand Valuntan pesos, that's over twelve thousand crowns, into *each* of your private accounts. All you have to do to get that money is to give us one truck and one hour. It's that simple."

Major Lichtenstein rolled forward in his chair. He planted both palms meatily on the table. "How about your life instead?" he said. His voice rode down the buzz of talk that had followed the mercenary's offer.

"Come on, now," the Major cajoled heavily, "that's a fair deal, isn't it? Man to man. We hide you, save your ass when the Rubes roll in—which you and me couldn't stop if we wanted to. You're clear. Your gear's gone, but that's gone anyhow. And Mary and the Saints, you won't have any trouble finding gallows bait to replace what you leave here, will you? Come on, man to man—what do you say?"

"Well, there's a whole lot of truth in that," Colonel Fasolini said. He leaned back in his chair, his tension apparently submerged by the new consideration. "A lot of truth," he repeated. "You know,

Major, I think I can buy into that. I mean, businessman's got to know when to cut his losses, don't he?"

Fasolini stood up. "Tell you what, gents—" he nodded to Brionca— "Captain, I'm going to my Operations Center now to pick up a few items. I'll be back in an hour and give my troops the order to disarm from here." He smiled. "Okay?"

"Take all the time you need, Colonel," Major Lichtenstein agreed. "Glad you're a reasonable man."

The mercenary closed the inner door behind him. Captain Brionca jumped to her feet. Lichtenstein's face was a mask of fury. He nodded to his Operations officer. "The bastard's lying," he said. "He's going to double-cross us."

Brionca caught the handle of the outside door just as it closed. She snatched it open, throwing her shadow forward on a fan of yellow light. *Kill him!"* she called to the guards.

CHAPTER FOUR

As they neared the warehouse, Albrecht Waldsten stumbled less frequently. He had recovered both his night vision and his poise during the march, despite Sergeant Ondru's frequent jabs. "You know," the tall officer said in a thoughtful voice, "you boys'd have to tie me up regardless, it'd be your asses if you didn't—"

"Never fear *that*," quipped Ondru. Because of the way his rifle was slung, he had to step very close to his prisoner in order to poke the weapon into his ribs. He did so again.

Waldstejn missed a half step. His voice was still friendly as he resumed, "But it strikes me that the knots might not be *quite* as tight if we all had a drink or two together first. After all, it's not much point worrying about liquor rations now, is there?"

One of the privates whistled, "Holy Mother," under his breath.

Ondru shifted his grip on his rifle. The looming warehouse had a rosy cast through his light-enhancing goggles. The visual cliche made him bark out a laugh. "You mean," the big sergeant said, "that you'll open the liquor cabinet if we don't try to amputate your legs with the ropes?"

Waldstejn turned his head, stumbling a little again, and replied, "Hell, yes. What did being a hard-ass get me? Look, I may be dumb, but I'm not too dumb to learn."

The Sergeant grinned back at his prisoner. "Guess we got a deal, then," he said. Ondru was thinking about how he would tie the sanctimonious bastard as soon as he opened up the booze. On his belly, with one cord looped from his throat to his ankles, that was for sure. That way if Waldstejn relaxed a muscle, the weight of his own feet would start to choke him. That for sure.

The Supply Officer had the magnetic key to the front door in his pocket. He swung the panel inward. One of his escorts felt a twinge of concern and brought his rifle up. Waldstejn was very careful to move slowly and to avoid any suggestion that he hoped to leap inside and lock the others out.

The lobby was even dimmer than the outdoors had been. The holes in the roof were brighter than the solid metal around them, but they served to illuminate the interior only for the escort with their night goggles. Lieutenant Waldstejn was thoroughly familiar with the lay-out, however. He walked without hesitation to the counter, knowing that there was nothing between it and the door to trip over. He swung open the gate. "Here," he said, "I'll just get the keys from back here and—oh, would one of you like to turn the lights on? The panel's by the front door."

Sergeant Ondru had stuck close to his prisoner's left elbow. "No!" he snapped. "Janko, get your goggles off." The night goggles issued to Federal troops had no built-in overload protection. The face-shields of Fasolini's mercenaries would hold a desired brightness setting, regardless of changes in ambient light. The Cecach-produced goggles, however, multiplied light by a set factor. They could dazzle their users with excess enhancement.

"Sure, no problem," said Lieutenant Waldstejn. He was trying to keep the fear out of his voice. The officer pretended to fumble beneath the counter for a key. The liquor cabinet had had a thumblock, keyed only to his fingerprint, ever since Waldstejn had taken over as Supply Officer.

Waldstejn's equipment belt was still looped over the back of the chair where he had slung it while talking to Captain Ortschugin. "There we go," Waldstejn said, jingling the keys from his pocket. His left hand, hidden by the chair, unholstered the little pistol.

"All right, you can turn on the lights, Janko," Sergeant Ondru said as he raised his own goggles.

Waldstejn stepped next to him, thrusting the pistol into the Sergeant's ribs as the lights flashed on.

The view of Doubek, behind the counter, was blocked by his own goggles and his sergeant's body. Janko, three meters to the side at the light switches, caught the motion. He gasped and threw up his rifle.

"Mother of God!" Ondru squealed to his subordinate in a high-pitched voice. "Don't shoot—you'll *hit* me!"

"Drop the guns, drop them!" Waldstejn cried on a rising inflection. He caught a handful of Ondru's tunic to hold the man close while he shifted the pistol in Janko's general direction. Janko dropped his rifle with a clatter.

The other private backed a step away from Ondru and the officer. He held his rifle waist high, advanced but not precisely pointing at the tight-locked pair.

"Drop it!" Waldstejn repeated, peering past the equally-tall man whom he held. He waggled the pistol at the uncertain private; and when it went off, Waldstejn himself was more surprised than any of the others in the room.

The muzzle flash of the little gun burned Ondru through his tunic. The Sergeant yelped but managed not to clap a hand to the spot. He stood as rigid as if he were a carcase on a meat hook. Doubek, by contrast, flung his rifle down as if it had burned him. He jumped backwards twice and banged into the wall. "I didn't mean anything, sir!" he bawled, holding out his empty hands. "I didn't mean anything!"

Blood was beginning to stain the left leg of his trousers, but he did not appear to notice it.

"Janko, come over here," the Lieutenant said. He gripped the sling of Ondru's rifle and jerked the weapon away. The Sergeant had not been able to drop the rifle as ordered because the sling was held by his shoulder strap until Waldstejn tore it.

Waldstejn stepped away from the non-com. "I'm going to lock you all in the liquor cabinet," he said with no awareness that the statement might sound

like a joke. He had not been sure his pistol was
loaded; he had no recollection of taking off the
safety; and he *certainly* had not intended to shoot
Doubek, thank God it did not appear to be serious.
Albrecht Waldstejn was more afraid of himself than
he was of any other facet of the situation. He had
made his plans, though, and he would carry them
out now even without real awareness of what was
going on in his head.

The door to the stores area banged open. "What
the hell's happening?" demanded Private Quade.
His eyes glanced angrily around the room until
they lighted on the Supply Officer. "My God!" the
Private gasped. He lowered the section of pipe he
held in his right hand.

"Go on, *quick!*" Waldstejn ordered. To the others,
his voice held a snap of command. "Into the back."
He pumped the assault rifle vertically. He was
afraid to gesture with the pistol lest it fire again.

Ondru and his two subordinates shuffled tensely
into the stores area. Quade remained in the doorway.
He frowned as the others moved past him. The
Lieutenant tried to wink at the black-haired man
when none of the others was looking. 'You too,
Quade," he said harshly. "Into the back." The Private obeyed slowly, still frowning.

The lights in the stores area threw crisp shadows down the aisles of racked supplies. The liquor
cabinet was actually a cubical shipping container
three meters on an edge. The sides were sheet
steel. Access was through a pair of fully-overlapping
hinged leaves in the front. The outer leaf was closed
by a hasp and lock. The cabinet was in no sense a
safe, but it was completely proof against unde-
tected pilfering.

It would also serve as a prison until someone opened it from the outside.

Waldstejn set down his rifle, then thumbed the padlock. He kept his pistol advanced toward the men of his escort, but he pointed the muzzle high—just in case. All three of them seemed to be in shock. Doubek was clutching at his wound with both hands and whimpering.

"In there, the three of you," the Lieutenant said as he wrenched open the inner leaf. More than half the container's volume was filled by cartons of spirits, but there was adequate room for the prisoners.

All three of them shuffled forward. Doubek was sniffling. "We won't be able to breathe," he said. "We'll die." His eyes were screwed shut.

Waldstejn stooped quickly to retrieve the rifle. "It isn't airtight," he said. "Besides, you'll only be inside for as long as it takes Private Quade here to cut the lock off."

When the three prisoners were inside the liquor cabinet, Waldstejn waved the rifle in Quade's direction. For the Private's sake in the aftermath, Waldstejn had to make it clear that his subordinate had nothing to do with what was happening. "Private Quade," the young lieutenant said loudly. "I'm deserting." He paused while he closed up the cabinet. The hinges squealed like the damned in torment. Winking again—he had to be sure Quade did not think that the threat was serious—the officer continued, "You can get bolt cutters and free them as soon as I'm gone, but if you move a muscle while I'm here I'll shoot you down like a dog."

Waldstejn's belt still hung on the chair out front, so he thrust the pistol into his side pocket. He stepped quickly to the arms locker—another shipping container—and opened it.

Private Hodicky slipped out from behind the ration boxes which had hidden him until the prisoners were locked in. "What can we do, Lieutenant?" he whispered.

"Go back to bed and pretend you were asleep," Waldstejn whispered back. He had to tug harder to open the arms' locker than he had the more frequently used liquor store. "On second thought," he said, glancing at the dark-haired Quade, "make sure he knows what's going on and doesn't get himself into trouble. I only need a couple minutes."

The arms locker held a variety of unassigned pieces and munitions, from anti-tank rockets on down. All Lieutenant Waldstejn needed was a canister of ammunition for the rifle he had appropriated. They were not going to be able to carry much, he and the mercenaries. The Company would probably have a spare weapon for Waldstejn, in fact. But the Cecach officer knew that he would be useless against the bruising recoil of one of the mercs' cone-bore guns. Better to carry an assault rifle and at least be able to spray the countryside with it if the need arose.

He turned back to his subordinates, clutching a ten-kilo can of ammunition by the handle. There was no time to worry about bandoliers and other gear, though he would pick up his belt as he went out. Hodicky was whispering with his mouth close to his friend's ear. Quade was no longer frowning. His face was quiet and as unexpectedly shocking as a razor blade in an apple. Waldstejn swallowed. "I told you not to move!" he shouted to prove to the prisoners that he had not left yet. He strode toward the door, weighted by the rifle and ammunition filling his hands.

Hodicky touched the tall officer's sleeve. "Good luck, sir," he whispered.

Lieutenant Albrecht Waldstejn, late Supply Officer of the 522nd Garrison Battalion, nodded back.

He did not trust himself to speak.

"Off and on, children!" cried Roland Jensen as he dropped into the gun section's double shelter. He slapped the sole of Herzenberg's right boot for emphasis.

The four troopers in the shelter jerked alert. The males had been playing a desultory game of Casino. They were using an infra-red signal lamp for light and reading the pips through their night visors. "Your weapons, *two* basic loads of ammo, and three days rations. Now, *now!*"

Jensen's own field pack was already strapped to the back of the gun seat. He swung back outside again.

Guiterez stuck his head and shoulders out through the end curtain. He was rolling the Casino cloth. "Where we shifting, Sarge?" he asked. "Is this a patrol?"

"For the moment, we're shifting to the OC on my own authority," the section leader said harshly. He locked a second can of ammunition into the one that was always loaded in the cannon. "Now shut up, get your ass in gear, and do *exactly* what I goddam tell you."

The Sergeant-Gunner loaded a third drum. That should be enough, a balance between functioning and the chance there would be no one alive to feed the gun after the first blasts of a firefight. He waited, breathing hard as he surveyed the compound through his visor. Bright needles of amplified light marked each of the locally-manned bunkers. They were constructed of earth over steel planking. That looked far sturdier than the Company's beryllium felt, but when the bombs had hit that morning, two of the heavy roofs had been shaken down and suffocated the troops beneath.

The necklace of Cecach dug-outs ended in a dark gap a kilometer south of the automatic cannon. Fasolini's shelters had no crowns of light, even on maximum enhancement by the visors. If Jensen had wanted to, he could have located even those by switching to infra-red. The plumes of body heat from the personnel would give away the positions even if no one inside were using an IR light source.

The gun crew tumbled out. Pavlovich held Herzenberg's pack as well as his own. The recruit was good, though; she would shake down. Another month of campaigning with the Colonel and she would be ready to shift at the drop of a hat.

Jensen twisted his seat forward into driving position. "Everybody aboard," he said. "This time you ride. And for God's sake, keep your eyes open."

The gun began to judder forward on its tracks even as the crew obeyed the unexpected order. Jensen never permitted anyone to ride the cannon as if it were transport and not a weapon. The extra load drained the batteries and strained the running gear.

Somebody looked out of the nearest bunker as they passed with the inevitable chatter of loose tracks. Jensen divided his attention between his course and the bulk of the local headquarters in the center of the Complex. Colonel Fasolini would handle things, he always did.

But if worst came to worst, nobody was going to take Gunner Jensen's crew without paying the price.

"Where's a pair of bolt cutters?" demanded Jirik Quade as the front door closed behind Lieutenant Waldstejn. Quade himself ducked into the open arms locker.

Private Hodicky looked in surprise at his black-haired friend. He and the Supply Officer had assumed that Quade would simply refuse to open the makeshift prison at all. Such a dereliction would implicate Quade in the incident needlessly, because a few minutes' start was all that Waldstejn required. "Ah, Q," Hodicky said, "let's don't be in *too* much of a rush, huh?" He pitched his voice low so that the prisoners could not hear his hesitation.

Sergeant Ondru's resonant threats from within the liquor store would have covered the words anyway. "Quade, you crap-head," the non-com was bellowing, "if we're not out of here in thirty seconds it'll be Morale Section for you, not just the glass-house. God be my witness, I'll have you *shot!* I know you planned this with him, and you'll by God regret it."

Quade lunged back out of the arms locker as abruptly as he had entered it. He carried a loaded rifle by the handle at its balance. "Pavel," he shouted angrily, "the cutters—I told you to get the—hell, never mind. I'll use this!"

"Hodicky, you little turd!" Ondru boomed. "It's your neck too, I swear on my mother's grave!"

The black-haired private snatched up the tubing

he had carried when he burst in on Waldstejn and his escort. The tube was about half his own height, a thick-walled section from a hydraulic suspension. It had made an excellent weapon; now it served as a crowbar as well.

Quade set down the assault rifle. While Ondru continued to shout threats from inside, the Private slipped his tube through the lock strap. He caught the end of the tube under the edge of the hasp riveted to the door. Using the hasp as a fulcrum, Quade tugged at the tube. Nothing gave. Quade braced his toes under the edge of the door.

"Q," said Private Hodicky, "wait, I'll get the bolt—"

"God *damn* it!" Quade shouted. Tendons sprang into high relief on his throat and wrists. The length of tubing flexed. Seams started at both shoulders of the little man's uniform. Hasp and lock bounced across the room as the rivets gave way. "Mother of God," Quade muttered as he slumped against the door. His lever, noticeably bowed, clanged on the floor.

"Get this *open*, you bastards," called the Sergeant.

Quade stepped away from the container. "Well, *do* it, Pavel," he ordered huskily. "Open the goddam doors."

Hodicky obeyed with a feeling of trapped fear. He spent his life skating over the thin ice of others' angers, others' needs, but this was an open abyss beyond his control or understanding. He pulled open the outer leaf. The inner one sprang back under the weight of Sergeant Ondru. On the floor behind him sat Doubek. The wounded man moaned and held the thigh which none of the three prisoners had thought to bandage. Janko waited hesi-

tantly as well. He was more than willing to let
Ondru carry the burden of informing their superiors of what had occurred.

Ondru's rage was bomb-fierce. It drove him out
into the warehouse with a roar. "*Now* you little
s—" he began. There was a pause. In a wholly
different voice, the non-com continued, "Quade,
what do you think you're doing with that rif—"

Quade shot the Sergeant through the center of
the chest.

The assault rifle had a burst control which disconnected the sear after five shots, even if the
trigger were still depressed. Quade squeezed the
trigger eight times to empty the forty-round magazine. Hodicky screamed and stared at his friend
to avoid seeing what was happening to the Sergeant.

The weapon fired light, glass-cored bullets which
had little accuracy or striking power beyond three
hundred meters. Point blank, as here, the bullets
burned holes in thin steel and pulped flesh like a
sausage mill. Liquor containers burst as the bottles within them exploded. The air stank of alcohol
and blood as Ondru fell backward. Quade's rifle
continued to spit round after round into the cratered chest. The limbs spasmed and the mouth
gaped until a bullet shattered the chin. With horror,
Hodicky noticed the gunman's fingers continued
to pump the trigger even after the magazine had
dropped automatically from the loading well to
make room for a fresh one.

Hodicky nerved himself to touch his friend's
shoulder. "Q," he said, "it's okay now. Loosen up."
His head ached with terror and the muzzle blasts.

Sergeant Ondru's head and shoulders had been
sawn away from his lower body. Liquor was gur-

gling from the ravaged cartons and was beginning to pool around the corpse. Neither Janko nor Doubek had been touched by bullets, though a shard of bottle had torn the seated man's face unnoticed. Both of them stared at the gunman. Their faces and clothing gleamed with their Sergeant's blood.

"Think I'm a faggot, do you, Ondru?" Quade muttered under his breath. He shuddered and turned from the carnage. "Pavel," he said in a normal voice, "I'm going with the Lieutenant. You and him are the only people who ever treated me decent, and I wasn't going to last here without him. You know that." Quade locked a fresh magazine into his rifle, then lifted a canister of ammunition. "See you around," the black-haired man said, using his full hands as an excuse to prevent an embrace.

"Hey, I'm coming too," Hodicky said brightly. "Sure, I'll—I'll come too." He turned to the door.

"Wait a minute," said Quade. He was frowning again. "Sure you want to do that?"

"Gee, it's like you said," Hodicky insisted. "With the Lieutenant gone, our ass was grass for sure."

"Well, get a rifle then," Quade said bluntly. "We'll need it."

"Q, I—" Hodicky began. He stepped into the arms locker, taking a rifle and canister as the others had done. "Let's roll," he said in the cheerful, brittle voice of a moment before. He had not loaded the rifle.

Janko and Doubek watched the two follow their lieutenant. Neither of Ondru's men spoke or moved from the open locker for over a minute after the others had gone.

*   *   *

"The hell that wasn't shooting," Churchie Dwyer insisted. He stepped to the front opening from which Del Hoybrin still surveyed the interior of the compound. "You heard it, Del, didn't you?"

"If you say so, Churchie," the big man agreed.

"It was somebody trying to start an engine," said Bertinelli as he loaded a chip viewer. "Too hollow for a gun."

A visored head thrust through the back curtain. In the voice of Hussein ben Mehdi, it said, "Doc, I want you to be ready in case something blows yet tonight," Then, "Dwyer? Is that you?" Churchie was recognizable with his visor down only because he stood next to the huge bulk of Trooper Hoybrin. It was pointless to direct a request for information to Del, of course. "Why aren't you two at your posts?"

"Sir," said Churchie with the deference which came easily when he was not looking for trouble, "Sergeant Hummel relieved us because of our wounds. They have to be dressed every four hours, you—*what the hell is that?*"

"It's Sergeant Jensen and the gun," said Del as his friend spun to see what was making the noise. The corpsman frowned and stepped forward, trying to get a look past the shoulders of the other men.

Lieutenant ben Mehdi backed out of the medical station to look for himself. The OC shelter was only fifty meters away. He had preferred to walk over with his directions to Bertinelli rather than to put his nervousness on the air. Now ben Mehdi called plaintively, "What are you doing here, Guns? Did the Colonel—?" He stopped.

Jensen braked the gun carriage from the fast

walk at which he had brought it from the head of the valley. The whine of its linkless tracks ceased. The Gunner stood and rotated his seat back into the firing position. "This will do for now," he said to his crew. "Dismount but stay close."

Only then did the blond sergeant walk over to Lieutenant ben Mehdi. He lifted his helmet visor so that he could speak without its muffling. In a very low voice, Jensen said, "Sir, I came in without orders. My boys were out in West Bumfuck and I didn't want them left if folks started climbing trucks in a hurry."

Ben Mehdi grimaced beneath his own face shield, then lifted it. "I would to Allah that Guido—" he began. He broke off when Dwyer called, "Visitors, people."

Someone in Cecach fatigues was panting toward the Operations Center from the direction of the Complex itself. Sergeant Jensen eyed ben Mehdi a moment. The Lieutenant paused uncertainly. Jensen gave a shrill, carrying whistle and unslung his shoulder weapon. "Over here," he called to the newcomer. "And you can leave what you're carrying, just for now."

It was unlikely that, however badly the Colonel's negotiations were going, the indigs were going to send a sapper to bomb the OC. It was also cheaper not to take the chance.

The newcomer dropped his burden. As the man approached at a staggering jog, both ben Mehdi and the non-com recognized him as Waldstejn, the local Supply Officer. He was blown from the half-kilometer run, but the exertion had also damped his nervousness. "Where's the Colonel?" Waldstejn demanded. "Need to see him fast."

Sergeant Jensen eased and ben Mehdi found his tongue. "I thought you might know," the mercenary officer said. "He was with your people." Ben Mehdi gestured toward the Headquarters building. "Or did you come from the warehouse?"

"Mary, Mother of God," Lieutenant Waldstejn wheezed. He bent over with his hands on his knees to draw deep breaths. The assault rifle which he gripped clattered on his right shin. "All right," he said, straightening abruptly. The eyes of the gun crew and the troopers who had been in the medical station were on him. "They're going to kill you, trade your lives for an easy deal themselves. Lichtenstein and the rest."

Churchie Dwyer whistled a snatch of tune under his breath, but no one interrupted.

"You've got outposts north and south on the ridges?" the Federal officer asked.

"North only," said ben Mehdi. "We've loaned your people the gear on the other side."

"Call them in, back here," Waldstejn said. "Like the gun, good, but you'll have to leave it because—"

"Who the hell are you to give orders?" demanded Sergeant Jensen.

"Look," Albrecht Waldstejn pleaded, "I won't have the bastards kill you. For *God's* sake, take my word for it till Guido gets back. I can maybe find you a way out, but we've got to *move!*"

Lieutenant ben Mehdi touched his commo key. "Black One," he called in a voice even tenser than usual under the circumstances, "this is Red Two. Bring in the Listening Post at once. Disable the gear, just bring them in."

"Sarge," called one of the gun crewmen. Two more figures were stumbling across the clear area between the Complex and the bunkers surrounding its perimeter.

Waldstejn stiffened. His goggles were not as efficient as the mercenaries' visors. "There were some guards," he began, "but I don't think they'd—*oh!*" The two short figures in Federal cammies could be only Quade and Hodicky, the *damned* fools. "They're mine," Waldstejn said, "it's all right."

The Privates approached the group around their lieutenant. They were in better shape than the run had left Waldstejn. The Cecach officer ignored them. He said to Jensen and ben Mehdi, "You've got a path through the mines besides the one along the pylons to the west, right?" The mercenaries nodded. "Right," continued Lieutenant Waldstejn. "You can create a diversion around the trucks—"

All the mercenaries stiffened as their helmets popped on the command channel. There were no words over the radio. The night suddenly flashed and crackled with gunfire in front of the battalion headquarters. Troopers spun up the electronic magnification of their gunsights and strained to see why half a dozen assault rifles had fired.

Del Hoybrin had been watching Headquarters even before the shooting. He flipped his face shield up and out of the way to keep it from interfering with his cheek-weld on his gun stock.

"Del!" Churchie shouted beside him.

The open door of the building five hundred meters away was a perfect aiming point. Hoybrin fired a three-round burst. His big body rocked back. Leaning into the weapon, he fired again. The yellow rectangle of light down-range smeared ragged as poured concrete shattered under the impact of the osmium missiles. One of the Federal riflemen

began spraying the night in nervous flickers. His
chances of hitting anything at the range were next
to nothing.

Del Hoybrin fired a third burst before Dwyer
wrestled up the muzzle of the gun. None of the
other mercenaries had tried to interfere. They had
gone flat on their bellies, watching the big man
with a caution born of experience. "Del!" Churchie
screamed, "don't shoot now!"

Albrecht Waldstejn and his men had dropped to
the ground a moment after the mercenaries had
done so. "God help us," the Cecach officer said to
ben Mehdi. "Let's get to your Operations Center
and try to sort this out fast."

"But Churchie," Del Hoybrin was saying in
surprise. "I was watching them. They just killed
the Colonel."

"The lights!" shouted Captain Brionca. "Turn
out the lights!"

Strojnowski might have been soldier enough to
risk it, but he was more interested in rolling outside to learn what was going on. The squad on
guard was from his own Third Company.

Lieutenant Dyk was cowering under the table
with the rest of the officers in Lichtenstein's office.
The young man leaped up with a cry and slapped
at the light switch. Then he stumbled over a chair,
scrambled to his feet again, and reached the panel
in the outer office just as another volley of projectiles ripped through the building. The overhead
lights flickered out as a gush of blue sparks
exploded from the shorted wiring. Dyk spun,
screaming. An osmium projectile punched a neat
hole in the partition wall behind him, having shat-

tered bone on its path the length of the Lieutenant's
outstretched arm.

Lime dust from pulverized concrete roiled in the
air within the building. Papers were burning on a
secretarial desk. Shorted equipment or a spray of
metal ignited by friction had started the fire, the
only illumination remaining in the Headquarters
building. The Federal soldier's return fire had
ceased also. Either the damned fool had emptied
his rifle or he had realized that he did not have a
snowball's chance in Hell of hitting anything at
the range.

The good lord knew why the mercs had stopped
shooting, though.

"Ondru, report," the company commander
growled.

"We got him," Sergeant Breisach's voice responded from the darkness. With his goggles on,
Strojnowski could just make out the forms of the
guards hugging the ground as he was doing himself.
Radios within the building were sizzling with un-
answered questions from the perimeter bunkers.
"Then, blooie!" Breisach went on. "Look, we can't
handle them at the range. You gotta bring in arty
or something, Captain."

As if summoned, the artillery lieutenant scurried through the door in a low crouch. "What
happened?" he blurted. "Did you get—" The young
officer tripped over Strojnowski's outstretched feet.
He pitched forward and screamed. The hand he
had thrown forward to break his fall had splashed
in what was left of Colonel Fasolini's thorax. The
mercenary had worn body armor that might have
saved him at a hundred meters. When the muzzle
flashes were close enough to burn his uniform, the

high velocity sprays had turned fragments of the backplate into missiles themselves. The air stank with the effluvium of ripped intestines.

From inside, Captain Brionca rasped orders slightly out of synch with her words over Strojnowski's belt radio. "All Boxer units!" she was saying. "All Boxer units! Fire at will at any off-planet troops you see. Do not leave your positions. Repeat, do not—"

An assault rifle stuttered briefly, pointlessly, near the eastern interface between Federal and mercenary positions. The bunkers were too widely spaced for the Federal weapons to be really effective. White flashes from the bunker, two guns and then a third, continued for several seconds. The shooting ended in a momentary orange ball in the midst of the muzzle flashes. The thump of the tube-launched mercenary grenade provided a coda to the chattering gunfire.

The artilleryman was trying to wipe his hand in the dirt. "Mortars," he was saying, "high explosives. We'll blast them out from a distance!"

Strojnowski punched his company push. "Ranger Six," he said, identifying himself to his troops, "to max Ranger units. Cease fire! Repeat, cease fire. Unless you've got a target in range and coming at you." The infantry captain paused to let that sink in. Then he added, "If you're fired at by mercs, reply with anti-tank rockets. Don't use your rifles, use rockets and wait till you've got something to aim at."

Screw Brionca and her stupid orders. The 522nd did not have to worry about a job they were not equipped for. All they had to do was to keep the mercs pinned down for the day or less until the

Rube tanks arrived. Strojnowski did not like the deal, but he liked it better than he liked having his ass shot away.

"Come on, Breisach," the officer ordered. "We'll crawl to my bunker and I'll use your squad as a reserve." The rest of the battalion officers could stay inside a targeted building if they wanted. Strojnowski only wished that he could intercept the mercenary communications as they almost certainly were intercepting those of the 522nd.

To the surprise of the infantry captain, the young lieutenant was crawling along beside him. It was probably a lack of any other direction. "But why aren't we shelling?" the artilleryman demanded. "Why?"

"Because we aren't soldiers, we're goddam prison guards!" the older man snapped back. "We're here to keep the contract laborers from breaking out, not to fight a war. The 522nd doesn't have a Heavy Weapons Company. No mortars, no heavy machine guns . . . Hell, the *mercs* were supposed to be our heavy weapons!"

The whole area was studded with bits of smelter slag. It passed unnoticed in the coarse grass, but it gouged at the knees and bare palms of a man trying to crawl across three hundred meters of it. Grunting, balancing discomfort against the risk of a bullet if he stood, Strojnowski said, "I felt sorry for them, getting the shaft that way. But if the Rubes need help executing them now, I'll shoot every off-planet SOB myself!"

CHAPTER FIVE

Two more mercenaries in battle dress scurried to the Operations Center from the east. They were hunched over with caution and the weight of their equipment. Lieutenant ben Mehdi leaned from the shelter to observe them in helmeted neutrality. "Team?" he called in a low voice.

"Black Twelve," one of them panted back. Both troopers knelt, keeping the hump of the OC between them and the distant Complex.

Ben Mehdi nodded agreement. "Right. We're forming up fifty meters north—" he pointed— "in a defile. Mboko's in charge there." He touched his helmet and ordered, "Black One, leapfrog your odd teams. Twelve is in." From the west, the Lieutenant could see two troopers from White Section already scuttling toward the OC.

Ben Mehdi's words echoed within the shelter

because the external speaker of the console was live. Albrecht Waldstejn was not on the Company net. He could no more listen to the necessary cross-talk as the escape plan went forward than could any other member of the 522nd.

And the escape plan was his, almost in its entirety.

"That's forty-two ready to jump," Waldstejn said, "plus us."

"Motion around the truck park," Trooper Dwyer reported from the back arch. "Somebody ought to spray them, one of the shelters do it when the team leap-frogs out."

"White Two," crackled the speaker, "leap-frog your odd teams. Twelve is in."

"That's it," said Sergeant Jensen. "Just the section leaders left. Time for the old girl to keep some heads down."

"Good luck, Sergeant," the Cecach officer said. "Ah, Communicator?" he went on.

Jensen was crawling out of the back arch of the shelter. Churchie Dwyer was there, watching the Complex with his huge partner. He nodded to the Gunner. It was a nasty job. Jensen could have told off one of his crewmen to do it. But by the White Christ of his ancestors, *he* was the Gunner in Fasolini's Company.

Communicator Foyle looked at Waldstejn with a flashing smile. "Sookie, sir," she said.

Waldstejn smiled back, tight as an E-string inside and furious with himself to be thinking what he was thinking about the plump brunette. Not *now*, Mother of God! "Right, Sookie. Time for you to leave too." Switching to Czech as the Communicator rose, the Lieutenant added, "Hodicky, you and Quade follow her. I'll be along in a minute or two."

"We better stay with you, sir," said Hodicky. He looked like a wren caught in a thunderstorm, huddled and miserable. "Not knowing the language and all, you know, sir."

Hodicky did actually have more than a smattering of English, but his friend did not. Private Quade had just finished stuffing a pair of mercenary cross-belt bandoliers with ammunition he and Hodicky had dragged from the warehouse. Ammunition for the assault rifles was packed in the form of loaded plastic magazines. When emptied, the clips were simply discarded like ration envelopes. The pockets of the cross-belts comfortably held pairs of Cecach magazines in place of the individual chargers of the mercenaries' own heavier ammunition. "There you go, Pavel," the black-haired private said. He proudly held out a bandolier to his friend.

A mercenary slid into the Operation Center past Lieutenant ben Mehdi. She flipped up her visor. Waldstejn had not met her before, so far as he knew, but he recognized the Sergeant's voice when she rasped, "I'm Hummel, Black One. You're in charge now?"

"Yeah, I guess I am, Sergeant," the young lieutenant agreed. His muscles were tensing involuntarily. Hussein ben Mehdi cleared his throat and shifted as if moving out of the line of fire. "And until we get our butts out of here, this isn't a democracy." Mother of God! how he wished that Sergeant Jensen were still in the shelter.

"Democracy?" Hummel repeated. "It's about to be a bloody morgue, isn't it? What's going to happen when we're half-way up the ridge—" she gestured; Hussein ben Mehdi flinched back— "and they start popping rockets at us? Think they won't? We need a diversion so they're not searching the north ridge till we're over it and gone!"

"Quade, cool it!" Waldstejn snapped. The little man had set down the bandolier and was watching Sergeant Hummel with a fixed expression. "Let's us cool it too," Waldstejn said to Hummel in a voice that was mild but which trembled. "We're all tight."

The mercenary non-com eyed Quade. Hodicky was gripping his friend's arm and whispering into his ear. Hummel grinned wryly. "I got enough Czech to manage," she said. "It'll keep the pins in if everybody understands."

Waldstejn swallowed. "Right," he said. "We've got a diversion. Sergeant Jensen's going to set his gun to sweep the Complex on continuous fire."

Hummel shrugged. "Won't work," she said. Another trooper stooped at the arch behind her, anonymous behind a lowered visor. Ben Mehdi edged even further away. "They'll volley rockets at the muzzle flashes—*some*-body will. Take all of ten seconds—all right, maybe a minute. How far do we get in a minute?"

"Gun ready," said the console.

"Column ready," it immediately echoed itself in Sergeant Mboko's voice.

Del Hoybrin turned. With his partner and Jensen, he was the rear guard. "You're going now?" the big man said, making a little shoving gesture with his left hand.

"Shut up, Del," Trooper Dwyer muttered. He was veteran enough to guess his chances of coming through the next minutes alive. Despite that, he wanted to get it over with.

Dwyer also wanted to piss; and that, at least, he could do something about. Unsealing his fly, the gangling man began to urinate loudly on a trunk of Fasolini's in the corner of the shelter.

"Lieutenant?" said Private Hodicky. His voice caught in his throat. He cleared it and said, "Q and me've got the uniforms. We could get in and get a couple trucks moving." He nodded back in the general direction of the truck park, north of the Complex proper. "They'd think we were going out that way in—" he swallowed— "instead of like we are."

"That won't work either," interjected Lieutenant ben Mehdi. The console spoke again, but no one in the Operations Center paid attention to it. "The uniform might work if they got close before they were seen, but they'll be tracked all the way from here. Once they're in range, all hell breaks loose."

"Flares!" Lieutenant Waldstejn whooped in sudden delight. Everyone else in the shelter jumped. "Our night goggles! They get overloaded. We set off a ton of flares, all at once, and everybody watching is blinded. By the time they've got their sight back, we're in the truck park!"

"We don't carry flares," Hummel pointed out. "Don't need them with—"

"God *damn* it!" Waldstejn snapped, as suddenly furious as he had been elated. He poked at the communications console, looking for the Send button. "Guns?" he demanded. "Guns? Do you read me?"

"Guns to Red One," Sergeant Jensen replied. "I read you. I'm ready to crank up. Aren't you ready?"

"You'll be given your orders when it's time, Sergeant!" Waldstejn responded in a tone that surprised him more than it did the others around him. Hodicky smiled wanly. "Ah, Guns," the Lieutenant went on, "do you have any illuminating rounds? Flares, you know? We can blind anybody watching through goggles if we can get a light bright enough."

There was a moment's pause on the other end of the connection. Then Sergeant Jensen said thoughtfully, "Flares, no sir. But light, now . . . I can make the whole compound bright as day if that's what you need."

"On the command, then," Waldstejn said. "Pointer Two-One, out." He had used his Cecach callsign without realizing it. It served as well as another.

Waldstejn swallowed. He turned to face the others in the shelter as well as he might and said. "All right. Privates Dwyer and Hoybrin—" he remembered the names; Del Hoybrin had resumed his search of the night and did not acknowledge the compliment, however— "you will act as the rear guard. Lieutenant, Sergeant Hummel—" nodding to them crisply— "you will proceed to the defile. Be ready to move as soon as the shooting starts, just make sure you've left a guide for the rest of us. My men and I will set out now for the truck park. I'll tell Sergeant Jensen to give us light as soon as the—as someone opens fire on us."

"Bullshit," said Jo Hummel

Everyone looked at her. The non-com gave a lopsided smile and went on, "I speak Czech, remember? Trooper Powers and me'll cover your boys." She glanced at the Federal privates with more appraisal than affection. "You'll go take charge of the Company. Like we all decided," Hummel added. She gave a snort.

"Your uniforms won't pass," Waldstejn objected sharply.

"I said *cover*, didn't I?" the Sergeant replied. "If it works, two's plenty to get a few trucks rolling. We got Gun's push—" she tapped her helmet— "and *we* got something that'll do some good when the shooting starts." She gestured in disdain at Waldstejn's slung assault rifle. "Which you sure as hell don't."

"Talk's cheap, lady," said Private Quade. His right hand was caressing the grip of his own rifle.

Hummel turned to him. "Then let's get a goddam move on, trooper!" she said. "Come on, Bunny." Sergeant Hummel began to stride toward the back arch, as squat and as powerful as the weapon she cradled.

Waldstejn caught her by the shoulder. "It's *my* place," he said quietly.

Hummel's anger was fueled by fear of the task she had just undertaken. "Do *I* know the way to this abandoned truck?" she demanded. "Your *place*, Lieutenant, is with your troops. And they're out there goddam waiting for you!"

Waldstejn released her. Del and Churchie backed away to let the three volunteers out to join Trooper Powers. The night covered them from bare eyes in seconds.

"Right," Albrecht Waldstejn said to no one in particular. "We'd better get out to the others, hadn't we?"

* * *

Lieutenant Stoessel sprinted the last twenty meters to the tunnel entrance of Gun Pit East. Since
the lasers were sited at opposite ends of the compound while battalion headquarters was in the
middle, it had been a toss-up which of his guns
Stoessel made for when the meeting broke up in
slaughter. The camouflage pattern of his tunic front
was smeared with sweat and real dirt. The right
sleeve was dark also, with the blood and wastes of
the murdered Colonel.

The gun pit was a figure-eight, partly dug down
and partly raised by a berm of the soil lifted from
the interior. The back lobe of the pit was the fusion bottle itself. It was connected to the gun platform in the larger front lobe by cables which were
virtually bus bars in their construction. At rest, as
now, the laser cannon lay flat beneath the lip of
the berm. Because the energy beam was recoilless,
the tube could be quickly raised and rotated at
any angle through a 360° arc.

The whole crew was present when Stoessel burst
in on them, but none of the gunners showed signs
of wanting to aim the weapon anywhere it did not
point already.

"Abel!" the Lieutenant said to his crouching gun
captain. "I radioed you to open fire on the e-enemy
cannon. You haven't even unlatched the tube!"

Yeoman Abel looked at his commanding officer
sullenly. "We've got power up," he said. The other
five enlisted men stopped talking and eyed each
other or the ground between their boots. That way
they could ignore the laser. "They did a bug-out
before you called us, sir," Able went on. "Besides,
I figure three seconds after that tube—" he gestured with a jerk of his bearded chin— "lifts over

the berm, it takes a round. If she's charged when that happens, there's gonna be shit flying all over here."

"I gave you a direct—" Stoessel began. He paused, then said, "What do you mean, they did a bug-out? They abandoned their cannon?"

"Naw, drove off with it," put in one of the crewmen who was glad of the change of subject. "We heard it."

"You can see for yourself, sir," the Yeoman agreed. "But I think I'd want to keep my head down. We're pretty well off, here— if we don't stir things up," he finished pointedly.

The Lieutenant scowled, first at his men and then at the laser in their midst. The automatic cannon had been emplaced only two hundred meters from Gun Pit East. He *could* take a look and perhaps have something to report to the Major.

Lieutenant Stoessel stepped again to the tunnel which sloped up through the berm. Distant sounds crackled. As Stoessel reached the outer tunnel mouth, he could see muzzle flashes winking near the Complex center. "There's shooting at the truck park," he remarked idly. "I wonder what's happening there?"

He might have chosen his words more carefully if he had known they were going to be his last.

Pavel Hodicky was desperately afraid that he was going to have to kill somebody in the next few minutes.

A little animal peeped and sprang away between the Private's feet. That frightened him back to immediacy. The four-man commando—properly a unit and not an individual designation—was spread in a line fifty meters across. The two Federal privates were in the middle. The mercenaries provided the end posts, checking the alignment and giving brief, angry whistles when one of the indigs straggled.

Face it; when Hodicky straggled, Q seemed to keep station instinctively, since his formal training had been as cursory as Hodicky's own.

They walked in a crouch, almost waddling. None of the four of them was up to crawling four hundred meters, but nature made them hunch over in anticipation of the shots that were certain to come. Hummel had been nonchalant in her brief instructions. The guards would shoot while their targets were well out of range, she had said. Hodicky's brief squint through his night goggles had shown him that the mercenaries were as bent over as the locals they escorted, however.

For the most part, Quade and Hodicky advanced with their goggles up over their foreheads. The promised illumination would otherwise blind them as well as the Federal guards. Afterwards, the deserters could dash forward, mingling with the guard detachment and getting among the trucks in the confusion.

The buildings of the Complex looked a single mass of geological proportions. Only the mercenaries' signals proved to the Private that he was really heading for the truck park. At its fence, he knew, were his comrades of a few hours before—watching his advance in rosy detail through the lenses of goggles he might have issued them himself.

Well, Hodicky couldn't complain. It had been his own idea, hadn't it?

Only Mary and the Saints, let him not have to kill—

The muzzle flashes ahead of him could have been the courting dance of a firefly. The bullets that snapped about his head had nothing of the same innocence. Pavel Hodicky threw himself down, knowing that at least one of his former comrades lacked his own unwillingness to kill.

The shots were Sergeant Jensen's signal. Hummel's call for "Light!" blatted over the radio as the blond man was already swinging onto the gunner's seat.

He had lain beside the automatic cannon lest premature motion bring a volley of fire on him before the commando was in position. The indigs had been willing to let a sleeping dog lie; now they would feel its teeth despite their forbearance.

Right and left pedals controlled the gun's traverse and elevation. Jensen worked them simultaneously while his left thumb flipped the sighting screen to its wide-field, acquisition mode.

The electric motors training the gun whined a friendly, familiar note to the Gunner. The slim barrel dipped only a degree under the lightest of left toe pressure, but the signal from Jensen's right heel aimed it back toward its previous position at the east face of the compound.

Toward, not to. The traversing pedal braked the muzzle to a halt as the mounded berm of Gun Pit East slewed across the sights.

Someone in the mass of buildings to Jensen's right had noted movement at the automatic cannon. An assault rifle began to spit at him from a window of the Complex. At this range, the gunfire was pointless; but the first anti-tank rocket could be only seconds away.

Sergeant Jensen had taken a professional interest in the laser cannon when his own weapon had been sited near it. Now he was betting a number of lives, his own included, that he remembered the lay-out correctly. The protective berm around the gun pit was a full two meters thick at its base. The earth comprising it was loose, however, heaped up by the digging blade and only cursorily stabilized. That would stop fragments and even normal shell fire; but what Jensen had in mind was something else again—or Saint Ultruda save them!

The sight screen zoomed to battle magnification, a three-meter field at this range. The central orange dot was at the base of the rear lobe of the pit. Hoybrin and someone else were now shooting from the Operations Center nearby. Hoybrin for certain, because the weapon was firing bursts. They were trying to suppress Federal gunmen from the Complex who were slashing at Jensen's life.

That did not matter now. All that mattered to the Gunner were the traverse pedal and the red switch under his right thumb. He pressed them together.

The blip of a rocket's sighting flare arched from the Complex toward the mercenaries' lines. Lieutenant Stoessel had just enough time to wonder what had set off the firefight when the sheaf of osmium projectiles plowed the dirt to his left.

The automatic cannon had neither tracers nor need for them. As with the laser itself, what you saw in the sights was what you got. Jensen's burst gouged the berm at a flat angle and at velocities

that made the earth itself a fluid. Jets of dirt were
spurting skyward even as the rounds clanged
against the fusion bottle which the berm had been
intended to protect.

The casing was heavy, even in comparison to the
sudden blows it received; but a hairline fracture
caused a ripple in the magnetic flux within. The
astronomical pressures did the rest.

The blast was in theory not a nuclear explosion,
only a jet of plasma from a relatively small fusion
chamber. The matter of the bottle, the inner surface of the berm, and everything else within either
lobe of Gun Pit East were stripped to ions. They
shot upward like a minor solar flare. Ravaged atoms
gushed up the access tunnel. Lieutenant Stoessel's
body did not so much burn as sublime at their
impact.

Bright as day, Roland Jensen had promised the
new lieutenant. The Gunner was grinning like a
skull as he threw the drive in gear. He cramped
the wheel hard, then jumped out of the saddle.
The self-propelled gun lurched noisily into what
had been the medical station. It crumpled the shelter roof as it passed. Jensen felt that he had to at
least jerk the old girl away from where she had
been targeted, even though he would abandon her
then.

Bright as bloody day!

Jirik Quade was up and running while the ground
still rocked from the explosion. Hodicky scrambled up to follow, pulling his goggles down with
his right hand. He was cursing his friend because
the curses were a normal thing, a frequent thing to

hear, and everything else around him was out of the Hell of his Grandmother's lectures.

The plume of charged vapor still hung over Gun Pit East, far to the left, but it was no longer a blinding flare. Night breezes were cooling and dispersing the pink glow. It was at once the pyre of seven soldiers and the only tombstone they would ever have.

Most of the platoon guarding the park was at the main gate on the west side. There were a number of troops on the north face of the woven-wire enclosure, however, much closer to the mercenary positions. These were the men who had been firing at the commando. One of them continued to do so. His blinded companions huddled at the base of the fence, where even amplified light could not separate them from the humps of earth and rank grass. A single soldier stood erect, screaming and spraying his personal darkness with an assault rifle. The muzzle was pointed up at almost a 45° angle.

The two mercenaries had stayed flat when Quade and Hodicky rose for the final dash. Now their guns cracked in unison. The limbs of the man at the fence splayed as if he had been electrocuted. There was a tiny fleck of light behind him as a projectile clipped a fence wire which was also in its path. The figure crumpled. There was no further sound or movement at the fence.

Quade reached the truck park before his friend did. Hodicky's body had moved at its best pace despite the terror filling his mind, but his lungs burned with exertion. The loaded bandolier was an anchor across both collarbones.

There was more to the operation, however, than the strength and stamina in which Quade excelled

most of the other men in the compound regardless
of size. He had the cutting bar out when he reached
the fence. Instead of using it to slash an opening in
the wire, the black-haired deserter waved it in his
left hand like a saber. His right hand prodded the
night with the rifle he held by its pistol grip, while
his eyes searched for someone to kill. The moonless
sky provided Quade's goggles with only a blur of
pinks and shadows. It had no targets for his
frustration.

The goggles affected depth perception seriously.
Hodicky bounced against the webbing of the fence
an instant before he had expected to reach it. "It's
me, Q—Pavel!" he shouted instinctively as he saw
his friend spin to face the sound. Someone atop
the main powerplant was volleying rockets. The
flare pots left pinkish trails across the sky over the
truck park. Pulverized concrete spewed across the
launching site as a mercenary replied.

Hodicky deliberately dropped his rifle in order
to unsling his own cutting bar. Like much of the
mercenaries' equipment, the principle behind the
tool was very simple. It was a light, narrow saw
with a blade fifty centimeters long. It cut on the
draw stroke, and its teeth coarsened gradually from
the hilt to the tip. The fact that the teeth were
razor thin and almost permanently sharp made
the bar effective whether one needed to cut tissue
or tank armor. The ten-gauge wire of the fence was
more a pressure against the blade than a real obstacle to it.

The little private slashed down, then across and
down again in an arc. Wires quivered discordantly
as a section of fence fell inward. "Come on, Q!"
Hodicky said as he hunched through the opening.

His sleeve snagged and tore unnoticed on a sharp end.

Quade threw down his cutting bar and reached for his partner's weapon. "You forgot—" he said.

From the darkness, someone whispered, "Janos? Is that—?"

The black-haired deserter turned and fired in a single motion. There was a horrible scream, above even the muzzle blasts. As if in echo of the initial burst, a soldier fifty meters away began shooting at Quade's back.

Reflex snatched Pavel Hodicky's hand to his rifle. Instinct froze it there while bullets cracked and sang in parting wires. The Federal soldier was flat on his belly along the fence line, an almost impossible target for Hummel and Powers. They were also prone and two hundred meters away. The mercenaries tried anyway. Truck bodies boomed as they were hit by projectiles that had passed over their intended target.

The Federal gunman was shooting high as well. It was the flash of one of his bullets hitting a post above Quade that snapped the deserter from his revery of slaughter. He whirled away from the screams which a second burst had not silenced. Still firing from the hip, Quade walked his shots into the opposing muzzle flashes. Again he fired until his rifle spat out its empty magazine.

"Come *on*, Q!" Hodicky cried. He ran to the cab of the nearest truck, still clutching his rifle. His trousers were slimed with feces.

"Forty-one," whispered the trooper as she reached Lieutenant Waldstejn. His slap on the shoulder sent her out to join the others who had preceded her, snaking single file behind Sergeant Mboko. This much was easy, though every step chanced a rocket or the fury of the remaining laser. At the ridge line, the risk of fire from the compound ceased, but a false step would shatter both legs on an air-sewn mine.

There were two cleared tracks through the mine belt surrounding the valley: west along the pylons, to permit the trucks to enter and leave the compound; and this one which Colonel Fasolini had decided to clear in case he needed a bolt-hole. The Colonel had not expected the 522nd to turn on his men; but neither had he expected the battalion to hold against a Republican attack. The truck route would become a killing ground for the locals rushing into it—and that, with luck, would have permitted the Company to slip out the side door and regroup.

It is impossible to foresee everything, especially during a war. Troops whose commanders try to provide for the dangers they *do* foresee, however, often are around afterwards to bury the less fortunate.

"That's the last," whispered Lieutenant ben Mehdi. The officer followed the trooper Waldstejn had just clapped forward by rote. "I'll stay and pick up the rear guard."

A rocket corkscrewed overhead, then plunged into the ground a hundred meters away. The white ball of the explosion was momentary but so intense that the shock wave a third of a second later seemed to be an echo. The near impact was chance. The federal soldier who launched the missile had lost control of it either through lack of training or because one of the mercenary rear guard had put a round close enough to the rocketeer to make him drop his controls.

Muzzle flashes lighted the face of the Complex and most of the Garrison Battalion's bunkers. Occasionally a soldier threw the switch on each assault rifle magazine which ignited the bullet jackets in a stream of blue-green tracers from the muzzle. That was rare, however, because it was certain to draw fire from one or a score of his ill-trained comrades. It was impossible to be sure what was going on at the truck park almost a kilometer away.

"Waldstejn?" ben Mehdi said, trying to prompt a response from the Cecach lieutenant.

Albrecht Waldstejn blinked beneath his goggles. Grit scooped from the ground by the near miss was drifting across the men. "Right," Waldstejn said. "Keep your head down." He scrambled off to join the last of the troopers following Sergeant Mboko.

Hussein ben Mehdi watched the firefight, trying to detach his mind from what was going on within the compound. When a stray bullet *brred* overhead, his hand tightened on the sweaty grip of his own grenade launcher. In general, the Lieutenant could pretend that it was a game, a light show.

He risked a quick glance up the way the other had gone. By daylight, they should all be clear, thanks be to Allah . . . and to the path that Fasolini's instincts had provided. "Allah receive you, Guido." the mercenary muttered. "If you were not a saint, then at least at the end you gave as much for your people as the Christ did for his."

*   *   *

Hodicky reached for the truck. Something cracked like a heart breaking on the side of it. That was surely a stray round, but the little private hunched over and ran to the next vehicle anyway.

Although the cargo bay of the ore hauler loomed high and wide behind it, the cab was only a step from the ground while the vehicle rested on its skirts. Visibility from the cab was not a factor since most of the time the vehicle tracked automatically across a line of pylons. For maneuvering in close quarters like the truck park, there were TV cameras at each corner of the cargo bay.

The cab lay-out was simple. Hodicky flipped on the battery switch to energize the controls and instruments. He did not turn on the lights. His goggles and the instrument glow let him see what he was doing well enough without drawing fire. Hodicky had driven induction-powered trucks before—never this big, and never in a lot so tight. But no one was going to complain about scraped metal tonight, the Virgin knew.

The little private twisted the joy stick to align the receiving antenna with the broadcast pylon at the gate. The cab door sprang open. Hodicky screamed and lurched around with his arms thrown up.

"You all right, Pavel?" asked Private Quade. His nose wrinkled. "Jesus Christ, what is it stinks in here?"

Hodicky licked his lips. "Go start the next one, Q," he said. "I'll have this moving in a bit." He could worry about clean trousers some other time.

"Hell, I never drove anything, Pavel," Quade admitted. He turned his head away. "I just came because . . . you could of got hurt."

"I—" Hodicky said. "Keep an eye out." He turned back to the antenna control, making a final adjustment and then pressing the switch that should transfer the vehicle to external power. There was a lurch as the drive fans beneath the bay came on line automatically. The blades began to sing as they ran up to idle speed. "Watch it now, Q," Hodicky warned. He twisted the knob which should increase the power and bite angle of the fans.

The air cushion which the fans built under the skirts lifted the huge vehicle a few millimeters off the ground. It skidded forward, not yet in perfect balance. The left side almost at once scraped down the next vehicle over. Metal screamed.

The would-be driver swore and twisted at the wheel while he fed in more power. He overcorrected and Quade, on the ground, had barely enough time to throw himself out of the way as the right side dragged.

If the wheel were released, the truck would swing itself onto the pylon corridor. It would ignore obstacles in doing so, however, and it would have locked itself against the adjacent vehicles. Hodicky twisted savagely at the wheel again, wondering if the auto-pilot could possibly have done a worse job than he was managing himself.

Part of the distant rear of the cargo bay tore free. The truck lurched ahead. Hodicky released the wheel and felt the vehicle swing with glassy smoothness. The windshield was fogged by acid grime from the smelter, but through it he could see the closed gate a hundred meters away. The rifle of one of the guards there flashed. The entire panel of the truck window disintegrated, spraying the cab with fragments of pin-head size and smaller.

Hodicky threw himself out the cab door. His toe caught on the coaming. The Private tripped and rolled with a skill he could not have managed deliberately. The fans of the truck blasted dust in his face as it slid past. Weeping, Hodicky scrambled to his feet and ran for the shelter of the remaining vehicles. His rifle and bandolier pounded at the bruises they had left when he hit the ground.

No one shot at him as he ran. Quade was hosing the gate guards with bright cyan streaks of tracer, knowing that would keep their heads down—and that it would concentrate what interest remained on him instead of his friend.

A rocket from the Complex hit the rear of the careening truck. There was a white flash that silhouetted the vehicle. The jet of gas and gaseous metal spurted across the empty cargo bay and out the other side in a dazzling spike. The ore hauler shuddered, but its drive units were untouched. The gyro stabilizer had brought the truck back on an even keel when the cab plowed through the gate.

Even empty, the big ore carrier weighed over twenty tonnes. The chain-link fencing was intended to keep humans out, not vehicles in. The guards were caught between Quade's snapping tracers and the onrushing truck. Some of those who thought they had scrambled clear at the last instant were killed by the gate itself. The hinges gave before the locking chain on the other side. The whole construct of steel wires and stiffening bars sprang away from the cab like a huge flail.

The truck staggered, but it surged on through. The right skirt was trailing and a drive fan screamed as it wrapped itself in wire.

Quade fumbled for a third magazine. He paused with his hand in an empty pouch of his bandolier. He looked around for his friend as he resumed the process of reloading, this time consciously. The door of the next truck in the line was open.

The black-haired man ran to the open cab. The truck bay was creased where Hodicky's first decoy had scraped along it. Soldiers in bunkers over a kilometer away were firing rockets into the truck park, acting more from instinct than awareness. Those which were aimed well enough to hit the broad target detonated with hollow booms. That drew additional fire.

"Pavel, come on, for God's sake!" Quade shouted into the truck cab. His left palm rested on the door jamb. He could feel the vehicle quiver as its fans came on. "One was enough! Come on, they're shelling us!"

"Get out of the way!" Hodicky cried. The truck slid forward as he spoke. The gap in the line beside him let the truck swing even as its drive nudged it into motion. Hodicky could not see for his tears, and his mind was filled with the intake roar of the fans.

The side of the ore hauler slapped Quade as he tried to jump away from it. Its pitted surface of steel and paint flakes bit and spun the little man, dropping him in the vehicle's wake. Hodicky, oblivious to that as he was to almost everything else, threw himself out of the cab as the truck picked up speed. As he did so, a pair of rockets from the gate slammed head-on into the cab. Both doors sailed away like bats startled from a cave. The sheet-metal front of the cab ripped upward, tangling the power antenna in shreds.

Only the back-up human controls had been
destroyed. The vehicle did not stop. The detuned
antenna dropped its power beneath the setting
and the vehicle slowed to a trot. As it glided through
the gap torn by the first truck, the sides of the ore
hauler sparkled like a display. Federal soldiers were
firing their assault rifles point-blank into the cargo
bay. The disintegrating bullets blasted holes in the
sides as they hit.

Hodicky picked himself up. He had scraped his
left palm badly on the ground. That pain seemed
to be all he could focus on as he staggered back to
the remaining trucks.

Jirik Quade lay crumpled on the gravel in front
of him. The right sleeve of his uniform had been
shredded from shoulder to wrist along with the
skin beneath. Quade's hand was still locked on the
grip of his rifle.

Hodicky's scrapes and dizziness washed away in
a rush of glacial fear. All external sounds sank to a
murmur as blood roared in the little man's ear-
drums. He knelt and gripped his friend's shoulders
in order to turn him face up. "Mother of God, Q,"
he whispered. "Mother of God!"

"Goddam, that truck hit me," Quade muttered
back. He opened his eyes with a start. "Christ,
Pavel," he said, trying to raise his torso and finding that his right arm did not work. "How long've
I been—*Christ watch it!*"

A Federal soldier had run toward them from the
wreckage at the gate. He had lost his helmet of
ceramic-impregnated thermoplastic, but his rifle
waved at arm's length as he strode. "Hansel!" he
cried, "are you all right?"

Hodicky twisted as he knelt, unslinging his own

weapon. The chill had returned. The Federal soldier was within ten meters. "*Hans!*" the man called again, skidding to a halt.

Hodicky raised his rifle. He froze. Behind him, Quade was trying to reach his rifle with his left hand. The sling was caught under Hodicky's knee.

"You bastard, you killed him!" shrieked the Federal. The muzzle flash of his rifle flared magenta in Hodicky's goggles. An impact sledged the little private backward over Quade.

The Federal's cheeks and eyes bulged momentarily. There was a tiny hole in the bridge of his nose and another, perfectly matching, in the back as he pitched forward.

"You sons of bitches coming or you going to wait for a private car?" roared Jo Hummel as she jerked Quade to his feet. Firing was still general now, but it seemed to be concentrated on the moving vehicles rather than on the truck park itself. Trooper Powers hunched in the angle of a truck body and cab. Her weapon was shouldered and ready for another target.

"Christ, Pavel," the black-haired man cried.

Sergeant Hummel knew that the three of them were in the open. Shots could rip lethally from the darkness before Bunny had a prayer of reacting to the gunners. But Hummel knew also that the deserters had saved the necks of troops they did not know when they started the truck careening westward. The Sergeant reached past Quade to lay her palm on Hodicky's chest. "Hell," she said, "the pump's fine and I don't see any blood. Gimme a hand and I'll carry him."

Quade was too battered to protest as the Sergeant raised his friend for a packstrap carry.

Hodicky's left cross-belt flapped around his knees. Powers stepped to them. She slashed the whole bandolier away with a knife she slid from Hummel's boot sheath. A bullet had struck the bandolier over the deserter's left shoulder. It had disintegrated on and with the two loaded magazines in the pouch. The loaded ammunition was electrically primed. It was as little affected by heat or shock as so much clay. The impact had ripped the tough fabric of the bandolier, however, and it had stunned the man wearing it.

"Well, we bought them some time," Hummel muttered as she handed her burden through the fence to Private Quade. Hodicky was beginning to drool, but he had not yet regained consciousness. "I only hope they know how to use it up there."

The three soldiers looked instinctively toward the northern ridgeline. Its dark silence was the best proof they had that their mission had succeeded.

"The Lieutenant says the lead team's through the mines, sir," Sergeant Mboko reported to Albrecht Waldstejn.

The Cecach officer gave a bleak smile. They were all accepting his leadership as if he had a real rank among them; and as if he knew what the hell he was doing. But one thing the tall officer had learned even before he was conscripted was that crises were best handled by people who were willing to make decisions. Fasolini's mercenaries might have gained only a day of life; but they did have that day over what staying in their shelters would have given them.

Sergeant Mboko was thinking along the same lines. Aloud he said, "I wanted to take a truck. The

Colonel said it'd be suicide. He was right a lot of the time."

After a moment, the mercenary said, "The background on Cecach looked pretty clean. Stalemate at the Front, that's not so bad. Real wackos on the other side, but the Federals who wanted to hire us about as decent as anybody in the middle of a war."

"Old data," said Waldstejn softly.

"Yeah," Mboko agreed, "about a year old. The Rubes got heavy armor, the Front went to hell. And the folks running things in Praha seem to have figured that if they're crazier bastards than the Rubes, then they'll *beat* the Rubes. Wrong both times, I guess. . . ."

From the modest height of the ridge, the two men had an excellent view of what was happening in the valley. There were a few riflemen firing uselessly from the Complex and outlying bunkers. Most of the garrison seemed to be concentrating on lobbing rockets into the two trucks. Both vehicles were beyond the westernmost bunkers of the compound, but only the first was still moving. The damaged second ore hauler had skidded and overturned when a rocket destroyed all the drive fans on its right side. Rounds continued to crash into it one or two a minute, now that it was immobilized. The white flashes reached the watchers in false synchronous with the booming of earlier warheads.

No one could have survived in the riddled cargo bay of the first truck, but Waldstejn thought for a moment that the vehicle itself might drift out of sight along the diminishing pylons. Then there was a hiss unlike anything else that had savaged the valley that night. The laser cannon had lifted from Gun Pit West, and its tube was cherry red.

Mboko cursed and shouldered his weapon. It was a long shot, but a large target and a fragile one.

The Cecach deserter touched Mboko's arm. "Let them," he said. "We're all dead, remember?"

"You know," said the Sergeant, "most times you get a really nasty war, it's planets that a couple different nations colonized together, different planets. You people here— one foundation, everybody Czech. . . . But you managed the job pretty well, didn't you?"

The laser drew a pale line across the night. The beam was pulsed so that metal subliming from the target would not scatter it in a reflecting fog, but the modulations were at too high a rate for human retinas to respond to them. Twenty-five square centimeters of the truck's plating flashed from red to white to black as the metal vaporized and the apparatus within the plenum chamber took the beam directly. Steel burned when severed cables shorted input from the receiving antenna into the hull. The gun continued to play on the glowing wreckage.

"You better go, sir," Mboko said without looking away from the spectacle. "I'll bring in the rear guard, never fear."

As Waldstejn started to move off, he heard the Sergeant say, "Colonel was right a lot of the time. But he still hired us out to these Federal sons of bitches."

CHAPTER SIX

The radioed summons had been to Ensign Brionca's office at the 522nd Headquarters building. Vladimir Ortschugin noticed immediately, however, that the real power there lay with the Republican chaplain. The holes punched during the fighting thirty-six hours before had been patched with plastic sheeting, but the building still smelled of burnt insulation.

For that matter, the Swobodan spaceman caught a whiff of Major Lichtenstein's body also. It hung as an object lesson from the boom of a crane parked just outside. The Major's neck had stretched so that his right boot drew little circles in the dust as his body twisted. Formally, the Republicans had executed Lichtenstein for failing to prevent the loss of much of the mercenaries' valuable equipment. Personally, Ortschugin wondered whether the Republicans would have deemed the offense punishable by death if they had been able to imagine any other use for the fat, drunken Major.

Ortschugin strolled into what had been the Major's office. He bowed and said, "Excellency, I am Acting Captain Vladimir Ortschugin, a free citizen of Novaya Swoboda. I am at your service."

Ortschugin had gained a few hours observation of the men who had conquered Smiricky #4. The Swobodan was aware now that his assumption of 'business as usual' had been seriously in error. Perhaps the very highest officers thought in terms of political and economic realities. Most Rubes, however, were on a mission for their Lord.

The slim, dark Republican officer did not speak. He rose from his chair instead and walked over to the spacer. The Republican uniform was taupe colored, a shade too dull even to be called black. Perhaps at base it was a yellow of infinite drabness, like a mole's hide. The Republican wore no insignia of rank, but Ortschugin did not need Captain Brionca's obvious terror to recognize the man's authority.

The Republican touched the chain which was barely visible at the throat of the Swobodan's tunic. He tugged out the small crucifix attached to it, still without speaking. With a single jerk of his hand, the Republican broke the chain and dropped the little icon on the floor. As his boot ground the silver against the tile, the Republican said, "On Cecach we no longer worship a dead god, Captain. We worship the One Who is Risen. This will be your only warning." He returned to his chair.

The back of Ortschugin's neck was stinging, but he was not sure whether the drops crawling down his vertebrae were sweat or blood. He swallowed to be able to say, "Yes, Excellency, I understand."

"You know your ship has been confiscated for trading with idolators," the Republican said as if he really did assume that would be obvious to the Swobodan. "What will be required to fly it back to Budweis?"

"Well, Excellency—" Ortschugin began.

"I am not an 'Excellency', foreigner!" the Republican officer broke in. "Only our Lord is excellent. You may refer to me as Chaplain Bittman, if you desire."

Ortschugin nodded obsequiously. What he *desired*. . . . But if he were to survive the next minutes, much less lift again from this *damnable* planet. . . . "Yes, Chaplain Bittman," he said aloud. "The hull damage will not prevent us from operating in an atmosphere, though of course we could not, ah, go off-planet under such circumstances." That was a lie—they could work ship in pressure suits if they ever got a powerplant. The discomfort would be a damned cheap price for a return to Swoboda. "But we still need a main fusion bottle. We can't lift on the auxilliary power unit, and we couldn't stay up for more than a few minutes on it alone if we did lift." And that was almost the truth, more was the pity, or the *Katyn Forest* would have been long gone.

"What about the broadcast antenna you rigged?" asked Captain—Ensign, now—Brionca unexpectedly.

The two men looked at her—Bittman in cool surprise, Ortschugin with an expression he prayed did not reflect his horror at the question. "Yes, tell us about that," prodded the Chaplain. "You have fitted an antenna to take you to Praha along the truck pylons?"

"We had, ah, considered, doing that, yes," the spaceman answered carefully. He decided that only the simple truth was going to work. That bitch Brionca was staring at him sullenly. Her uniform looked as if she had slept in it. Her eyes looked as if she had not slept for a week. "The power hook-up proved possible—" they could check the ship and see that— "but there are delays in the alignment controls. The program is simple compared to our ordinary navigational work, of course, but it's very different. . . ." Ortschugin let his voice trail off. Sweat from his forehead made his eyes sting, but he was afraid to raise his hand to wipe them. Saint Nicolas be with us now!

Bittman stood again. He was showing the first signs of real interest since his eyes had stopped measuring Ortschugin for a rope. No one had suggested that the spaceman sit down. His knees were beginning to quiver with the unaccustomed brace in which tension was holding him. "You mean that your whole huge starship can run on broadcast power in good truth?" the Chaplain demanded.

"We, ah, thought perhaps so," the Swobodan agreed. "We didn't test it before the Complex, ah—"

"Yes, was liberated," Chaplain Bittman finished for Ortschugin. He added, in a voice which had no more expression or mercy than the clack of a trap closing, "I advise you not to 'test' the system now, either, Captain. The idolators are attempting to make a stand along the line between here and Praha—they know how important it will be to the future of the Return to God. Elements of the three armored regiments are pushing them back. Major elements." Bittman permitted himself a smile at something he probably thought was funny. "What do you suppose the concentrated fire of, say, four Terra-built tanks would do to the hull even of your starship, Captain?"

"We're at your service, E-Chaplain Bittman," the spacer said through dry lips, "but the pylons do lead only west from here."

"For the moment!" the Chaplain retorted with a zeal that shone across his slim, swarthy face. "Do you know why this line is crucial to the Lord's work, Captain?" he demanded rhetorically. "Because the fusion plant here, for the mining and smelting operations, was more than big enough to energize a broadcast system as well. That means that when we complete a temporary link from our own system east of Bradova, we have a channel for the heaviest, bulkiest supplies straight to the idolators' capital! Our armor is the head of the spear plunging into the heart of schism and idolatry!"

For the moment, Ortschugin's mind made of him an engineer again and not merely a victim. He understood the situation perfectly. Pylons were easy enough to raise and align. They were, after all, little more than lattices with two pairs of antennas. The lower alignments beamed power to whatever vehicle was equipped to receive it, while the upper alignments charged the system itself. Cutting a pylon would prevent vehicles from proceeding until the gap was repaired, but the other parts of the system would continue to function.

If it were energized from both sides of the gap.

Republicans and Federalists both had criss-crossed their sides of the Front with branch lines to supply their troops. The power and load capacity of the branches was limited, however. The working, full-scale fusion plant of Smiricky #4 could very well tip the scales. The next Republican thrust would not outrun its supplies and so be contained, the way previous victories had been.

Ensign Brionca understood also. She was looking at her hands, interlaced on the desk in front of her. Her fingers were not moving, but each nail left a bloodless white halo on the back of the hand where it rested. For the first time, Captain Ortschugin felt a twinge of sympathy for her.

"Well, that's good news—that we'll be able to repair your vessel," the Republican chaplain was continuing briskly. "But that was only one of the things we needed to discuss with you." He sat down. His voice was cool again, his face composed. Bittman had become a human being who no longer wore the mantle of the Lord. "I am informed that you had personal contact with the mercenaries who were stationed here and with the—" He paused, with his mouth quirked in irritation.

"The Supply Officer," Ensign Brionca said. She did not look up. "Lieutenant Waldstejn. Albrecht Waldstejn."

"Yes, the Supply Officer," the Republican agreed with a sharp glance at Brionca. He turned his attention to the spaceman. "What do you know about their intentions, where they planned to go?"

Ortschugin's face went blank in surprise. "Go?" he repeated. "Well, Praha, I suppose. . . . But good Christ, you don't mean that—"

"Never curse again on the soil of Cecach!" Bittman said.

Ortschugin nodded and swallowed. "Yes, Ex-C-

Chaplain. I, ah, I was very surprised that any of the—of them had survived. We watched the trucks being blasted on our screens, you see."

"There was no one in the wreckage," the Ensign said dully. "No sign of anything human, not even a driver. They all walked out while we were shooting at empty trucks."

"Yes," said the Chaplain with another look of appraisal, "we may have executed Major Lichtenstein more painlessly than his actions deserved. But as for you, Captain Ortschugin—" the voice was the voice of a computer, balancing accounts for the Lord— "I would not have you think that this is a minor matter, a few heretics. We *will* find these—persons, with the Lord's help. Even now we are searching their most likely hiding place. If you can help us, well and good."

Like a yo-yo, Ortschugin thought as the Chaplain rose again, but there was no humor on the spacer's face or even on the surface of his mind.

"If you know something of their intentions and you do not tell us," Bittman continued, his face like wood and his voice like steel, "then be assured that the prisoners we take will speak, will tell us everything they know before they die. If you have hidden anything from us, you will join those you tried to protect."

"I know nothing of their plans," the Swobodan said. He cleared his throat. "I didn't know they *had* plans, and I thought they were all dead." He paused. Then he added, "I suppose that was right, wasn't it? They are dead, Waldstejn and the rest. They just don't know it yet."

* * *

"*Christ*, what a place to be buried," muttered Churchie Dwyer.

"I didn't think there'd be whores," Del Hoybrin agreed sadly. Even his long-time comrade had to turn to be sure that the big man was serious.

Before the outbreak of fighting, ore from Pit 4B had been rich enough to employ eighty to a hundred miners. A branch line connected the pit with the truck route between Praha and Smiricky #4. A line directly to the smelter complex would have been shorter, but there were two severe ridges in the way. Loaded trucks did not like hills. Neither did Churchie, but nobody was asking him. . . . The muscles of the veteran's shins burned with climbing as badly as if they and not his back had been broiled two days before.

The pylons leading south-west toward the main line flared their bract-like antennas not far above the scrub which had recovered most of the area. "The old man was really pissed when they dumped the truck here," Pavel Hodicky remarked shyly. "I can see why, now. Even if everybody in the convoy was asleep, they should've heard the branches hitting the trucks, shouldn't they?"

Dwyer grunted as the trooper ahead of him released one of those branches. "Hell," he said, "Lichtenstein was always pissed. Pissed on brandy." His voice changed, taking on a reverential note which was blasphemous when applied to the images Churchie polished in his mind. "I know just how to sweat that brandy out of him, too. Sweat the marrow right out of his bones, for what he did to us."

"Ah, I meant the Lieutenant," Hodicky explained. "*He* was our boss." He squeezed Quade's shoulder, trying to bring the black-haired man into the conversation.

The four of them, two veterans and two deserters, had been together since the escape. By the time Sergeant Hummel's commando had stumbled back to the Operations Center, the 522nd's aimed fire was concentrated on the truck line westward. All a rear guard could do then would be to draw the indigs' attention to the real escape route. Del and Churchie had joined their section leader unharmed. A rocket had sailed over them to demolish the front of the shelter, however. The Company's cone-bore weapons had no true muzzle flash because the propellant was fully consumed in the barrel. After continuous fire, though, a miasma of faintly-glowing sabot material had drifted in front of their position. It was that which had marked them for a Federal rocketeer who was a damned sight better than belonged in the 522nd.

Well, so were Quade and Hodicky in their ways, though that black-haired runt gave Churchie the creeps when their eyes met.

The company was straggling down to the over-turned truck. It loomed out of the brush like a fish cast up with other flotsam by a high tide. Troopers were clambering over the vehicle. At its side stood the new command group. Sergeant Jensen was already leading his small section toward the build-ings at the pit head. The Federal lieutenant was obvious for his sand-mottled fatigues among the woody blurs of the mercenaries around him. A bloody supply officer. Well, Mrs. Dwyer hadn't raised her sons to get their heads blown off like generally happened to leaders in this business. Churchie didn't give a hoot in Hell who was in

charge, as long as they knew what they were doing.
Officers who put men and bullets in the same
category of fungible goods did not last long in
mercenary units.

One of them had not lasted through his first
firefight when he commanded Churchie Dwyer.

"Suppose there's anything worth having in the
buildings?" the veteran asked, nodding through a
gap in the brush.

"Doubt it," Hodicky said, glancing to the side
also. He was enough shorter than Dwyer that he
could not see the pit head at the moment. From
the hilltop, six grueling hours before, however,
they had all gotten a glimpse of the shaft cover
and the paired barracks. While the mine was in
use, the valley was defoliated periodically just like
that in which Smiricky #4 lay. Now from an angle,
a sea of brush lapped the roofs. The regrowth of
the brush was taller though still less dense than
some of what the Company had just marched
through miserably.

Between lyceum English and the blend of Slavic
languages Dwyer had picked up during a life of
slaughter and chicanery, the two men could com-
municate fairly well. Hodicky was pathetically
grateful for the attention. The chance to actually
give the veteran useful information was a delight.
"The place was abandoned two, three years ago,"
he explained. "There was still ore, but they couldn't
keep workers. They'd bug out over the next ridge
where there's a big farm, ride back to Praha in
produce trucks. Or if they were Rubes, and a lot of
them are sentenced to the mines instead of—well,
sentenced to the mines . . . some of them would try
to slip across the Front."

The little man grimaced. He had known a few Reformed Brethren in school, though his home neighborhood had been almost solidly Catholic. The Rubes were all crazy, besides going to Hell for sure when they died. "They stationed troops around the Complex," Hodicky continued, "that's what we were doing there. But it wasn't worth it for the outlying pits, it'd take too many guards for how much they were getting out of them."

Waldstejn had often lectured his two subordinates in the warehouse for lack of anyone else in the 522nd for him to talk to. Hodicky, nearly as lonely himself, had listened to his present benefit.

They were close enough to the truck now that the press of troops standing around it hid more of the vehicle than the foliage did. The stream down the middle of the valley could be heard just beyond. "Well," said Churchie Dwyer, "there might at least be some booze in there, right? Only fair, after this goddam hike that we ride back—"

And then, with reflexes that not even the thought of liquor had dulled, Dwyer was clearing his weapon.

"Well, nothing structurally wrong," Lieutenant Waldstejn said. The drive fans rotated freely under the impulse of Sergeant Mboko's hand.

The convoy had been reversing manually in the dark, and one of the vehicles had managed to slip its skirt over the skirt of the next ahead. Because the branch to 4B had less than half the available power of the main line, the fans had not responded as the driver had expected when he tried to correct the tilt. The whole business had demonstrated

an ineptitude striking even for the Transport
Service.

Now, though, as dusk blurred the far slope to
gray suede, there was a chance that the accident
would save everybody in the Smiricky garrison
who deserved saving.

"What's it loaded with?" asked Lieutenant ben
Mehdi. The voices of troopers echoed from the
back of the vehicle.

"Hey, everybody out!" ben Mehdi added. "I don't
want people screwing around when it may be stuff
we need. Bastien—" he waved to a Leading Trooper
in Mboko's section— "get your team together and
start off-loading the cargo."

"It was all supplies for the Complex, so I wasn't
really concerned," said Waldstejn, walking toward
the back himself. Sergeant Jensen had gone off to
find a cable to right the truck. The other three
mercenary leaders appeared to drift with him.
"From the codes on the manifest, it wasn't food,
dammit. Probably drill bits for—"

"Jesus Christ, *watch that!*" screamed Sergeant
Hummel as two soldiers swung a case from the
truck to the ground. "That's explosives!"

The packing case was banded with gray plastic.
It hung from the fingertips of the men who had
just released it. All their efforts could do was to
drag them after the case. It hit the ground with a
thump and a spurt of dust. There was dead silence
around the vehicle.

"Well," said Lieutenant Waldstejn testily, "I don't
know what the problem is. They weren't going to
pack detonators in with the explosives, after all."
Tense faces loosened as the Cecach officer stepped

to the case and rubbed grit from its warning label with his open palm.

Johanna Hummel looked a little embarrassed also. Without hesitation, however, she said, "Lieutenant, I've been places where they tried to stabilize nitrogylcerin with mica. When I saw the red star—" she nodded at the label—"I didn't wait around."

"Well, on Cecach we use plastic explosives," Waldstejn retorted defensively. "We're civilized, even if we don't have all the high tech electronics—" He stopped and turned back to Hummel. "Forgive me, Sergeant," he said. "You were obviously right. And if we're civilized, then the way we've treated you and the Company gives little enough proof of it."

"Well, we still need to get it the hell out of the truck, don't we?" remarked Sergeant Mboko. "It's going to be a bitch to right anyway." In a louder voice he ordered, "Carry on, Bastien, but make a chain, will you? Don't just toss the stuff around like so many sand bags."

"Ah, Sergeant Hummel," Waldstejn said, "start your troops cutting brush on the far side of the truck." The Cecach officer forced himself to face Hummel. He felt awkward about giving orders to any of the mercenaries, but it had to be done—for all their sakes. Hussein ben Mehdi and the two male sergeants made it easy with an acceptance that met him more than half way.

Jo Hummel made nothing easy. Her attitude was a challenge, while her sex—and her apparent sexual preference—aggravated Waldstejn's discomfort. Now she said, "Look, Lieutenant, I hope to God you don't think you can turn this low

crap—" she waved a hand— "into levers to help
pry the truck up with. My section's tired. Since
there's no straight branches as long as your dick, I
don't see—"

"I believe, Sergeant," Waldstejn interrupted,
grasping the nettle, "that we can wedge a mat of
brush under the side as soon as we get it off the
ground. That way if the cable slips, we don't start
over from the beginning. Now, if you'll give that
order, I want to talk with you in private." He
jerked a thumb to the side, away from the vehicle
and the troops around it.

Hummel pursed her lips. Beside her, Trooper
Powers squatted on the ground. She had taken off
her helmet and was kneading her temples wearily
through her bright blond hair. "Yes sir," Hummel
said. She raised a finger to key the radio.

The reconnaissance drone, jinking around brush
scarcely three meters above the ground, sailed over
them like the first of the shells it surely presaged.

Trooper Herzenberg's light-wand trembled, throwing the shadow of the mine elevator over the far
wall in a quivering circle. She was exhausted with
the long march. Sight of the cable they had been
sent for brought no elation, only a shudder at the
new job it presented. "Guns," she called, "here's
one that's still up. Want me to climb out and cut
loose the cage?"

There were three shafts at the pit head for reasons which no one in Jensen's section could fathom.
All three were covered by a single high, sheet-
metal building over fifty meters long. Two of the
elevator cages were at or near the bottom of their
shafts. The third, which Herzenberg had been sent

to check, had a winding drum full of cable. The newly-recruited trooper still found the difficulties attending the mass of braided steel to be insoluble.

Guiterez strolled over to her before Sergeant Jensen himself arrived. The big building was unlighted except for what entered through rust holes and the pairs of windows high in either roof gable. To eyes adapted to the daylight outside, the small patches of brightness were more dazzling than useful. Guiterez took the dim light as an invitation to lay his hand on Herzenberg's solid hip. The gesture was more of a caress than a pat. The female trooper was almost too tired to bat him away, but she twisted and the butt of her slung weapon cracked Guiterez across the knuckles.

"Hell, honey," said the veteran, ignoring the rebuff, "you don't need to risk that sweet little ass of yours." He knelt, resting his gun barrel on the shaft railing.

"Hold up, Tilly," Jensen replied on the radio. "I'll take a look at it." The whisper of his words followed their radio shadow through the air of the big room.

Guiterez flipped the holographic sight picture up to full magnification. The braided elevator cable shimmered at an apparent fifteen centimeters from his right pupil. Four orange lines rayed from the center. The greatest advantage of the electronic sight over an optical one was that there was no tube for heavy recoil to slam against the shooter's brow ridge.

The cable quivered across the field of view despite Guiterez' attempts to steady it. The picture slowed as he took a deep breath.

"Look," Herzenberg said, "Guns says—"

The shot blasted. There was a momentary fluorescent tremble of sabot material and a flash from the cable. The needle-slim projectile was far too small to sever a one-centimeter cable. Instead, it drilled a neat hole which made no significant difference in the strength of the multiple, redundant strands.

"God *damn* it, Dog," one of the approaching crewmen shouted, "will you stop clowning around?"

"Well, I thought—" Guiterez said, standing up sheepishly. He lowered his weapon and massaged his shoulder.

"If you'd thought," said Sergeant Jensen harshly, "you'd have known we could do without the last—" he eyed the angle of cable from the take-up drum, through the support pulley, and down again to the elevator itself— "four meters with what there is on the drum." The tall section leader reached up with his cutting bar. He positioned it carefully on the highest part of the cable he could reach with his hip supported by the guard rail. Then he slashed downward and parted the cable with a single stroke. The short end of the cable flew up with a twang of released tension. The cage dropped a centimeter or so before its automatic braking system locked it to the guide rails with a horrible scrunch.

"That," said the Sergeant-Gunner, "is what you'd have done if you'd thought." He was taking quick breaths which belied the apparent ease of what he had just done. Almost anyone else in the unit would have needed several strokes to cut the braided steel. "Now," Jensen continued, "you and Herzenberg cut through the axle on both sides." He tapped the drum. It rocked a little now that its ratchet no longer supported the weight of the elevator. "We'll roll the bastard down the hill and save ourselves the trouble of dragging the cable."

There was a shot, then a crackling volley from outside the shed. The veterans slipped their weapons into their hands. Herzenberg followed suit a moment later.

"Guns to White One," Jensen called on the command push. "Give me a sitrep."

Instead of the requested situation report, there was an crackle of static and a few words in what might have been Sergeant Mboko's voice.

The Gunner looked around at the sheet metal and dim tracery of girders surrounding them. "We've got to get outside to hear anything," he said. "You two—" he pointed to Guiterez and the newbie— "get cracking. We may need the truck ready yesterday if somebody's caught us." With the other two members of the gun crew at his heels, Jensen began sprinting for the distant door.

Herzenberg and Guiterez looked at one another. Swallowing, they laid down their guns and unclipped their cutting bars. As their blades rasped against the axle in distinct rhythms, the firing beyond the walls ceased.

The first trooper to fire at the reconnaissance drone missed by a country mile. The drone had a three-meter wingspan and a speed of less than a hundred kph—but it was as unexpected as a bomb in a flower basket. Satellite recce was impossible amidst laser cannon and stratosphere-launched penetrators. Satellites became orbital junk within minutes of starting their first pass over hostile territory. High altitude aircraft were in an even worse plight.

But a vehicle which whirred along near the ground, tacking often and randomly as it ran its programmed course, was preserved by terrain irregularities from the weapons that wrecked its higher-flying brethren.

The drone was powered by an almost silent high-bypass turbofan. The intake cowling looked large above the slim, armored cigar carrying the fuel and instrument package, but the engine had been deliberatedly understressed in the expectation that it would pick up trash and bullets in the normal course of its existence. Still, the drone was slow enough that almost anyone in the Company could have demolished it, despite its twitching changes of direction, if there had been a clear field of view. The trooper who glanced up to see the rotor sailing toward his face at a hundred klicks went straight over on his back. For navigational purposes, the drone treated the soldiers as if they were bushes. The drone lifted to clear the truck behind him as it would have cleared the man himself—by a meter. His shot was scarcely into the same sector of sky as the fog-gray wings that flashed above him.

"Maria!" Waldstejn blurted as the drone flicked overhead. Around him more experienced troopers were snatching at weapons whose slings were entangled with the straps of cast-off packs. Shots thrashed the brush as the drone skipped away downstream. Then somebody planted a boot in the small of Waldstejn's back and thrust him out of the way without ceremony.

Private Quade, fifty meters away with the last of the Company, had more warning than the soldiers around the truck, and his assault rifle could spray rounds toward what seemed a hopeless target for

aimed fire. The right wing lifted as the drone
banked left, its body out of sight below mounds of
coarse scrub. The gray-brown camouflage mottling
of the upper surface was suddenly puckered by
three bright specks—holes punched by Quade's off-
hand burst. The right wingtip dropped and the left
one rose, further away as the drone threaded its
way out of the shot-spitting pocket. It was effectively undamaged, and no further shots could be
expected to—

A gun went off directly above Albrecht Waldstejn's
head. He twisted on the ground to curse the shooter
who was both wasting ammunition and threaten-
ing to deafen him. Out of the corner of his eye,
Waldstejn saw the drone again. It was flipping
skyward, end over end, in a spray of sparks and
fuel which then ignited in an orange flash. A projectile had coursed the cylindrical body the long
way, taking no more account of the armor than it
had the brush through which it had drilled to
reach its target. The drone spun, shedding its wings
as it did so. Open-mouthed, the Cecach lieutenant
watched Iris Powers put a needless second round
through the center of the fireball. The drone blew
up on the ground, another flash above the scrub
and a pillar of black smoke.

Powers began to switch magazines. She had
braced her trim buttocks against the top of the
truck's plenum chamber when she shot. By leaning forward at the waist, she had avoided having
her shoulder broken between the recoil and the
immobile mass of the truck.

"How in the hell did you do that?" Waldstejn
demanded as he got to his feet. "It was out of
sight—the body of it, I mean."

The section leaders were still shouting into their radios to stop troopers from firing toward the smoke.

Powers blushed. A wisp of blond hair curled from beneath her helmet and across her cheek. "From where the wing was, the body had to be—where I aimed," she said. She spoke so quietly that Waldstejn had almost to read her lips since the shooting had partly deafened him.

"Goddam good work, Bunny," said Sergeant Hummel as she hugged her friend. Powers was slipping two loose rounds into the magazine she had just taken from her weapon. "I think we're clear, Lieutenant," Hummel continued. Her tone was businesslike but no longer hostile. "We're low enough here—" she gestured in the direction of the stream and the fuming remains of the drone—"that it can't have been in radio contact with its base when Bu—Trooper Powers hit it." Hummel and Waldstejn exchanged tight smiles. "So they don't know we're here."

"Well, we may not be so lucky the next time," Waldstejn said. "Pick the six best shots in the Company and put them on look-out until we get moving." He smiled again, his lips as taut as his guts. "And Private Quade, he should be among them. Mboko, let's get moving on this truck. We need—"

Waldstejn fell silent. Soldiers were throwing themselves down. And after surviving the bombs that had hit Smiricky #4, even an ex-Supply Officer could guess the meaning of the howling from the western sky.

*   *   *

Horobin had time to slip the glossy pornography under a stack of log books when Director Piccolomini opened the door. He did not, however, have time to scan his instruments before his superior could do so. "Everything normal, sir," said the Reconnaissance Technician, taking a chance that would have paid off nineteen times out of twenty. His blood in his ears roared against the purr of the score of monitors in the room with the two men.

Director Piccolomini's face darkened to a shade in ugly contrast with his taupe uniform. He pointed at the inked tape curling from one of the top row of monitors. Peaks jabbed at five minutes intervals against the pre-printed time scale along the edge. There was no peak during the latest six minutes. As the Director of Reconnaissance and his subordinate watched, the tape continued to crawl out of the monitor with only the flat line that indicated no signal had been received from the drone keyed to that machine. "What do you mean *normal*, Technician Horobin?" Piccolomini demanded.

"I—" Horobin stammered. His skin prickled with sweat, as if Piccolomini were a furnace and not a short, balding man.

"Well, do your *job*, you fool!" Piccolomini shouted. "You only have two drones out. Surely you know what to do if there's an anomaly on one of them!"

Horobin had not bothered to read the glassine-covered Special Procedures sheets when he took over the watch. Normally the trailer housing the monitors was the quietest, most private place in General Yorck's headquarters. Now the Technician fumbled for the sheet marked Monitor 7, feeling as if he were about to melt away and wishing to the crucified Lord that he could. He turned to his superior. "It say—" he began

"Don't tell *me*, you idiot!" Piccolomini cried. "Do it! *Do it!*"

The handset slipped from Horobin's fingers when he picked it up, but on the second try he managed to punch the correct combination into the key pad. Reading the data through the glassine and the blur of perspiration clouding his eyes, the Technician said, "Echo to Landseer."

"Go ahead, Echo," replied the artillery controller through a burst of intervening static.

"One of our drones has failed to report in segment Apache," Horobin continued. "That is, ah—yeah, Apache. Execute Apache soonest."

"Roger, execute Fire Order Apache," buzzed the controller's voice in apparent disinterest. "Landseer to Echo, out." The speaker clicked and went dead.

"Well, aren't you going to log it in, Technician Horobin?" Piccolomini asked. "One of your drones has disappeared while flying a high-risk pattern, hasn't it? Do I have to tell you *all* your duties, man?"

Dear God, if you'll only get him out of here, the Technician thought, I'll make it up to you. I *swear* it. And he slid out the log book, having forgotten completely what he had hidden beneath it only seconds before. The photographs flopped to the floor, glossy side up. The blonde woman of the top one appeared to be smiling, though it was difficult to tell since most of her mouth was hidden by the labiae of her brunette companion.

Piccolomini looked from Horobin to the photographs. The Director's face momentarily relaxed from anger to puzzlement. His mind was struggling to find a present referent for the picture, as if it were an enlargement of the internal structure of a molecule.

The expression that replaced puzzlement would have been suitable for someone who had stumbled upon a pack of dogs devouring an infant.

Technician Horobin felt faint. He was holding himself in a tight brace and vainly willing an end to his vital functions. The trailer shuddered under the hoarse blasts of the alarm the Director had pressed to summon a squad of the interior guard. "Is this how you serve your Lord?" Director Piccolomini shouted. "Swilling the foulest poisons of the adversary while the enemies of the Lord's Church sweep clear of his vengeance? Do you know what this means, Horobin? It means death! Death!"

The tape from Monitor 7 was still flat. A series of peaks sprang up on the other working monitor, however. It was keyed to a drone with the column advancing toward Praha. It had picked up the first salvo of the battery executing Fire Order Apache. Six twenty-centimeter shells were in flight toward what Republican analysts had determined to be the most probable hiding place along the segment of its path where the drone had disappeared.

"Death!" Piccolomini repeated.

The bars sang against the axle. It was awkward cutting up from the bottom, but otherwise the weight of the reel bound the notches against even the ultra-slick sides of the bars. Between strokes, Guiterez panted, "I don't know where you get off on this high and mighty crap. Don't I helped you? Girl, you don't know shit when you came here. Me and the boys, we save your ass a lotta times, a lotta times. So what's the harm you give us the time, huh? You give us the time, we give you the time."

Herzenberg had closed her eyes, as if that would somehow lessen the effort of sawing. Her breath burned her throat, and her voice caught the first time she tried to speak. "The only time I want from you," she said, "is time to myself. Goddammit, Dog, if I was looking for a dick I'd have—"

"Christ Jesus, get clear!" blasted Sergeant Jensen's voice from their radios.

Both troopers dropped their cutting bars and turned. The tall section leader stood in the doorway, silhouetted by the outside light. Jensen's face was hidden. His voice held the horror of his realization that Guiterez and Herzenberg would not have been able to hear the sound of incoming shells as those outside could.

A rosette opened in the roof of the great shed. For a microsecond, the interior blazed with six clean shafts of sunlight. Then the salvo detonated.

Without specific reconnaissance—the data the drone would have broadcast if Trooper Powers had not shot it down—Republican intelligence units had no way of knowing about the overturned truck and the troops clustered around it. They did have pre-war maps and imagery from the last minutes before the satellites spilled down in gouts of fire, however. From these materials, spurred by the chill, righteous fury of General Yorck, they had plotted likely escape routes for the mercenaries; suitable search patterns for the drones which would track them down like the beasts they were; and probable shelters from which the pursued might ambush a drone before it could report them.

Pit 4B had been one of those shelters.

The shell that went off in an air burst on the ridge girder perversely saved Trooper Herzenberg's life. The high-capacity shell ripped its casing into a sleet of fragments that seemed hideously dense; but the pattern was spherical and Herzenberg, fifteen meters beneath its heart, was missed by any shrapnel large enough to be lethal. The shock wave flung her down in a red blur—the flash of high explosive and the blood surging in the capillaries of her eyes.

The shell that lanced into the ground beside the mine shaft did not, as a result, cut the trooper in half on its way.

Earth and steel gouted across the huge mine shed, red flashes and the reeking black smoke of combustion products swaddling the fires that gave them birth. The shell that knocked Herzenberg to safety rolled back the roof in a thirty-meter ulcer. Bare girders sagged with the ends of the ridge pole, saved from collapse by the fact that their burden had been stripped away from them.

Someone was screaming. After an instant of disorientation, Herzenberg became sure it was not herself. She opened her eyes.

The cavity in the roof was no bar to the sunlight, but smoke and dust swirled surreally over the skeletal girders. It blurred and scattered the twisted scene below. The elevator cage was warped. The shaft on which it stood had lost all definition on two sides to a shell crater, but the tubular frame of the cage had not offered much purchase to the blast. The flat, heavy ends of the cable reel had caught the force squarely, however.

When the shock wave hit it, the reel had torqued

and snapped the axle where the troopers' cuts had weakened it. It now lay up-ended across both of Guiterez' legs.

Herzenberg wobbled to her screaming companion. She was obscurely troubled to find herself five meters from where she had been during the last moment she could remember. Nothing was clear in her mind or her vision. Grit and long-chain molecules racked her lungs even more than the sawing had.

Upright, the drum was as tall as the stocky woman. It was tilted by the flesh it crushed beneath it. Herzenberg strained to tip it clear, bloodying her hands on frayed strands of the cable. The reel shuddered. Guiterez' mouth closed and his eyeballs rolled up as he fainted. Weeping with frustration, Herzenberg looked for a lever. She found her companion's weapon. She thrust the barrel under the drum and pried with the stock. The light barrel shroud crumpled onto the diamond core.

"Get out of here!" someone shouted. "Christ Jesus, get out!"

Herzenberg did not look around. Tears of rage and effort blinded her. Her brain was not capable at the moment of processing further information anyway. Sergeant Jensen surged around her. He gripped the gun butt with one hand. With the other, he plucked the woman away for all her hysterical determination could do to hold her to the lever.

The trooper fell backward as her sergeant straightened. His hair was a sun-struck halo rimming the gray metal of his helmet. The dense plastic gunstock sheared with a crack like nearby lightning.

The reel began to topple away from the man it imprisoned.

The roaring in Herzenberg's ears was not blood but the second incoming salvo.

The last image that Herzenberg's eyes carried with her into blackness was that of flame fountaining from a shell burst. At the apex of one red tendril, silhouetted against the sky, was a ball which had recently been a human head.

"Fucking A," muttered Marco Bertinelli as he started to run up-slope. The pit head buildings were in tatters. The end of one barracks was ablaze, and a sooty pall rippled turgidly over the shed covering the shafts. Someone in the gun crew was screaming over the radio for a medic, though.

"Team One to me," Sergeant Mboko ordered, jumping up as well. "We're going to get them out and get our own butts out of there too." He began to stride after the Corpsman. His gun was in his hand instead of being slung.

"Black Section, off and on," said Jo Hummel. The high points of her bandolier had been frayed and dirt-smeared by the speed with which she had hit the ground moments before. "We'll take up a cover position on the next ridge and wait for White. Move it!"

Fire Order Apache had been a simple Battery Three—three shells from each tube of the battery, with no delays or follow-up shellings scheduled. But no one in the Company knew that. Every move had to be made in the gut-crawling awareness that Rube artillery had the area targeted.

"Wait, dammit!" said Albrecht Waldstejn desperately. "Mboko! Cancel that, we need the truck clear now!"

The black sergeant ignored the call. Half his section was beginning to follow him as ordered. The troopers glanced at one another and the smouldering impact zone.

"Forget it, Lieutenant," Sergeant Hummel said off-handedly. She was checking the response of her own troops and not bothering to look at Waldstejn. "It was a good idea, but if the Rubes've got us taped, there'll be a ground patrol along any time. That thing—" she turned to wave at the truck— "can't outrun a tank, and we can't fight a goddam tank either, not with what we got on our backs. Come *on,* Black Section!"

"Hold up, I said!" shouted Waldstejn. The troops nearest him looked back in concern, but they continued to file off after the section leaders familiar to them. The Cecach officer's voice was only a murmur without authority in the brush a few meters away.

Sookie Foyle's helmet was flexed to a five-kilogram backpack. The plump-looking Communicator unclipped the microphone from that pack and threw its red toggle switch. At once, the sending units of every commo helmet in the Company were locked out, keeping all channels clear for the command set. In a clear, dispassionate voice Foyle announced, "Max units, freeze in place for orders from C-captain Waldstejn." She handed the mike to the startled officer. Through a half-smile she whispered, "Should I have made you a colonel?"

"All right, people," said Albrecht Waldstejn with the appearance of calm. "Those shells came from the west of us. We're already surrounded, so we're not going to run after all."

He paused. Troopers had halted in place, startled by the command but too unsure of the situation not to obey. Their uniforms shimmered in shades of gray and brown as the fabric picked up nuances of its immediate vicinity.

"You goddamned stupid hunkie!" roared Sergeant Hummel, furious most of all at the realization that only Waldstejn had access to the radio net now. She strode back toward the officer, holding her weapon muzzle-high as if a banner fluttered from it. "We're not going to surrender now, they'll feed us our *balls* if we do!"

The young Cecach officer had the disorienting feeling that he was standing on a chess board and that a giant version of his own hand was reaching for him. His face was as still as chiseled steel. Into the microphone he said, "We're going to fight our way out, people. We're going to give the immediate pursuit a bloody nose to buy us some time, and then we're going to ride home in style. I swear by the blessed Virgin!"

Hummel had stopped in her tracks. She sucked in on her lips as part of an expression which was not wholly a frown.

As Waldstejn paused the second time, he caught the eye of one of the mercenaries—Dwyer, the gangling fellow who appeared to have taken Hodicky and Quade under his wing, thank God. The trooper grinned knowingly and shook his head in mock exasperation.

"First," Waldstejn said loudly, "White Section empties that truck, and I mean *fast*. Sergeant

Mboko, report to me when you've got that organized. Second—"

As he continued to thump out orders with the unhurried aplomb of a drop forge, Waldstejn found himself noting the warmth of the Communicator standing close with the command set. He did not let himself look directly at her, though. Not yet.

Gunner Jensen's face and hands were black. His torso was white and unmarked though the tunic had been blown completely away from it. Cooper and Pavlovich knew their section leader too well to bother arguing with him. They slashed at the springy brush with their cutting bars, clearing a path downhill to the truck as Jensen had ordered. They grunted with exertion. The faster they worked, the further away they would be when the follow-up salvo arrived.

Marco Bertinelli hopped beside the Sergeant. The Corpsman carried only the two extra helmets and his own medical pack, but he still had difficulty keeping up with the burdened Jensen. "Guns," Bertinelli pleaded, "for God's sake, let me check you out, will you? We can get a stretcher party up here and—"

"Said I'd do it and I'll do it," the blond man repeated flatly. He cradled the still form of Trooper Herzenberg. Her right arm and leg were bare except for splints and mauve patches of Skin-Seal over the abrasions. They had set the femur first. Jensen had extended her thigh muscles with as much force as was necessary to bring the ends of the fractured bone back into alignment. Herzenberg had been mercifully unconscious when they set the broken humerus a moment later.

"Shouldn't have forgotten they couldn't hear incoming, working inside like that," Jensen said. There were cracks across the surface of his scorched lips, but he had not let the Corpsman treat even those. "Can't help Dog, but I won't leave her up there for the next round."

They were nearing the frantic activity around the overturned truck. Pairs of soldiers were dragging cases of explosives into the brush. Some of them carried their pack-shovels already extended in the hand that did not grip the case. "They'll learn Dog didn't come cheap," the Gunner said. "A lot of them'll learn that."

CHAPTER SEVEN

"You got a rummy team checking you out, Captain,"
whispered what had been Guiterez' radio helmet.
"Smile for the camera."

The warning meant that there were a pair of
drones this time: low-ball on the deck, high-ball a
kilometer behind and three hundred meters in the
air. Instead of transmitting its information in bursts
when it lifted higher into the air, the low-ball
drone had a constant link with its companion. The
higher bird transmitted the data to Army HQ for
processing. It was safe from small arms because of
the distance it trailed the lead unit. It was still
cold meat for more sophisticated air defenses, but
the system was a good one for pin-pointing hot
spots in a generally cool environment.

"All right, it's working," said Albrecht Waldstejn
to the two privates who had escaped with him.

They stood carefully on top of the truck box, resisting the impulse to leap up in an access of nervous energy. Waldstejn began to wave. From their vantage point, four meters plus their own height, the trio of Cecach soldiers had a good view over the top of the scrub. There was a ragged path down which the reel of cable had been rolled. At the other end of the path, the pit head oozed a thick smudge. The dust lifted by the shellbursts had settled out of suspension, but fires still burned there and among the brush piles ignited by the mercenaries.

The cable lay in tangled sections beside the upright truck. Some lengths were still reeved through holes punched in the side. By looping the cable around braces and putting men on both ends to pull, the Company had managed to right the truck with a concerted heave. Waldstejn had supposed that they would need to double-loop the cables, using sturdy vegetation for mechanical advantage in lieu of proper blocks and tackle. Fifty strong, disciplined humans had proved to be all the advantage required.

There were no obvious signs of what had been the truck's cargo.

The low-ball snapped past the three of them, close enough that a puff of exhaust from its engine dried the corneas of Waldstejn's eyes. It was moving much faster than the ordinary survey drone which Trooper Powers had brought down. Even from his height, Waldstejn could follow its course with his eyes for only a second or two before it was gone. He lowered his arms, but it was a moment before he remembered to relax the rictus

into which his face had formed itself when he tried
to smile.

"Goddam," muttered Jirik Quade. He was knuck-
ling the muscles of his own taut belly with his
head bent over. Quade's pain was real enough, but
it had nothing to do with physical fear. The black-
haired soldier had to become an actor in a few
minutes. He was out of his depth, part of a complex scheme at which all of his instincts rebelled.
He did not understand the whole plan, and he was
desperately afraid that he would not be able to
handle his role. But the stakes were clear: the
certainty that Pavel and the Lieutenant would die
if he did not carry out the act.

Pavel Hodicky had been waving also. "They'll
make another pass," he said in a fast, detached
voice. "The drone approached from the east, so the
ground units will come from the east too. Even if
the drones have infra-red, they won't pick up anyone but us, because Lieutenant ben Mehdi says
Cecach technology isn't up to—"

Waldstejn put a gentle hand on the little private's
shoulder. The younger man was shivering. "That's
right, Pavel." the officer said. "See, the high one's
orbiting already—" he pointed. "In a few—sure,
here it comes."

Water sloshed against both narrow banks of the
stream. The drone angled back up the valley so
low and tight that its wing-tips trailed twigs. Its
nose cap was flat black, uncamouflaged and per-
meable to the full assortment of sensors which
might be included in its instrument package. For
an instant, the drone pointed directly at the truck.
Waldstejn saw a blurred flash of the terrain behind the aircraft through the cowling of the turbofan.

Then the drone pitched and was gone, whipping soots and smoke from the fires high enough to make the men cough.

Then there was silence in the valley, and nothing moved except by pressure of the wind.

Private Hodicky took a deep breath. "You know, sir?" he said in a normal voice. "I thought they'd shell us when they found us. Shell us first, I mean. I know they'd send somebody by to pick up the pieces later. . . ." He gave Waldstejn a wan grin.

The young officer laughed. He thumped the heels of his hands together in an instinctive attempt to loosen his muscles. "Tell you what, soldier," he admitted, "I was guessing fifty-fifty myself on that. Eagles, a patrol checks us out, crowns they target the next salvo on this truck instead of up there at the mine." He waved.

"Hell, shells or no shells, what's it matter?" asked Private Quade off-handedly. "We're sitting on a bomb, ain't we?"

It was an honest comment, not a gush of pessimism forced into words by fear. Jirik Quade's fears had little to do with the lethal hardware they were juggling. But his words tightened the insides of his two companions.

Churchie Dwyer had expected the induction roar and the higher-pitched howl of the fans themselves as they pumped air into the plenum chamber at pressures so high that steel floated on it. He had not expected the oncoming tank to shake the ground beneath it without any direct contact.

"Black Three," he said, touching his key. He was not sure the tiny transmitter in his helmet would carry down to the Lieutenant, not with him flat on his belly in a slit trench like he was. "Vehicles approaching, estimate thirty kph—" that was slow, must have backed off the throttle when they got close— "estimate several vehicles."

Beside Dwyer, Del Hoybrin stretched out his arms to grasp the forward corners of their cover sheet. Churchie had carefully strewn the top of the microns-thick fabric with loam and foliage before they crawled beneath it into the cramped trench. The sheet would blur to match its surroundings more slowly but with even greater delicacy than their uniforms did; but the veteran figured that in a pinch, nothing looked more like dirt than dirt did. Now gusts eddying beneath the skirts of the approaching vehicle swept across the light soil and caused the sheet itself to flutter.

Tanks were hideously expensive and in short supply for exploiting the main breakthrough. Therefore, Waldstejn's quick appraisal had left the Company in reasonable hope that the pursuit would be limited to light, indigenously-produced armor, vulnerable to their shoulder weapons. But they could handle a tank also, so long as—

"Lead vehicle is a tank," Churchie reported, but he was unable to hear his own voice. The muddy daylight through bare patches of the cover sheet was blotted out. The roar was palpable as the huge armored vehicle slid across the trench on its cushion of air. The cover sheet molded itself to the mercenaries like a coat of body paint. It rammed them down with a pressure which though uniform forced a wordless scream from Dwyer's throat.

Then it was past. Brush whanged and popped against the skirts of the next vehicle, an armored personnel carrier which slipped along at a respectful distance from the tank. Equally large, the APC lacked the tank's massive armor and weaponry. Its crew and infantry complement scanned the brush through vision blocks, uneasily aware that because the tank was proof against most weaponry, a band of cornered fugitives might hit the APC first in hopes of dying with their teeth in a throat.

The personnel carrier slid over the trench. Its fans were powered by gas turbines and not by a fusion bottle like that of the tank. Its passage was a caress by comparison with that of the heavier vehicle. With the hatches buttoned up, it was difficult to see the ground even at a distance from the vehicle. If anyone aboard tried, whirling dust hid the outlines of the mercenaries.

It did not occur to Del Hoybrin to try to report. Churchie handled that sort of thing. Dwyer was only half conscious. Blood drooled from his left nostril.

There were five more armored personnel carriers ripping stolidly through scrub already bulldozed by the lead tank. Then, closing the column with the scarred, brutal assurance of the town bully, came the one they could not count on dealing with.

The Rubes must really want them bad, Dwyer thought muzzily, to send *two* tanks after the Company.

"Ooh, Daddy Krishna, that's a big mother," murmured Trooper David Cooper.

"Tell me about it," agreed his shelter-mate, Grigor Pavlovich. "You know, if we hadn't left the gun behind, they'd be expecting us to do something about that bitch ourselves. And goddam if I know what we'd do except get eat up."

The troopers who had been actually overrun by the Republican armor had a worse view of the vehicles than many others in the Company. As the Cecach lieutenant—was he a captain?—had said, there were Rubes any way they moved, so it was a toss-up where a patrol would be vectored in from. The Company was strung in one and two-man shelters no deeper than body thickness, in a circuit three hundred meters' radius from the truck. Twenty-odd shelters in a kilometer or so made the bunkers around Smiricky #4 look as dense as a phalanx . . . but the guns would carry, and the chances of the entire Rube unit being in range of somebody were very good.

With what was rumbling down the hill now, though, that put them in the place of the frog that swallowed the bumblebee.

"Whooie," Cooper said. He was able to look over the lip of his trench at the armor because of the distance intervening. "I tell you, buddy, if that's indig manufacture, then you and me hired onto the wrong side in this one."

"Naw," Pavlovich explained, "they were built by Henschel on Terra. The Rubes bought tanks, the Feds bought men. Us." He turned his head to spit tobacco juice over the side of the trench without raising his head further. "I still think we hired on the wrong side."

"Hell, there's two of them," his companion whispered. The tense half-humor was gone, leaving his voice flat. The grip of Cooper's weapon felt sweaty and very frail beneath his palm.

The tank wallowing through brush at the head of the column was painted taupe to match Rube uniforms and their outlook on life. It gave an impression of enormous solidity, but it did not look particularly large—certainly not at six hundred meters, not even through the magnification of Cooper's gunsight. As a matter of fact, the tank was only about nine meters long and four wide. The height was almost greater than the width, because the plenum chamber and drive fans had to underlie the entire vehicle.

There was a stubby muzzle on the bow slope flanked by lights, sensors, and vision blocks. It would be an automatic weapon of some kind, probably a light cannon. The ball mounting would limit it to 90° of arc or less, but the tank itself could spin like a top on its air cushion. The gun thus had all the traverse that a turret mounting could have offered.

What *was* mounted in the turret was a reflector-beam laser as powerful as the pair which had been emplaced at Smiricky #4 for air defense. For the heaviest anti-armor applications, a cannon firing shot of high kinetic energy was still superior to a laser of the same bulk. The great advantage of a laser—when it was coupled with the fusion plant which a tank required for mobility anyway—was that the laser never ran out of ammunition. Instead of being left defenseless after twenty, forty, even a hundred discharges in a hot battle, a laser-armed tank could continue ripping so long as an opponent shared the field with it. Especially for tanks built for export to worlds which might lack the materials or technology to produce osmium or tungsten-carbide penetrators, a laser main gun made sense.

But the most lethal weapon in the world was useless if it could be knocked out before it was used. To the mercenaries lying in ambush, the most frightening thing about the tanks was that their armor made them virtually invulnerable to any weapons the Company had available. Indeed, the tanks were very possibly invulnerable even to hits by the automatic cannon that Cooper and Pavlovich had crewed before bugging out of the Smiricky compound.

The tank was faceted with blocks of sandwich armor. The hull and turret had no curves, but neither did they have any shot traps or plates vertical to a probable angle of attack. The sandwich was faced with sloped, density-enhanced steel, up to ten centimeters thick on the turret and bow slope. The central layer was a mat of monomolecular sapphire, its interstices filled with a high-temperature gum which acted to equalize mechanical stress. The sapphire filling was far inferior to steel in terms of stopping high-velocity projectiles, but under battlefield conditions it was impenetrable by lasers or shaped-charge warheads.

Behind the sapphire was a second layer of steel as thick as the first; and the first layer alone would shrug off rounds from the Company's shoulder weapons like so many drops of rain. Two tanks. Krishna.

One of the armored personnel carriers swung out on the column. It doubled back around the tank at the end, returning to squat at a point on the ridge overlooking the valley. The other seven vehicles continued to rumble down toward the truck. They kept a ten-meter separation and probed the brush with nervous twitches of their weapons.

The APCs were designed to carry a half-platoon of troops apiece. They were as large as the tanks

and mounted an automatic cannon in a small turret forward. They were not significant threats as
vehicles—their light armor would stop shell fragments and rounds from indig assault rifles, but the
mercenaries' guns could penetrate them the long
way. The danger of the APCs lay in the fact that
they carried twice the number of troops as lay
awaiting them. Nobody had to tell the Company's
veterans how lethal a short-range burst from an
assault rifle could be.

"Well, I'll tell you one good thing," Cooper said
to his partner. "It isn't us up there with that APC,
waiting for somebody to step out and take a leak
down our necks. . . . And it isn't us down *there*,
either."

The motion of Cooper's eyebrows sufficed for a
gesture toward the stationary supply truck. The
three figures in camouflage fatigues looked very
small atop it. And against the bow and the pointing weapons of the lead tank, they looked hope-
lessly vulnerable.

"Fine, there's two of them," the radio said in the
attentuated voice of Albrecht Waldstejn. "Ignore
the APCs. Your only target is the farther tank. Ah,
farther from the truck, the second tank."

There was a whisper of heterodyne in Sookie
Foyle's ears as her command set rebroadcast the
message. The radios woven into the helmets of the
Company were short range. Under ideal circumstances, they were good for a kilometer. The fact
that everyone's head was stuck below ground level
made the present circumstances far short of ideal,
and there was no damned room for error. One
channel of the command set was dedicated to

Waldstejn's helmet. Anything he said over the radio was banged out to the whole Company on a separate frequency.

Sookie was alone in a slit trench on a knoll to the northwest of the ambush. It was the direction from which it had seemed least likely that the Rubes would approach. That was not because Foyle was a woman or the Communicator *per se*. There were seven other women in the Company; and like those others, Sookie Foyle carried a gun and was expected to use it goddam well. At the moment, however, her duty was more important than that simply of a gunman. She had to set off the ambush itself.

The armored vehicles were dark blotches against the yellow-green of Spring foliage. From a slight elevation, the armor was as obvious in its approach as ticks crawling across a sheet. The few troopers huddled low in the notch of the valley had a view of only a few meters through the scrub. It was one of them who would have to detonate the make-shift mines on which the Company's prayers had to rest.

One of the figures below on the truck brushed his head in what could have been a wave toward the oncoming tank. "Don't think I'll dare key this again," whispered Albrecht Waldstejn. "It's all in your hands, Sookie. For God's sake, don't give the word until a tank is in range. Whatever happens."

She could not see the Cecach officer's fixed smile as he greeted the hostile armor. His back was to her, and the distance was long for that sort of detail, even through the gunsight. Waldstejn's transmission had clicked off at the last half vocable, suggesting more than reason permitted Foyle to believe.

Sookie tried to wet her lips with a tongue that was almost equally dry. Let him live, she prayed silently. Dear God, let the others both die but let him live.

Her hips moved in the narrow trench, pressing her groin tighter against the soil in an instinctive search for relief.

Sergeant-Gunner Roland Jensen could see nothing but the dirt just in front of his eyes. Enough light seeped through the cover sheet for that. Even without the cover, there was nothing to see above his shelter except brush, and he had seen enough of that during the march from the compound. Like much Cecach vegetation, the scrub that had retaken this valley dangled roots at intervals from the tips of branches. That had made the Company's flight an obstacle course, but at least it meant now that their pursuers were unlikely to notice the hiding places before they were intended to. . . .

Jensen was singing to himself, mouthing the words soundlessly as he always did to pass time. It was a habit to disconnect his brain until it was needed again. The blond man had a reputation for patience, for perfect stolidity.

"If in the field your grave you find," he sang, starting the fourth stanza.

He was not at all patient, not with the ox-like torpidity of a Del Hoybrin, at least. But Jensen had learned to wait. The supply truck had contained caps, detonating cord, and the explosives themselves; but there had been no provision for initiating the explosion except electrically. It was a load of fungibles, after all. The Smiricky Complex had no need of the ignition hardware itself.

"That is not cause for crying. . . ." The ground was trembling. Part of Jensen's mind could hear the snap of branches springing up against armor plating. His helmet's commo worked. He had heard without difficulty Waldstejn's final relayed instructions. That meant Jensen would be able to hear the Communicator's own instructions as well, and there was no reason in the world to try to see anything for himself.

"In the green, green grass, just rest your ass. . . ." It had been easy to fuze the truck, easy enough, but the daisy-chain had to be initiated separately for the plan to have a prayer of success. The device chosen to set off the daisy-chain was Sergeant-Gunner Roland Jensen.

"And watch the clouds go flying!"

It was his own fault, but Allah save him from the fruits of his stupidity!

Lieutenant Hussein ben Mehdi pressed his knuckles against his brows as if he could somehow force out the awareness of what he had to do. He had hung the bundle from his pack only seconds before leaving the Operations Center for the last time. It only weighed two or three kilos, after all, and it might be useful. *Use*-ful! Allah save him from the Hell he had earned, it was that indeed. And who but Lieutenant ben Mehdi, the foresightful officer who had brought the bundle—who but he should be trusted *with* its use?

There might have been no reconnaissance drones accompanying the patrol . . . but not even ben Mehdi had been able to think that it was probable that the ground forces would not have that support. He alone of the Company—save for the Cecach trio, might Allah requite them!—was placed within the daisy chain. If there were drones at all, they were most likely to orbit the center of affairs, and even a few meters could make a crucial difference.

Ben Mehdi had no overhead shelter except his cover sheet and the acrid smoke. They had lighted a brush fire a few meters away from where he lay. It should confuse vision and the possible heat sensors on the Republican vehicles. Whether or not it hid the mercenary, the smoke certainly punished him with its smouldering lethality. His gas filters made each breath agony, but they did nothing to prevent smoke tendrils from making his eyes burn.

As Allah willed, but might he not will so terrible a thing! prayed Hussein ben Mehdi. Beside him in the trench lay the bundle of five, broomstick-slim anti-aircraft missiles. To fire them accurately, he would have to stand with the bundle extended on its launching staff. He would be as obvious as if he were waving a Federation flag. Ben Mehdi had both the experience and the imagination to picture how the Republican gunners would react.

Allah preserve him!

The lead tank came to a quivering halt twenty meters from the waiting truck. Behind the tank, the six vehicles which had followed it down from the ridge formed a hedgehog. Each armored personnel carrier pulled close to the vehicle ahead of it, then rotated 30° to one side or the other. That way the heavier bow armor and the turret weapon faced attacks from the flank, but the troops within the rear compartment could still use their weapons through the firing ports provided for them. The tank at the rear did a slow 180° turn on its axis so that its heavy laser covered the track the vehicles had just ripped through the scrub.

"Too far," muttered Quade, kneading his thighs with hands that left sweaty patches on the fabric. "Goddam, won't get neither of them."

"We'll work something out," said Albrecht Waldstejn. Moving sideways so that he continued to face the armored vehicles, the Cecach officer stepped down to the roof of the cab. He used the edge of the microwave dish as a handhold. It was warm with use. The truck had a live feel though it was motionless in any gross sense. Hodicky had run the fans up to speed and then locked them flat while the trio mounted the truck. That way they could be seen. The fans were still spinning without load, ready to boost the vehicle on its air cushion as soon as someone dialed up their angle of attack.

There was presumably a radio discussion going on among the officers of the Republican patrol. No sign of it reached Waldstejn as he clambered down. He stepped on the driver's seat, then to the ground.

The armored vehicles had no external loud-speakers, and it was quite obvious that their crews were not anxious to unbutton until they better understood the situation. The tank's main gun followed Waldstejn on silent gimbals with the same precision that it would have tracked a target worthy of its ravening power. The automatic weapon on the bow slope occasionally moved. It was clearly ready to sluice the truck body with a stream of explosive bullets.

The patrol was halted, but all the vehicles still hovered a finger's width above the ground. A fire that had smouldered near to death now quickened with a gush of sparks. The draft beneath the skirts of the lead tank bathed the Federal troops with smoke and dust blown across the stubble of cut brush. The fans roared as they sucked air through protective gratings to replace leakage around the skirts. Because it was omnipresent, Waldstejn did not realize how loud the noise was until Hodicky tried to speak over it. The little private had followed Waldstejn to the ground, but he still had to shout to ask, "How close, sir? You see it now. How close?"

Staring at the dark bow of the tank did not put Waldstejn any nearer to being able to judge how thick its armor was. Too damned thick, almost surely.

The mass of the tank was an aura about it, and its three-meter height was no longer a statistic but a lowering presence. It was not the armor that mattered now, just the angle, and that number was not changed by Waldstejn's fear of the reality whose laser glared at him like the path to Hell. "Half this," he said to his subordinate, "or a little less if you can, but—don't startle them whatever." The tall officer began to walk toward the tank. His hands were in plain sight and his body was so tense that he was near to fainting.

Hodicky yelped at the change in plans, but it had taken Waldstejn's action to break the silent deadlock. There was a swish and a clang as a side-panel of the lead personnel carrier hinged down. The section of troops which the vehicle held moved nervously onto the ground. They blinked in the sunlight with their rifles pointed in various directions.

The real value of armored personnel carriers lies in the troops they carry. From their inception, however, there has been a tendency to use them as fighting vehicles rather than as infantry transporters. Even brave men hesitate to leave their dark cocoon for natural terrain searched by an enemy's fire. Rationally they may know that the metal box encasing them is more a magnet for fire than a protection in a hot engagement; but reason dies when the first bullets rake the field.

Republican designers had developed a simple solution for the problem. The troop commanders could throw switches and drop either or both side panels of their APCs. The thin armor-plating became a ramp which neither hindered the troops' deployment nor encouraged them to stay with their vehicle. Most of the present unit knelt, coughing at the smoke in the air. Six of the soldiers trotted toward Waldstejn. One of them was an officer marked by a pistol and a belt-slung radio. "Hold it right there!" he ordered Waldstejn.

Someone came to a decision. There was a change in the medley of the drive fans. Republican infantrymen turned in alarm. Waldstejn's own heart leaped in fear of the unexpected modification. Then the background noise died away as all the vehicles settled to the ground. Their fans slowed to idle on descending notes. The difference was as abrupt as that of walking out of a stadium where amplified music was being performed.

"Thank God you've found us, sir!" Lieutenant Waldstejn cried to forestall the Republican officer. The troops in dark uniforms clustered about their captive. Others from the group still near their vehicle moved uncertainly toward the two Federal privates. "My men and I were kidnapped from Smiricky #4 by a band of bloodthirsty cut-throats—off-planet dregs, every man of them and their whores too! Now that you're hot on their trail, we have a chance to get revenge. Why, you can *see* how the beasts used us."

Waldstejn waved back toward the Privates. Quade and Hodicky certainly looked the hang-dog remnants of brutal torture. Quade's uniform had one sleeve. The scabs on his arm had opened again when he climbed from the truck. Red cracks seamed the dried blood. They looked to be one stage removed from amputation, though the scrapes were trivial compared to the bruising Quade had received at the same time.

For his part, Hodicky had washed his trousers at the first spring they came to. He had then marched in them wet. Dust had fused to mud that seeped into the fabric as indelibly as the original dye. That, together with gares ripped in the cloth by the brush and an expression of stark terror, made Pavel Hodicky look as battered a victim as his black-haired friend.

"But where—" the Republican officer began. His radio broke in on him. Its demand was a buzzing snarl, audible in full only through his earpiece but easy enough for Waldstejn to reconstruct from his own experience with anxious superiors. "Sir, they say they were capture—" the Republican tried to explain.

"Is your commanding officer in the tank, Major?" asked Lieutenant Waldstejn pleasantly. He could not identify Republican rank tabs. If he could have, he would have bumped the harried officer two grades for certain rather than by estimate. "Here, it'll be simpler to do this directly, won't it? I understand, I'll keep my hands where everyone can see them." As he spoke, the Federal officer began to walk forward at an easy pace. He was striking for the right side of the tank that faced him squarely. He held his hands at shoulder height, their bare palms forward.

"No!" shouted the Republican officer as his radio buzzed again. "No sir, I didn't—"

"That's all right, boys, keep me covered and we'll all be safer," said Waldstejn to the two infantrymen who seemed ready to block him without direct orders. Retaining his calm smile, Waldstejn nodded in the direction he was moving. The tank laser and the automatic cannon of the nearest APC were both trained on him—and on the Republican troops around him. One of them leaped back with a look of horror and an oath.

From what Waldstejn had heard, swearing like that in the Rube forces was good for six months solitary—or death, if your unit chaplain was hard-nosed. Even so, the Federal officer thought the oath was a reasonable response to the imminent likelihood of being blasted by friendly weapons.

And Albrecht Waldstejn was well able to empathize with that concern at the moment.

"Ah, none of you guys'd have some water, would you?" asked Private Hodicky. He gave the Republican soldiers a nervous smile. The Federal private had learned years before that bullies found his smile a good reason to kick him. That was fine. These troops could like him or despise him, it was all the same. What they had better *not* do was fear him and watch him closely.

"Ah, back in the can," one of the Republicans muttered with a gesture toward the personnel carrier. There was the usual tendency of troops being moved by vehicle to strip gear from themselves. Packs and web gear prodded uncomfortably when you were one of eighteen or twenty men being jounced in a cramped troop compartment. Of course, that meant that when something happened, your gear was in a tangle out of reach. None of the six men clustered around the Federal captives carried a canteen. Only two of them had slung belts of ammunition before spilling out of the vehicle.

Not that that mattered. Two shots would be quite enough for Hodicky and Q. Their hands were as bare as Waldstejn's.

"This your truck?" one of the Rubes asked. He nodded. The taupe-clad men were uncertain. Their covert glances toward the rear showed it was not action by their prisoners that they particularly feared. The 522nd Garrison Battalion had been typical of second-line Federal units in having little or no discipline. Its officers were for the most part despicable; certainly they were despised by the troops they nominally commanded.

The situation in the Republican forces was wholly different. Rigid control was exerted downward from all levels. Breaches of discipline were corrected with a rigor which seemed harsh even by comparison with the standards set for civilians by the theocrats of Budweis. There was a basic flaw, however, in Frederick the Great's dictum that soldiers should fear their officers more than they feared the enemy. That stifles initiative and causes men

to look up the chain of command instead of themselves taking even the simplest measures.

Measures like deciding what to do with a pair of
Federal privates they had been told to watch.

"We fixed it," croaked Jirik Quade. He gave the
skirt of the supply truck a thump with his hand.
The contact felt good. He hit the metal again.
"When, when we got away from the, yeah, the
guys who, ah. . . ." Quade thumped the vehicle a
third time and watched it carefully. He had not
made eye contact with any of the Rubes since they
approached the truck. He was going to screw up,
he was going to get Pavel and the Lieutenant killed,
and he did not even have a gun!

"Right," said Hodicky with enthusiasm. Lieutenant Waldstejn was walking toward the tank, now.
He seemed to be drawing with him a cluster of
Rubes including the protesting infantry officer. "We
fixed it up, but then we waited for you guys. You
know, we tried to j-join the Lord's forces be—"

Waldstejn turned. He looked worn and lonely
amidst the taupe uniforms. "Private Hodicky," he
called in a clear voice, "show the Major how the
truck works. Just back it up a little."

"But *sir*!" the little private cried.

Waldstejn ignored him. The tall, slim officer
stepped around the bow of the tank, out of Hodicky's
sight.

"One of you guys want to get in with me?"
asked Hodicky. His mind was neatly calculating,
chosing words that clicked out engagingly through
his fixed smile. He climbed the step, then slid into
the cab through the door that they had left open.
"Not that we could run anywhere," the Private's
mouth pattered on, "jeez no, think what that—"

waving at the armored bow, thirty steps away—
"would do!"

"Hey, hold on," said a dark-clad soldier. "I don't
think. . . ." His assault rifle was of a pattern different from those issued to Federal troops, but it had
the same sort of hole in the muzzle end. More or
less without thinking, the Republican began to
point the weapon for emphasis.

Private Quade undid his fly.

The dark-haired private was supposed to call
attention away from Hodicky by counterfeiting an
epileptic fit. He *couldn't* do that, could not act any
better than he could have flown a starship. But
there had been no one else to use, because Quade
could not drive the truck, either. . . .

"Hey, *watch* that!" a soldier cried as he leaped
away.

Quade's urine splashed audibly from the skirt of
the truck, gouging away at the grime on the steel.
As Hodicky boosted the power, air squirted out
beneath the skirts. The side-draft caught the urine
and atomized it across Quade's boots and those of
the Republicans on the ground with him. "Whoops,
should've looked for the lee rail," the little man
cried happily over the intake whine. The others
cursed.

The truck slid away at a slow, non-threatening
pace. Hodicky was backing and turning simultaneously so that the open tail-gate of the truck
swung toward the bow of the tank.

"Hey!" shouted a Republican. He fired for emphasis. His bullet cratered the door of the cab.

Hodicky chopped the fans, grounding the truck.
"Hey, *guys*!" he cried, raising both hands to his
startled face. "Hey, it's *over*!"

He was going to have to wash out his trousers again, he thought sickly. If he survived.

From the foreshortening of her sights, it looked to Sookie Foyle as if the supply truck had been swung into direct contact with the lead tank. Despite the optical exaggeration, that meant that the deserters from the 522nd had done their job well.

That left Foyle with her own problem.

There had been almost four tonnes of explosive aboard the overturned truck. The mercenaries had buried it in a rough hundred-meter circle about the truck. That meant there were five meters or more between each thirty-kilogram case and the cases to either side of it . . . and the second tank was still outside the daisy-chain entirely.

"Control to Guns," Foyle whispered into the mike. "They're halted out of position. Don't do anything—" God, she shouldn't have started this, Jensen didn't need to be told by a Communicator to follow the plan set down ahead of time—"when the truck goes off. C-control out."

There was no reply. Well, Guns would tear a strip off her when it was all over, and she deserved that or worse.

The daisy-chain was for the moment only a construct of Foyle's memory. The individual mines had not been marked. They were merely covered with friable soil from the holes in which they were laid. Excess dirt had been scattered in the brush where the breeze picked it up and mingled it with dust from kilometers away. There was little chance that the Republicans would notice the explosives, even if they dismounted. More possibly, someone might stumble over the chain of det cord which connected the cases of plastique, but the thin cord blended well with the yellow-gray soil.

Sookie Foyle had to read the daisy-chain like the dial of an invisible clock. It was flattering that the Company's command team—ben Mehdi and the sergeants with whom she had worked for years—had assigned her the task without hesitation. That flattery was small recompense for the horror into which a screw-up would plunge her.

Foyle had spread her sight picture to survey the whole Republican column. Now she tightened the magnification again, focusing on Albrecht Waldstejn. His head was visible above the fender of the lead tank. Nothing would happen for some seconds, at least. The trench which would protect the Cecach soldiers was twenty meters from where the Captain now stood. It had been hidden beneath the cab of the supply truck until the vehicle moved. The charge would surely not be fired before Waldstejn too could reach a place of safety.

The Federal officer turned from the Republican tanker to whom he had been speaking. Waldstejn's face had in the past days lost a garrison softness that could never have been called fat. He had deliberately left a stubble of whiskers which suggested privation. Now he was shouting something back toward the truck. His face smiled as he stood waiting, but his blue eyes were closed.

Republican soldiers began running. They were crying things unheard as Foyle furiously traded magnification for field of view.

Then the blast blotted out everything in the center of her sight picture.

* * *

A hatch, invisible beyond the facets of armor, opened on top of the turret. A furious Republican officer looked out. He had to bend forward to see Waldstejn. "Ensign Farrago," the tanker shouted to the officer from the APC, "are you a complete idiot? And what is that *truck* doing?"

"Sir, I—" the infantry officer said yet again.

There was a shot. Waldstejn's heart leapt but he did not turn. From where he stood, close to the side of the tank, the truck and his two companions were hidden by the massive armor.

"Hey, it's *over*!" Hodicky cried.

He was alive, thank God, and Waldstejn's smile never slipped as he said to the tanker, "Sir, it was only an earnest of our good intentions, I assure you."

"*Lieutenant!*" Hodicky cried, "they're dragging me—"

"Go ahead!" Waldstejn shouted over the steel and sapphire barrier between him and his men, between him and the trench that was to have been his shelter from the blast.

Men were shouting. He rested his left hand on the armored flank. Waldstejn was in the dead zone, so close to the Republican tank that its laser could not be depressed enough to hit him. The builders had cured that problem very simply by embedding a line of anti-personnel charges in the armor at waist height. By throwing a switch, the tank crew could spray the ground outside their vehicle with shrapnel that a mouse could not hope to hop through.

Ensign Farrago gripped Waldstejn by the shoulder, bellowing something unintelligible. There was a burst of shots nearby.

Waldstejn's eyes were closed. "Dies irae," he whispered through smiling lips. Not the hymn for itself but as a return to childhood and the problems of a choirboy. "Dies illa—"

And perhaps as a prophecy.

"Solvet saeclum in favilla—"

Day of wrath, this day that rips the ages into ash.

He did not hear the explosion. The shock wave had already stunned him before his brain could have perceived it as noise.

Their eyes had followed Pavel and the moving truck. For the moment, at least, none of the Republican infantrymen seemed interested in the deep trench which had just been revealed beside Jirik Quade. The black-haired private closed his fly. For the first time since he had heard the Lieutenant's plan, Quade was at peace. His duties were complete. He was too pleased with the success of his own improvisation to notice anything else which might be occurring.

There was a shout and a shot. All the world moved in a gunsight as the Private turned. His mouth and eyes were open and his mind was searching for a target. In the air hung the *crack*! of a high-velocity bullet exploding on metal, sharper than the muzzle blast that spawned it.

"Hey, it's *over*!" Pavel blurted, white-faced in the cab.

Quade grunted with relief. The Rube nearest him had stepped back in shock as the little private turned. Now the guard, too, relaxed; but he did not lower the rifle he had aimed at Quade when the Federal spun like a breech closing.

The Rube who had fired pointed his rifle in the air and turned half away from the vehicle. He looked embarrassed. Two of his companions pushed past him to the truck. "Hey, out of there," one of them demanded. A taupe-clad tanker was now leaning from the tank and shouting toward men hidden by the tank's own bulk.

Hodicky had rotated the supply truck around an axis just in front of its cab. He was only three meters from where he had started, but the truck was closer by its full length to the tank. A Rube reached into the cab and caught Hodicky's ankle. The dark-clad soldier slanted his rifle up in his free hand, a threat in fact if not by deliberation.

Everything was according to plan, except that the Lieutenant was squarely in the line of fire.

"Listen, you idolator!" said the Rube holding Hodicky, "I said to get *out*!" He jerked at the ankle he held. Pavel gripped the door jamb and the steering wheel. The gun muzzle jabbed at his ribs.

"*Lieutenant*!" the Private cried, "they're dragging me—"

"Go ahead!"

"I'm coming," Hodicky gasped to the soldier who held him. The other's finger twitched toward the trigger of his rifle. Quade, two jumps away, was a weapon himself now, but the guard nearest him was watching the drama at the truck instead.

Hodicky released the steering wheel and let himself be pulled down from the driver's seat. His right hand reached under the dashboard as the guard hauled him forward. Only Quade understood what his friend had just done.

They had twenty seconds.

Pavel cried out as he bounced on the pressed-metal step. The soldier holding him dragged the little man a pace further from the truck, then kicked him. "Does that help you listen?" the Rube demanded. "Does that?"

Sergeant Mboko had improvised the delay switch with sand and a ration can. When the can was flipped over, the sand ran out until it no longer had enough weight to depress the switch which had originally flashed the headlights while it was held down. Now the switch waited to send current to an electrically-primed blasting cap in the back of a thirty-kilogram shaped charge.

The Republican soldier spat and turned from Hodicky. He faced Quade, half his size and as bedraggled as a cat caught in a rainstorm.

"G-go, Pavel," Quade said. Blood droplets jeweled the cracked scabs on his taut right arm.

"You want some of this?" the Rube shouted. He waved the butt of his rifle in the smaller man's face.

Quade ignored the weapon. He leaped for the Republican, gripping him by both biceps. The man screamed. Quade's fingers compressed his muscles as if they were clay in a potter's hands.

Pavel Hodicky was dizzy with pain. He had not felt the boot hit him. It had been lost in the hot rush of his lower spine hitting the cab step. Even as Quade spoke, Hodicky was rolling through a red blur. He was not rational enough to be scrambling toward the trench—or even scrambling away from the imminent blast. He was simply moving because his last conscious awareness had been of the need to move. The ground dropped away beneath him.

Another of the guards cried out. The man Quade held was gasping and staggering backwards. Dark-clad soldiers were leaping to their feet with curses. The two nearest men were battering at Quade with their gun butts.

Quade wrenched his head back with a gurgle of triumph. His opponent fell away as if propelled by the blood jetting from his throat. A Republican screamed again and fired with his rifle almost touching Quade's back.

The soldier trying to hold Quade from the other side gaped down at his left arm. A bullet had struck the elbow and disintegrated, amputating the limb within the sleeve. Quade turned toward the man who had killed him. Shock has no effect on a berserker. The black-haired Federal had ceased to be human seconds before the shots ripped his heart and lungs to pulp.

Quade gripped the gun muzzle with his left hand. He reached for his killer with his right. His snarl was silent because he had no diaphragm to drive the sounds. The blood on his teeth was not his own. The Republican shrieked and turned away just as the world dissolved in a red flash.

For all its simplicity, the shaped-charge principle was discovered by accident. An engineer tested a small block of explosive by detonating it against the side of a safe. The safe was not structurally injured. In its steel side, however, was stamped in mirror-writing the logo of the explosives manufacturer. The logo had been impressed in the block, and on detonation the gases propagating along the sides of that shallow impression were focused at their mid-point. They struck the safe with greatly-multiplied force, stamping themselves into plating which would have resisted the impact of much larger unfocused blasts.

Shaped charges were gleefully adopted by the military as soon as armor became a commonplace of war again in the Twentieth Century. If the face of the explosive were hollowed into a long, conical throat, the blast could be focused in a pencil-thin jet of unimaginable intensity. A thirteen-kilogram charge could blast a hole through fifty centimeters of hardened steel. Sergeant Mboko, with practically unlimited quantities of explosives to work with, had molded his charge from a full thirty-kilogram case. Even with the imprecisions involved in such a field expedient, Mboko's weapon could have ripped through any practical thickness of steel armor.

Unfortunately for the mercenaries, the sapphire core of the Terran armor would shrug off a jet of white-hot gas that vaporized metallic armor.

Unfortunately for the Republicans, Albrecht Waldstejn had allowed for that when he made his plans.

The supply truck blew up with a deep red flash. Quite apart from its focus, the thirty kilograms of explosive were comparable to the bursting charge of a large shell. The rear half of the vehicle disintegrated. The cab and some shredded remnants of the body lurched forward, crumpling with the acceleration. The trench that sheltered Private Hodicky was two meters deep. Despite that, the shock wave slammed him from one end to the other. The men struggling at ground level were killed instantly by the unimpeded blast, even before the shrapnel tore their hurtling corpses. The face of Jirik Quade was smiling with perhaps as much happiness as it had ever shown in life.

Instead of the tank's invulnerable frontal armor, Mboko's shaped charge was directed toward the skirts around the plenum chamber. The drive fans were buried in the floor of the vehicle, out of the way of possible assault. They had enough extra power to keep the tank floating on its air cushion even if there were some holes in the heavy steel skirts that focused the cushion downward. What happened this time was not merely a few holes.

Centimeter-thick steel vaporized like ice in a gas flame. A ragged twenty-centimeter circle was gone from the bow skirt. Almost the entire rear skirt ballooned away. The jet, spreading but still powerful, had punched the metal there after traversing the hollow length of the plenum chamber. Brush flared at the touch of white-hot gases. The tank driver had started to lift his vehicle immediately before the explosion. Now the tank lurched to the ground again. Though its drive units were undamaged, they could not pressurize a plenum chamber that gaped like a barn in a whirlwind. The fans roared, whipping the nearby brush into a sea of orange flames.

The armored personnel carriers were protected by the tank from any serious effects the blast might have had on them. Inside the APCs, men were bounced against equipment and each other; but both the vehicles and their complements remained combat ready.

Waldstejn and his companions had done their part. The rest was up to the Company.

CHAPTER EIGHT

Churchie Dwyer knew the APC was close. They had heard it returning as a lookout from the direction the column had taken. He had been cursing as he recovered from the pounding the tanks had given him, and this too was reason to curse. But it was also reason to lie still and pray that their cover remained adequate.

The look-out vehicle had approached at a leisurely pace. That might, of course, have meant that it was taking its time to get into a perfect firing position from which to rake the trench. The pair of mercenaries could not even bump up the lip of their cover sheet to watch. They lay on their bellies with their heads toward the approach to the valley. If they tried to turn around now, they would be seen unless the Rube driver was blind. All they could do was to listen to the fans and feel

their sheet quiver above them from air spilled
from the plenum chamber.

Even so, when the huge blast in the valley signaled them to action, Churchie was shocked to
find that the side of the personnel carrier was
within arm's length of him. That meant that if
somebody dropped the sides, the two mercenaries
would be knocked silly without anybody knowing
they were there.

The APC was starting to lift from an idle. Dwyer
fired. He was trying to angle his shot forward
toward where he thought the driver must sit. The
muzzle blast rebounded from the flat side with
stunning force. The steel puckered inward where
his projectile had struck it. The hole in the center
was rimmed with lips of metal white-hot from the
impact. The APC started to rise. Churchie fired
again, letting the vehicle's incipient turn change
the angle for him. Then his partner began to rake
the personnel carrier with fully-automatic fire.

Republican APCs had five firing ports in each
side panel. The troops within could spray their
surroundings through the ports without dismount-
ing. When the shooting started, however, none of
the soldiers had inserted his rifle in a port. Hoybrin's
burst gave them no opportunity to correct that
error.

The big mercenary walked his fire from the rear
hinge forward. He leaned into the first shot so that
his gun muzzle almost touched the armor. At the
end of an eight-round burst, the recoil had pounded
him erect and lifted his point of aim from waist
height to shoulder height. Del slid his bracing right
foot against the back wall of the trench. The vehicle was still up on its fans, but the gyros which

balanced it could not prevent it from beginning to slide down-hill. It would have required a living hand at the controls to stop that drift. The thin armor echoed with screams and curses as soldiers tried to clear weapons while their dying comrades thrashed in the same cramped quarters. Aimed shots from Churchie's weapon punctuated the human sounds with high-velocity cracks. Breathing deeply with the exertion of absorbing recoil, Del Hoybrin ripped the remainder of his twenty-round box through the front portion of the troop compartment.

At such short range, most of the osmium projectiles punched neat exit holes in the far sidewall of the vehicle. One of the wounded or dying men inside clamped on the trigger of his assault rifle. That burst multiplied casualties inside in a way that a dropped grenade could not have equalled. The light bullets spalled fragments from the armor. Everything sailed around the riddled crew compartment, flaying and burning where the osmium bullets had only punctured.

The APC was nine meters long and weighed over fifteen tonnes. The murderous delight of having so huge an opponent at his mercy blinded Churchie Dwyer to the significance of its uncontrolled drift. Del was kneeling to insert a loaded magazine in his weapon, but Churchie was fully erect. The personnel carrier was four or five meters away, still broadside to them. The mercenary had just fired at the rear compartment, trying to smash the turbine, when the automatic cannon in the turret opened up on him.

Parallax and the breadth of a finger saved Dwyer's life. He had forgotten about the cannon because the shooting started when the big gun was too close to bear on the troopers. The range had opened almost enough when the gunner squeezed the trigger. Churchie was still so close that the electronic sight failed to compensate perfectly for the angle between the gun muzzle and the fiber-optics sensor beneath the tube. The shells which should have taken off the mercenary's head instead blew up on the brush fifty meters beyond him.

The sheaf of twenty-five millimeter cannon shells did not crack like the lighter, faster projectiles of the infantry weapons. Their shock waves slapped Churchie across the forehead, lifting off his helmet. The gout of propellant gases from the muzzle stung like a spray of hot sand. Screaming, the tall mercenary threw himself flat again. The recoil of his weapon was dangerously liable to break the collarbone of anyone firing from a prone position. Eyes stinging, deafened by his own shots even before the cannon blasted in his face, Churchie began shooting at the turret he had previously ignored. At his second round, a white spark beneath the gun tube marked his hit momentarily. The hot metal was quenched by a spray of vaporized oil as the cannon's recoil compensator blew up.

The gun jammed at once. Churchie continued to fire at it until his own weapon spat out a plastic clip to announce that it needed to be reloaded.

There was a moment's silence. Cannon recoil had speeded the vehicle's drift and had swung its bow away from the mercenaries. Gray smoke was leaking from the ports and bullet holes in the troop compartment. Hydraulic fluid which had splashed on the turret face was sustaining a sluggish fire. As the APC crackled into unbroken scrub, Del Hoybrin fired a long burst into its engine compartment. Fuel exploded. It blew off an access plate and sent flames rocketing twenty meters into the sky.

"Churchie, what do we do now?" the big man asked.

Not all of them were dead. You could feel the screams as a high component of the roaring fire. No one seemed to be healthy enough to release the side panels, though.

Nothing grated in Dwyer's right shoulder as he locked home a fresh magazine. "Now," he said, "we move to where we can see what's going on down there." He nodded curtly. The Rube vehicle was fully involved now, a blotch of flame and black smoke. It warmed bare skin and blocked all view of the valley. "Could be the beggars need us," Churchie added. A level of hearing was returning, as it always did; and always less than the level he had had before battle. "Just could be."

Mingled with the shots and grenade bursts in the valley was the unmistakable hiss of a laser. At least one of the Republican tanks was still in business.

The shots mean all three of the indigs are dead, thought Hussein ben Mehdi, please Allah, may it mean that they are all dead and I don't have to—

The ground rippled. The air went orange as the charge detonated. The shrub nearest the mercenary bowed away from the shock. His cover sheet lifted, then was jerked back by the implosion that echoed the blast. The whole valley rang with the savage crash of the tank skirt hammered and dissolved by superheated gas.

The Lieutenant sprang to his feet. He generally wore body armor in action, but he had known he could not pack it out on his feet. Ben Mehdi's clamshell was somewhere back at Smiricky #4. Colonel Fasolini's set was there too, shattered uselessly into his body in all likelihood . . . but Lieutenant ben Mehdi wished that he had his anyway.

The sunlight undimmed by the cover sheet had drawn him up. Now ben Mehdi's whole focus was on the bright sky. His mind tried to close off everything his peripheral vision showed. The reconnaissance drones were still in their tight, fluttering orbits. Ben Mehdi raised the air defense bundle. Its telescoping staff gave a meter of stand-off between his face and the five tiny rocket motors. The bracing strap was looped around his right shoulder, and the wire sighting ring was clicked into place.

Please Allah!

The lead tank squatted in a sea of fire only thirty meters away. Closer yet to the Lieutenant's right were the nearest of the dark APCs. Three of the five gun turrets pointed more toward him than away, and the flanks of all the vehicles could mow the scrub clean with whips of automatic fire.

The drones were both within the sighting ring. Screw them all! Ben Mehdi jerked the release cord with his left hand.

The sky to the mercenary's rear was fouled by trash from the explosion, bits of the truck roof and a plume of the light soil sucked upward in the following seconds. It would not affect the missiles' infra-red homing, but it gave ben Mehdi the unnecessary feeling that Death lowered at his shoulder. The five plastic tubes at the end of the staff chugged in rotation. Felt recoil was mild, comparable to a large-bore pistol rather than to one of the Company's armor-piercing shoulder weapons. The first four missiles each left the launcher with a hiss and a puff of black smoke. The last tube ruptured at the base. The missile sizzled skyward, a bright spark, but the backblast scorched ben Mehdi's hands and the skin of his throat beneath his face shield.

The Lieutenant threw down the empty launcher and flopped back in his shallow trench. The valley rang with bullets striking armor and the startled, enormous, return fire of the Republican vehicles. No one had shot at ben Mehdi. None of the enemy had even seen him through the brush in his self-camouflaging uniform. Surprise and the concentration of fire from higher up the slopes had saved the Lieutenant where a hard suit could not have.

There was a bright flash overhead. The drones' turbofans were mounted high and they had a low infra-red signature besides. There was nothing else in the sky to confuse the missiles' homing systems, however. The maneuvers built into the drones' stacking programs might have helped them against a human gunner, but they were useless against the air defense cluster. The tiny missiles were short-range and not particularly fast, but for targets within their capabilities they were hell on wheels.

The drone closest to the flash continued to fly, but it trailed a white mist. The second flash and the report of the first, lost in the gunfire, were almost simultaneous. The wings of the other drone folded abruptly like those of a hawk preparing to swoop. The third flash was followed by the red glare of atomized fuel igniting in the wake of the drone damaged by the first warhead. It drew the last two sparks as well, decoyed but decoyed without harm because there were no proper targets for them.

Praise Allah! thought Lieutenant ben Mehdi. He had done all that any of them could expect. Now he could lie flat until the fighting was done, and no one could think him a coward.

But his right hand had already drawn his grenade launcher, and his left arm was tensing to raise him again over the lip of his trench.

Trooper Dolan sat up in her trench, throwing back the cover sheet. A cannon shell hit her squarely in the chest. That was bad luck—the burst continued to climb the hillside, blasting rock and brush far above any of the mercenary positions. For Maxine Dolan it would have been the worst of luck anyway, whether or not the round had been aimed at her deliberately. Her arm separated from the offal that squelched back into her trench. Twenty meters away there were speckles of blood on the gun Jo Hummel had leveled at the Rube column.

The Company's weapons and gunsights made three hundred meters a clout shot for a steady hand. Sergeant Hummel had been there too often already to think that her hands would be steady at the start of a firefight. After the first magazine, after instinct took over and her gun slammed the shoulder of an equally-mechanical gunner, then Hummel could equal her firing range accuracy on the battlefield. For now she kept her sights open to the point that the nine meters of a personnel carrier just fitted the field. The orange bead jumped against the taupe background as she opened fire.

Every trooper in the Company had a number

and warning of a field court—a bullet behind the ear, mercenary companies had no time to waste on frills—if they were caught engaging the enemy in any other order. White Section was emplaced north of the stream, Hummel's Black Section had the south. Each trooper was to divide his section number by the number of vehicles in the column, then fire at the one whose number resulted. That would put a multiple cross-fire on all the Rube armor, rattling the tank gunners—God help us! —and shattering the APCs.

If you were unwilling to violate orders, you had no business leading a section of Fasolini's Company. Jo Hummel blasted away at the second armored personnel carrier, not the first. She could not hope to hit the taupe-clad soldiers who had dismounted from the leading APC. The buttoned-up second one was a big target, its alert gunner had begun raking the hill before most of the Rubes had responded to the explosion, and besides . . . it had been Dolan's assigned target, so one of the bastards was going to be shorted whatever Hummel did.

The veteran sergeant jerked the trigger, angry as always at her clumsy technique as she tried to keep the sight bead centered. The armored vehicle was quivering. Smoke and muzzle flashes continued to burst from its automatic cannon while rifle fire sparkled on its flanks. The punishing recoil of her weapon drove from Sergeant Hummel's mind the awareness of the blood spattering her gun's barrel. Almost, she could forget the warmth of Trooper Iris Powers, kneeling in the trench beside her and firing at targets which could pulp her as surely as they had Dolan.

*   *   *

The gunner of the second Rube tank saw no need to pulse his laser for the present targets. The weapon drew a line of slag and brush exploding into fire across the northern slope. The sparks of projectiles flickering against the tank's armor may have endangered troops in the personnel carriers and dismounted. They constituted no danger at all to the vehicle from which they bounced—but Cooper continued to fire.

The tank was fifty meters further from him than the nearest of the APCs, but Dave Cooper was too good a shot for that to matter. Cooper had started firing with the hope that he *could* pierce the tank's armor. He had a downward angle on the vehicle's back deck where its plating was thinnest. The fusion bottle was separately enclosed, no chance of harming that in any case. But a fighting vehicle is such a dense assemblage of hydraulics and wiring, of ammunition and black boxes, that a round which penetrates anywhere has a real chance of doing disabling damage. Designers' instinct crowds equipment together so that the armor need not be spread thin to cover the volume. That ensures disaster on those occasions when the armor is nonetheless thin enough.

Henschel of Terra had won their gamble this time. A chance image as Cooper's gunsight rose in recoil proved his failure. The tank was turning but its deck and turret were still partially aligned with the mercenary. He caught the flash on each as a single round ricocheted from deck to turret and off again skyward. It left little more than a scar on the paint at either impact.

The tank was sliding forward, perhaps to shield the line of lighter vehicles from the shots tearing at their right flanks. The mercenaries' slit trenches were raggedly aligned, wherever overhanging scrub gave shelter and a field of fire low among the stems. The line of geometric exactitude which the laser drew across the slope could not directly threaten more than a few positions. The gunner was firing blind in an attempt to cow the ambushers with volume in place of precision.

The attempt was working very well. Even Cooper, focused on his own business, could tell that the shots coming from the northern slope had slackened abruptly. A trooper leaped up screaming as the beam passed by. The brush behind him and his own uniform were both afire, though the laser had not struck him squarely. Slag and ash exploded around the mercenary as a score of Republican riflemen finally found a target. The trooper dropped again, sawn apart by multiple hits. The blood soaking his fatigues quenched the fire the raving beam had lighted.

There were the sensor pick-ups, Cooper thought; redundant but at least vulnerable to his shots as the hull and turret proper were not. He was swinging his weapon, following the tank's motion and aligning with the cupola vision blocks when Pavlovich screamed in frustration, "God*damn* that laser!"

Without really thinking about it, Cooper shifted his sight picture a meter further down range and fired. It was a good shot. The release broke cleanly and the recoil was a surprise as it always is when the shooter concentrates on his sights and lets his muscles act on instinct. It was the last round in the magazine, though, and Cooper rolled sideways to hook out a fresh one without bothering to see what the effect had been. He and his fellows had bounced so many shots from the tank with no effect that his mind retained only duty in the place of hope.

The massive vehicle slid on past the fourth, then the third personnel carrier. The squat tube of its laser continued to traverse the hill slope. But there was a tiny, glowing dot where the tube and its mantle joined, and no beam issued from the weapon.

Trooper Powers shifted aim and fired twice more. Those were her ninth and tenth rounds. She had just run out of the targets she had chosen with the tacit agreement of Sergeant Hummel.

The only automatic cannon still firing was the bow gun of the lead tank. The turrets of the five armored personnel carriers each had a pair of holes in them. The holes were centered in whichever surface happened to have been facing Powers at the time she fired. She did not bother to check her results. It was conceivable that a projectile or two would be turned by the armor. It was even possible that the white-hot osmium needles would fail to destroy anything vital in the gun mechanism or gunner as they lanced through the compartment. The chances of either were vanishingly small, and there was plenty more ammunition in Powers' bandolier to deal with them if the need arose.

Beads of sweat quivered on the Trooper's upper lip when recoil shook her body. Her blond elf-lock was darkened and glued to her forehead. Blinking, she increased the field of her gunsight and swept it over the brush near the leading personnel carrier. A swath of darkness among the twisted stems was not shadow but taupe fabric. Powers dialed up the magnification again, concentrating wide-eyed on the holographic display.

The boots were obvious, and the dark blur lying foreshortened in front of them had to be the soldier's torso. Body shots were uncertain with the Company's weapons, though. All the theories about velocity effects and hydrostatic shock could not change the fact that sometimes an osmium projectile would drill straight through a man without discernible result. Better to—

A hard line, the front rim of a helmet, twitched beyond the foliage. The soldier's eyes were closed but his lips trembled in silent repetition. Powers squeezed off.

The helmet sprang out of her sight picture as the gun recoiled. She traded magnification for field again. Not to check the results; that would have been a waste of time.

To find another target.

The lead tank was planted for good. Its bow gun streamed shells across the valley floor, endangering no one but the dismounted Rubes who might have survived the shaped charge. Albrecht Waldstejn was crumpled near the lead personnel carrier, where the explosion had thrown him. The officer whose attention he had held through the last seconds was sprawled face-upward on his turret. His hips and legs dangled down through the hatch at an angle which would have been impossible if the shock had not broken his spine. The laser was silent, either damaged or without a conscious gunner at the moment.

None of which put Sookie Foyle nearer to accomplishing her own task, but the chance was coming.

Three of the APCs had lifted, but the rear tank was the only vehicle actually in motion. The whole valley floor was a killing ground. None of the APC commanders seemed willing to choose a route out of it when all routes were bad; and the Commanding Officer of the unit lay dead on his turret.

Ten meters—but the tank was accelerating. "Now!" Foyle screamed. "Guns, *now!*"

Only the disdain with which it shrugged off osmium projectiles made the mass of the tank credible. Gracefully, accelerating at a rate which must have rocked the men inside her, the tank approached the daisy-chain of high explosives. Dirt loosely mounded over a mine now squirted to either side, driven beneath the skirts by the fans.

Then it was past. The uncovered case of explosives gleamed in the sunlight behind the Republican tank.

"Guns, *now!*" Communicator Foyle was shouting as Sergeant-Gunner Jensen reached out of his trench and crimped the grenade fuze. No Republican saw the motion, an arm thrusting full length, then withdrawing beneath the sheet which had covered it until then.

The five further seconds which Jensen waited were as long as any block of time he could remember. He held his shoulder weapon tightly by its grip and barrel shroud. Jensen was not very good with the individual weapon, not like he was with the splendid automatic cannon he had abandoned. At this range, it would serve very well, though, if no stray round or ricochet—

The grenade went off ninety centimeters from Jensen's head. Then the world exploded.

The field expedient the Company had chosen to set off the daisy-chain was simple and effective. An ordinary mini-grenade would be set off next to a blasting cap, which would in turn be crimped into the first link of det cord. Concussion of the grenade would set off the lead azide primer in the cap, and the initiation cycle would proceed in normal milli-second course.

The problem was that the grenade itself had a five-second fuze. The tank, the target which *had* to be in the killing zone, had dialed on full power by the time it reached the daisy-chain—and passed it.

The ring of explosives went off like a read-out dial around the streak the shaped charge had already burned across the landscape. The individual blasts were squat and black and so huge that they completely hid the train of det cord that spurted between them at almost ten kilometers per second. To the mercenaries posted higher in the valley, there was a perceptible delay between the first case to detonate at the northern tangent of the ring and the last on the south toward which the blasts raced in mirror image from either side. The delay was in no sense significant.

Most of the explosives were wasted. Only three of the cases had any real effect on the Republican column. The remainder blew the ground into a gigantic funerary wreath, strewing brush and pulverized soil harmlessly over a square kilometer. There had been no assurance of where the Republicans would come from; and there would have been three cases, ninety kilos of plastic explosive, adjacent to any column which approached the bait.

The third armored personnel carrier blew straight upward, flattening and opening like a steel flower. Its self-sealing fuel tanks ruptured and were wrung like sponges by the blast. The sprayed fuel ignited in a great orange banner. It drifted north and started to settle before it burned out. Plating and the heavier contents of the vehicle tumbled over the black tendrils. The gun turret, squarely above the case of explosives, hung thirty meters in the air for the fraction of a second while inertia struggled with gravity. Then it fell back into the crater which gaped to receive it.

The fourth APC flipped over on its right side under the impact of blasts in front and to either flank. The angle it had taken in the hedgehog formation determined the details of its fate. Its fans shrieked. They were spinning at full throttle without the brake of an air cushion now that the plenum chamber was sideways. Several mercenaries on the south slope found the hubs irresistible bull's-eyes. The fan motors began to dissolve in cascades of blue sparks.

By contrast, the second personnel carrier was skidded twenty meters forward. Its nose grounded, then bucked upward when the rear drive fans lost all power. Heavy screens prevented trash from being sucked into their ducts, but the cubic meters of dirt excavated by the daisy-chain flooded the rear intakes and cut off the air flow completely. The vehicle began to wallow. Its driver and most of its infantry complement—those still alive—had been battered unconscious by the see-saw impacts. Like its overturned sister or the windows of an abandoned house, its defenselessness drew redoubled fire.

If the Republican tank had been directly over a charge the way the third APC had been, the tank would have been surely disabled and very possibly destroyed. Its mass and five meters grace saved it from either occurrence. Gimmicks had failed. Only stark courage remained.

Shock waves travel faster through ground than through air. When the daisy-chain went off, the little creek froze in a pattern of tiny white-caps at the intersections of the profusion of ripples. The floor of Lieutenant ben Mehdi's shallow trench bounced him up as he had not quite chosen to do willingly. Twenty meters away, the front elevation of the second tank was back-lit by the explosives it had just cleared.

The red flash was momentary, but not even the huge mass of the tank could ignore the blast entirely. The looming bow nosed down. Its skirt plowed a furrow four meters wide in the soil and brush. The grate-covered intakes along the upper deck sneered at ben Mehdi for an instant. All the anti-personnel charges ringing the hull went off together.

The crackling discharge was inaudible, but a diagonal line sawed off flanking foliage like wind sheer over a sand dune. The dirt rolling in front of the low skirt spewed higher, shot through the blue-white light like static electricity. Then the stern slammed down, the tank slewed, and tonnes of choking grit swept across it and ben Mehdi.

The Lieutenant fought upright in grim terror. His face-shield trapped air for his lungs, but the mass that blanketed him was lethal and blinding. The weight slipped away as ben Mehdi rose. The heat and grimy prickling remained. The first thing that the mercenary saw as soil cascaded off his face-shield was the tank, bucking and howling and broadside, less than three meters away.

The tank's skirt was crumpled. That increased the difficulties posed by the choked intakes. The driver was expert, however. First he had deliberately grounded his vehicle. He was clearing his fan ducts with short bursts where full power would have burned out the drive motors.

"Come on!" roared somebody else. Beside Lieutenant ben Mehdi loomed Gunner Jensen. He had lost his helmet again. His face and bare torso were gray with dust.

They ran toward the bellowing vehicle together. Jensen's left hand was on the Lieutenant's shoulder, but ben Mehdi was being guided rather than pulled. His own mind had disconnected itself in the maelstrom. Its hopes and prayers were void.

Jensen used his companion's shoulder as a post when he leaped to the deck of the tank. Ben Mehdi staggered. The vehicle was rocking from side to side. Shrieking, the turret began to rotate though the laser itself was silent. Beside the Lieutenant, the armor rang and a crater the size of a demitasse splashed out of the steel. The inner face of the crater gleamed with its new osmium plating. That was a molecular film of the projectile. It had vaporized with the steel as kinetic energy became heat in a microsecond.

The Sergeant fired down into a fan duct. His body recoiled upward as if he were riding a jack hammer, once, twice, and there was a shower of blue sparks from the intake as the laser tube brushed Jensen off in a flurry of limbs.

Lieutenant ben Mehdi acted with the passionless intellection of a computer. It was all he had, now that Jensen had stirred him into motion. Ben Mehdi ducked, craning his right arm and his grenade launcher up over the tank's deck. The pocked armor burned where his chest pressed against it. As the steel surged and air pumped down the intake past his weapon, ben Mehdi fired. The contact-fuzed grenade burst on the grating, lifting the mercenary's weapon but not tearing it out of his grasp. The tank's own armor protected his flesh, and the centimeter or so belled from the muzzle of the launcher tube did not impair its effectiveness. The Lieutenant thrust the weapon back and fired again. This time the blast was on the drive motor itself. The searing crackle of a short circuit extended the explosion.

When a second red light winked from his control panel, the Republican driver plunged into the panic he had resisted until then. He rammed the throttle forward and held it there, though the four rear intakes were still clogged. Even with the damage of its plenum chamber, the tank managed to skid sideways in a triumph of over-engineering. Ben Mehdi was knocked down. Jensen scrambled away from the steel Juggernaut. Then three fans failed explosively. The tank ground to a halt. It was alive, but it would be immobile until it could be hauled to a dock capable of repairing something built more massively than a starliner.

Sporadic shots were still being fired. All the armored personnel carriers were wrecked or burning. The few surviving Republican infantrymen were throwing down their rifles, praying to be allowed to surrender.

Captain Albrecht Waldstejn was not fully conscious. His hands were pressed against the ground, but he did not have enough coordination to push himself up to a kneeling position. "Got to move before they spot us again," he was whispering. "Got to go where they won't be looking...."

CHAPTER NINE

"Look, baby," said Churchie Dwyer on the vehicle-to-vehicle push, "it's all one with me. But if you people don't come out now, you don't get asked again."

The interior lights of the lead tank were on. The mercenary could not claim that it was the darkness of the fighting compartment that made him claustrophobic. Dwyer did not like it, though, even with both hatches wide open. Mrs. Dwyer hadn't raised any turtles, no sir. A bunker was bad enough, and bunkers weren't usually targets three and a half meters high.

The commander of the other tank responded with a volley of what were literally curses. The Rube officer took delight—or at least, such pleasure as anything gave him at the moment—in cataloguing the torments due Dwyer and the rest of the Company in Hell. Just fine, the gangling trooper thought. He snapped off the radio. There were some people whom it was more than a business to blow away, and a lot of them on Cecach seemed to wear taupe uniforms. Churchie levered himself up and stood on the tank commander's seat. His head stuck out in the open air again that way. "All right, Del," he shouted. "Let's do it."

The Rube gunner stared nervously at Churchie from the other seat in the turret. He had waved a rag from his own hatch instead of trying to drag his CO clear and button the tank up. That had saved his ass, but he was obviously uncertain as to whether or not it would stay saved. For the moment, his mercenary captors needed him to identify controls in the disabled tank. That was a short-term proposition.

Trooper Dwyer bumped his knee on the turret controls. "Goddam if I know why anybody serves in a coffin like this," he grumbled in Czech to the prisoner in the seat below. "Only goddam thing I can see they're good for is shooting the hell out of other tanks—and we can't even do that since some dickhead put a couple rounds through the laser."

"I, I'm sorry," the gunner said. He nodded his head as if the bruise on his forehead had not left it throbbing in agony. The prisoner would have agreed or apologized in response to anything the mercenary said to him. Not only had the gunner seen the bodies outside before his captors ordered him back within the tank, he could also smell the men who had been aboard APCs which had burned.

Churchie craned his neck to watch Del. The job had fallen to Dwyer because he spoke enough Czech and he was not involved in further planning the way Hummel and ben Mehdi were. It would be a relief when it was over, but that ought to be soon.

The crew of the second tank refused to be reasonable, and they had a bow gun which still worked even though it did not bear on anything in particular. The Rubes could watch Del Hoybrin dragging the power cable toward them from their captured consort, twenty meters away, but there was nothing they could do about the fact. For that matter, if they even thought about it at all it was probably to make sure they were not touching metal.

Del clamped the cable to the stub of the second tank's radio antenna. The big man waved to Churchie, then ran back to cover behind the captured vehicle.

Churchie dropped back into the turret. "All rightie, sweetheart," he said to the captive gunner, "you do it." Frightened but willing to do whatever he was asked, the Republican flipped a switch on the control panel between the two seats.

The tank generator could be used to supply six-hundred volt DC current through a reeled cable at the stern of the vehicle. The tanks' fusion bottles made the heavy vehicles useful power sources for units in bivouac. Now it gave the Company a means of eliminating die-hards whom they could not reach otherwise.

When the captive gunner threw the switch, all the instruments in the second tank flickered and the electrically-primed ammunition for the bow gun detonated. There were about a hundred and fifty rounds in the metal loading drum. When they all went off together, the driver's hatch blew open and the huge turret lifted its trunions from the track on which they rotated.

Inside the captured tank, the explosion was only a thump. Churchie Dwyer raised himself again to look at the results. Gray smoke was boiling out of the fore-hatch and around the turret base of the other vehicle. There were no screams from the crew; nor, of course, were there survivors. Del Hoybrin was watching as he waited for further directions. "Right," said Churchie to his prisoner. "Up and out, baby. You just earned yourself the chance to be tied up and left at the pit head, what's left of it."

The Republican obeyed, using the hydraulic lift on his seat instead of clambering out as if it were part of an obstacle course. He had a sick expression on his face.

"Cheer up," said Dwyer as he swung his own legs clear. He gestured toward the other tank. The smoke from its hatch was now black and occasionally touched with the flames which were cremating the bodies within. "Think of the alternatives, hey?"

"That was Black One at the pit head," said Communicator Foyle. "They've secured all the prisoners and they're following on."

Albrecht Waldstejn had a radio helmet, now, but he had made no response to Sergeant Hummel's call. He did not respond to Foyle's prompting, either. The savior and by God commanding officer of the Company was trudging ahead in a daze. The Communicator touched him on the shoulder. "Sir?" she said.

"I'm all right!" the Cecach officer snarled. When

he turned toward the contact, he stumbled. There was a curse from the line of troopers behind as they bunched. A stretcher bearer stumbled in turn.

"Oh, Maria," Waldstejn prayed as Sookie Foyle's arms helped him straighten and resume his place in the file. Most of the Company had their night visors locked down, though there was still enough afterglow to see the back of the trooper marching in front of you. "Sorry, Sookie," the officer muttered. "I was . . . I'm not very alert."

"My fault to bother you, Captain," Foyle said. She took pleasure both in Waldstejn's use of her first name and in the opportunity for her to call him by the rank she herself had conferred. When they got back to Praha, it would be over; but they were days short of Praha at best. Days and nights. "Sergeant Hummel said the rest of Black Section is following along," the Communicator repeated. "And she said it worked just like you said it would with the tank."

"Damn, I should have stayed with them till they got clear," the young officer muttered. "I don't like—" he shrugged— "running out that way." Shrugging had been a bad idea. It pulled at the scabs over his shoulder blades and the torn fabric sticking to them. Waldstejn had skidded on his back very hard when the explosion hurled him down. Marco Bertinelli had looked at him, but he was not the sort of medic who would spend time on a scraped officer when there were real wounded around. And even from the first, before a trooper had handed the logy Waldstejn a canteen and amphetamines, the Cecach officer had been alert enough to prevent *that* misuse of the Corpsman's time.

"So you could slow them down while they try to catch up with the rest of us?" the Communicator asked bluntly. "Sir, a few people had to take care of the prisoners and the last tank. We've got stretcher cases, we've got people like you who ought to be in stretchers. Right now, Jo Hummel needs you like a hole in the head. Tomorrow night we'll *all* need you. After all, it's your plan."

"My plan," Albrecht Waldstejn repeated in a dull voice. He hoped he had explained it in detail to somebody else. Because right at this moment, it was unbearably difficult to remember how to walk in lock step with the trooper in front of him.

Pavlovich's hands were on fire.

"Look, Guns," Sergeant Mboko was saying behind him, "I can tell off a couple of my people if you need a hand with the stretcher."

The trouble with the stretcher was not just the weight. Herzenberg's boots caught Pavlovich's thighs every time an irregularity in the ground threw him off stride. Also, a stretcher pole bit the hands differently from anything else. The calluses at the base of the trooper's fingers had already worked loose. One of the resulting blisters had burst stickily. The rest would follow before this night—much less this march—was over.

"No," said Sergeant Jensen. The poles trembled with the violent shake of his head. "We'll take care of our own for now, Stack. You'll need all you've got left unencumbered if the Rubes manage an ambush."

Sergeant Mboko snorted, but he did not state the obvious. The Company would need more than his leading fire team if they stumbled into the enemy yet tonight. "Well, don't forget the offer," the black sergeant remarked. He shouldered brush aside to pass Pavlovich and Cooper on his way forward.

Take care of our own! The gun crew was part of the Company, wasn't it?" Pavlovich's arms felt at each stride as if they were going to pull out of his shoulders. Cooper, ahead of him, was crumpled under the weight of two packs and weapons. At least he did not have the stretcher poles flaying his palms.

Of course, they already *had* flayed Cooper's palms. Cooper had taken the first half hour on the front of the stretcher, while the gun slings had cut against Pavlovich's collarbones and the two packs ground his vertebrae together. In a few minutes, they would switch off again. It would have been nice to have a couple of the under-loaded troopers of White Section lending a hand.

Grigor Pavlovich continued to stumble forward silently. It would not have done him any good to speak to the Gunner. Besides, Roland Jensen still carried his own pack and weapon as well as the back of the stretcher. And so far as either of his conscious crewmen could tell, Jensen intended to carry the stretcher without relief until the column halted at daybreak.

"God *damn* it," Pavel Hodicky burst out through his snuffling. "It isn't fair!"

Instead of agreeing with the younger man, Churchie Dwyer said, "Well, I don't know it's ever fair, baby. But it was going to happen, if that's what you mean. Hell, it was bound to."

Hodicky spun. The tall veteran, last man in the

column as usual, waved him onward with the ration bar he was chewing. They had full rations again, courtesy of the stocks in the two APCs which had not burned. "March or die," Dwyer said, and his grin did not make the words a joke.

The deserter fell into line again. They had lost a pace or two on the next ahead, Trooper Hoybrin. Del carried two packs like the troops of the main unit with the four stretcher cases. The spare pack was Hodicky's, though the little private had not realized the fact yet. He had accepted the rifle and bandolier they had handed him, but in the shock of Quade's death he had not been able to think about the rations and field gear which should have been his responsibility also. Hodicky would have been up with the main body, except that Dwyer had tipped Sergeant Hummel the wink as she told off her rear guard.

"Look," Hodicky muttered as he trudged forward, "I know Q didn't talk much, but he wasn't dumb. He wasn't!"

"No argument," the veteran replied mildly around the last mouthful of ration. Ignoring orders, he pitched the foil wrapper into the brush. If the Rubes were sophisticated enough to track them by that, they were too sophisticated to need to do so. If Captain Waldstejn didn't like it, Captain Waldstejn could police up all the crap himself.

"Well, I suppose you thought it, though," Hodicky replied. He was calmer but still defensive. "I've heard what he did, stood there to keep them away from me till the bomb blew him up. But it wasn't because he was stupid, it was for *me*! Because I got myself in a hole, didn't know what I was doing . . . and Q gets killed."

"Look, sweetheart," said Churchie Dwyer. He had carried around a three-legged cat for a year until a quarantine official on Rereway had killed it. "Del's dumb, right? You tell him to stick his arm in a drive fan to jam it and he'd likely try. But he's not going to go out of his *way* to kill himself. Now, there's times you're going to go West no matter what you do. But even in this business, you can die in bed if you don't spend too much time looking for someplace else to do it. I don't have a word to say against your friend Q . . . but baby, he was going to buy it before he was much older. In a bar or a barracks—or hell, in the kitchen when his old lady put a knife in him. I'm sorry, but he was the kind who finds a way."

They marched along without speaking further for several minutes. Hodicky had made sure that his issue boots fit when he was assigned to the supply room, but the unaccustomed marching had raised a blister on his right heel anyway. "Churchie?" he said at last.

"Umm?"

"What would you do if somebody ordered *you* to stick your arm in a drive fan?"

The gangling trooper laughed. "Well, kid," he said. "I've knocked around a bit. One of the reasons I've stuck with the Company is it's not the sort of outfit you hear orders like that very often." After a pause, he added in a somewhat lower voice, "I don't guess you'll ever hear an order like that twice from the same guy."

The brush whispered against their uniforms as they continued to march toward the objective Albrecht Waldstejn had set for them.

*   *   *

"Stupid bastards," muttered Sergeant Mboko toward the distant gleam of light. Pressing the bulge on his helmet to key the command channel, he said, "White One. I'm on the last ridge. The outpost's manned, I can see light there."

"—got to rest here," Hussein ben Mehdi babbled, his words stumbling over the last of Mboko's. "We're all beat, we're wasted. There's no way we can—"

The voice cut off. Either someone had physically removed the Lieutenant's finger from the transmit switch, or Communicator Foyle had cut him out of the circuit. Damned right, the chickenshit . . . though the Lieutenant had earned his pay with that tank, so you never could tell.

Brush crackled. Mboko had ordered a general halt, but Dubose had decided to squirm up beside his section leader. "That it?" the Leading Trooper asked. His voice was muffled by his face shield. Minuscule leakage from the shelter two klicks away made it a beacon under the shield's enhancement.

"Why—" the Sergeant began. His radio interrupted him.

"Top to White One," said Albrecht Waldstejn's voice. It was thinner than radio propagation alone could explain. "Will the brush where you are cover us in daylight?"

The black sergeant looked around him. Light enhancement, no matter how effective, robbed you of real depth perception. Still, Mboko had been using a night visor long enough to make more than an educated guess about the present surroundings. "Yeah," he said, "it's no different from the rest of what we've been hiking through. Stay low, stay twenty meters back from where the ridge drops away, and I don't see any problem. If they send a drone over, we've got problems irregardless."

"If they think there's a reason to search for us here," Waldstejn agreed, "then we've got problems." There was a pause and a crackle of static. The Captain's voice resumed with a difference in timbre which marked the general push, "Top to max units. We'll bivouac on this ridge. White One will give assignments left to his section, Guns will assign his people and the wounded center, Red Two will assign Black Section right until Black One rejoins. We'll be here all day with no smoke and no movement."

There was a pause, but it was for Captain Waldstejn to clear his throat. "Get your rest now, soldiers. Tomorrow night we come down to it. Over and out."

"So that's really it, huh?" Dubose said, waving again toward the light on the far ridge.

"Why the hell ask me, trooper?" replied Sergeant Mboko testily. "Didn't you spend just as much time as I did at Smiricky #4?"

CHAPTER TEN

The five of them did not need to look at one another while they hashed things out. The command channel would have worked, would have permitted the non-coms and the two officers to lie with their separate units while they made the final dispositions.

Human nature beat technology in straight sets, as it usually does. The command group lay on its individual bellies, facing inward like a dry-land version of an Esther Williams routine. They were as tired as any of the troopers they commanded, and the sun that spiked down through the bush above them was just as hot as it was elsewhere on the ridge. When Gunner Jensen saw someone crawling toward them, making the shrub shiver, he snarled, "What the *hell* do you think you're doing,

trooper? Get back where you belong, and if you
disobey orders again I *guarantee* you won't move a
third time." Jensen's hand was tight on his gunstock, but the real threat was in his hard blue
eyes.

Sergeant Hummel looked back over her shoulder.
The strain made her squint. "It's Dwyer," she said
to the command group. More sharply, she called,
"Spit it out, soldier, and get your ass back where
it belongs." The section leader did not care for
Trooper Dwyer. She knew a good deal about him,
and she guessed more. But Dwyer was not the sort
to need hand-holding or to call his superiors' attention to himself without reason.

"Look," Churchie said. He was speaking toward
the soil rather than to the command group. If
there had been a way to hand this to somebody
else, he would have done so; but Del could never
do it, and nobody but the pair of them knew.
"There's another goddam route through the mines."

Hummel rolled on her side so that she could
look at Dwyer more easily. Alone of the five
listeners, she understood the veteran's self-directed
anger. Dwyer was in the process of volunteering
for a particularly nasty job. He must have figured
his chances of survival were even worse if he remained silent. Perhaps Del Hoybrin's life also had
a place in Churchie's calculations. Hummel was
quite convinced that the survival of the rest of the
Company had not been a major factor.

Lieutenant ben Mehdi craned his neck to see
past a branch and say the wrong thing. "What do
you mean 'another route', trooper?" he demanded
in a voice that cracked for dryness.

Trooper Hoybrin carried four extra canteens. Churchie's response had all the sneering range that he would not, save for anger, have lavished on a superior. "Hey," he snapped, "we march in by the way we came out, that's the plan? Right over the fucking mines even a dickhead'd have sense enough to lay there after we did a bug-out? Or maybe you were figuring to waltz in along the pylons, where there's still a working laser and a half dozen bunkers with a clear field of fire?"

"Calm down, soldier," said Albrecht Waldstejn hoarsely. "Tell us about the better way."

The gangling veteran was right. Hummel and Mboko had insisted—with a parochial contempt for indig forces—that the Company's escape route would not have been sealed, not in three days. Waldstejn, with the mild agreement of Sergeant Jensen, thought that even Lichtenstein would have mined the corridor before the surrender. That way, the Major would have had *something* to offer his new masters in place of inertia in the face of failure. The real problem was that there was no way to determine who was correct. The corridor would only be scouted in the dark, when whoever was making the reconnaissance was likely to detonate a mine if there were any.

The casualty was acceptable, under the circumstances. The warning the blast would give to the garrison was not.

"There's an old fuel tank on the slope," Churchie said. He was mumbling again, and the others had to strain to hear him. "It's still there, I checked before I broke in on you guys. There's a cleared path, narrow but they didn't know about it, so I figure it's still there. I can flag it. Other end's the OP."

"That observation post's still manned," said Sergeant Mboko. "They had a light on last night."

"Campbell said he smashed the monitors before he leap-frogged in," Jo Hummel responded. "Unless they switched gear from the south OP, then it's visual only. And I doubt any of the indigs could figure out how to connect Class 3 sensors even if they did try." Hummel was still looking at Dwyer. He would not meet her eyes.

"Well," said Sergeant Jensen, "I like it better than trying to enter along the truck route. And that was the best choice *I'd* heard."

"Even if the sensors aren't working," said Sergeant Mboko patiently, "there are guards there. If anything happens, we've still got to get down the back slope and through the bunkers after they're alerted. That's just what you were afraid of if they'd mined the Colonel's corridor."

"No, it'll still work," said Waldstejn with sudden animation. His headache had dulled to a background level after they halted. The muscle cramps and bruises were almost a pleasure by comparison. "I'll be the first one through. If anything happens, a shot or somebody hits the alarm, I'll be right there at the radio. Nobody on night duty in Headquarters is going to worry if he's told in Czech it's all right."

"God dammit, you are *not* going to do that," Sergeant Hummel insisted with real anger. "No goddam body but you has a prayer of making a deal with that spacer. Things are tight enough anyway without a bunch of us trying to introduce ourself while all hell breaks loose." She paused, breathing hard. "Nothing wrong with the plan, though," she muttered. "I'll go first instead."

The Cecach officer sighed and struck both his palms against the ground. A thorn jabbed the heel of his right hand. "Sergeant," he said, "we aren't talking about being understood. If the first thing the duty officer hears after a shot at the OP is somebody muttering pidgin on the radio, he's not even going to *wonder* what happened. He's going to know, and he's going to hit the general alarm so fast his hand blurs. This isn't hero time, this is business."

"Well, hell, your kid can do it then," said Churchie Dwyer.

They had forgotten him. The command group turned in surprise to an unexpected voice. The muttered statement made sense only to Waldstejn anyway. In the brief pause, the Cecach captain said, "Private Hodicky? Ah, I don't think—"

"Well, why not then, dammit?" Jo Hummel interrupted. "He's a native speaker and he's damned well expendable!"

The Captain's mind flashed red, but no retort was called for. In the present circumstances, 'expendable' was a technical term, like 'dead'. A factor to take into account.

In any case, it was impossible to object to Sergeant Hummel's characterization when she had just volunteered to take the lead position herself. Waldstejn said, "I think we've got to class Private Hodicky with the walking wounded. His friend, you know, Quade—that was a bad shock to him."

"It's going to be a worse shock if they're waiting and kill us all!" Hussein ben Mehdi burst out. "The only way we got out alive was they were all looking the other way. And this is the *Rubes*, not the bone-brains in the 522nd!"

"Hey," said Trooper Dwyer.

The others ignored him. "That's right, Captain," said Sergeant Mboko. "They need that big a garrison if they're going to keep the Complex going with all those civilians."

"Ten to one odds if we crash in," Hummel agreed harshly. "And them in bunkers, likely with heavy weapons this time. Who the hell do you think we are, an armored division?"

"Captain!" said Churchie Dwyer. For the first time, the veteran trooper had lifted his head toward the command group and had spoken distinctly. They looked back at him. "Captain," Dwyer said, reverting to his normal whining tone toward superiors, "the kid'll be OK. He's coming around. And he'll be OK."

Waldstejn sighed. He began picking at the thorn in his palm. "We've got a lot of choice, don't we?" he said to his hands. Then he looked up. "All right, Hodicky will be with the leading element to cover in an emergency," he said crisply. "Thank you, Pri-Trooper."

Churchie Dwyer dipped his head in response. He slid backward, looking for a place more clear of brush so that he could turn around. Albrecht Waldstejn called after him, "Trooper? We'll brief him later, of course, but—would you tell Pavel about this? Give him a little more warning."

Churchie nodded again. As Dwyer crawled away,

the Cecach officer was saying, "All right, the observation post is nearer where we want to go; but do we have details of the bunkers along that section of the compound?"

CHAPTER ELEVEN

The markers were stakes of brush split lengthwise so that their white cores faced the oncoming troops. Tape would have been better, but they did not have tape, did not have wire—did not even have cloth which would not determinedly blend in with its surroundings. Directly ahead of Pavel Hodicky, Churchie Dwyer grunted as he thrust another stake into the ground. He began to crawl forward, angling to the right this time.

The Cecach private had not thought about the mines at all during the time he was stationed at Smiricky #4. The mines had been strewn around the valley years before in much the same way that the cluster bombs had been dropped during the Republican attack. They were laid on the reverse slopes instead of being targeted on the valley itself, of course; and unlike the bombs, they did not arm themselves until they had been exposed to the air for an hour or two. After that, they slowly weathered to the look of rocks the size of a child's fist. They remained lethal until they were detonated, and a kilogram's pressure or less was quite enough to set them off.

"Another stake!" Churchie whispered.

Hodicky passed one to the veteran, taking another in turn from Del Hoybrin behind him. Colonel Fasolini's escape route had been a genuine corridor, cleared to a minimum width of two meters. It had a single dog-leg in it so that a fortunate intruder could not simply follow his nose across the minefield; but the escape route had been intended for fast use under adverse circumstances.

Churchie Dwyer had not needed such a corridor, nor could he have have cleared one without being caught. Wherever possible, Dwyer had skirted mines which lay in his immediate way. Only when chance had sewn an area too thickly to be avoided had he actually removed mines. There was no safe way to do that except by blowing them in place. Trooper Hoybrin had carefully dropped a hundred-kilo sack of dirt on each mine while his partner prayed that both the blast and the noise would be adequately absorbed.

The path which resulted from the troopers' combined labors was a snake trail. Churchie himself was muttering gloomy appraisals. Pavel Hodicky would have been terrified of what he was doing, except that he was even more terrified of what he might be about to do.

Hodicky had been issued a helmet salvaged from one of the four dead. It had blood on the inner lining, but that was not why he did not wear it now. Bareheaded, with the darker Woodland pattern of his uniform turned out, Hodicky might for a moment pass for a Rube soldier. The off-planet precision of the metal-fiber helmet would mark him at once to anyone who saw it; and Hodicky had learned very early in life that the top of his head was generally going to be the first part of him people saw.

Dwyer paused again. Hodicky had been following by watching the veteran's boots and pretending there was nothing else around him. Now Churchie was gesturing forward with one crooked finger. The Cecach private forced himself to look.

Slightly above them and less than three meters away was the sand-bagged end of a shelter. Two narrow firing slits had been left in the facing wall. The light from within the shelter made the slits glare at Hodicky like the eyes of a predator.

Cautiously, concerned now with noise alone since they were beyond the mines, the mercenary began to crawl toward the slits. Hodicky also began to edge forward, a little more to the right to bring him to the blank side of the beryllium arch instead of the bags. He could hear whispers of movement behind him but he dared not look around. After swallowing hard, Hodicky unslung his rifle and began to waddle up the final slope. He could not crawl as Churchie did without the weapon scraping on the ground. A noise like that here, and—

The back curtain of the shelter brushed open. Light bloomed about the soldier who had just exited. The man was reaching for his fly, spitting distance from Hodicky, when he stopped and cried, "What—"

The Cecach private stood up. "It's all right, Ser-

geant Breisach," he called in a loud voice so that
no one in the shelter would panic. "We were sent
to relieve you." Hodicky walked toward the tall
man whom he had expected never to meet again.

The curtain shuffled. Hodicky could not see it
yet from his angle, but a voice called, "Hey, they're
relieving us?" It was easy enough to visualize the
face turned hopefully out toward the darkness.

"What do you—*Sergeant*!" Breisach said, closing
with a snarl and a snatch toward his rifle. That
movement stopped. The turncoat did not have
enough visual purple to see the hedge of weapons
aimed at him, but Del Hoybrin's looming bulk was
itself a death threat. Breisach backed toward the
curtained entrance again, driven by Hoybrin's gesturing rifle. Dwyer and Trooper Powers had thrust
their weapons through the firing slits. When the
soldier within turned in sudden confusion, it was
to face the muzzles of a pair of guns aimed at his
chest and right eye. His hands rose silently and his
jaw began to tremble.

Sergeant Hummel stepped past Hodicky and
tugged the slung rifle from Breisach's arm. The
captive was still in Federal uniform, but his collar
wings were ragged. All the non-coms of the 522nd
had been publicly stripped of their rank tabs as
part of the restructuring process of their new over-
lords. A few soldiers had been hanged as incorrigi-
ble idolators as well, but that had been a ploy to
get the attention of the rest. The Council of Deacons knew as well as anyone else did that religious
partisans were assigned to shock units, not sumps
like the 522nd Garrison Battalion.

"In there," Hummel rasped to their captive. "And
don't move except I tell you."

Breisach obeyed with a look of sullen hatred. Hummel opened her mouth to send Trooper Hoy-brin in to watch the prisoners. Pavel Hodicky was already following the ex-sergeant. The section leader blinked, but she had more important things to worry about at the moment. Standing outside the shelter for the sake of radio propagation, she began to report the situation to the rest of the command group in urgent tones.

The shelter was cramped by three men and the tension. Pavel Hodicky did not know the other captive though he also wore a Federal uniform. The little private only glanced at that man, however. He was focused on Wolfgang Breisach, just as the big ex-sergeant glowered at Hodicky alone instead of at the weapons pointed at his back.

"You're gone, you know, you little bastard," Breisach said. "You got nowhere left to run." His torso was angled forward, lowering his head. The shelter was deep enough to clear Breisach's hair along the arch where he stood, but anger was tugging him forward against the chain of fear.

"Didn't think they'd leave you all here," said Private Hodicky. His mind was widely separated from his voice, from the present world. "Lot of things I didn't think."

"You know what they're going to do to you and your little faggot friend?" Breisach continued hoarsely. "The—the Deacons, they don't like queers, no. They'll—"

"Quade's dead, you know," Hodicky said. He was smiling. "It was really because of you and Ondru that he, that he had to go off the way he did."

"Kid!" Churchie Dwyer whispered from the firing

slit. Del had pulled aside the curtain, but he was viewing the interior of the shelter with no more than his usual mild interest. The other prisoner was openly terrified. He had backed into a corner. He did not notice the radio until his hip brushed it. Trooper Powers was twisting her own weapon to keep it bearing on the nervous man, unable to intervene through the opening in any other way.

"Hey, that's too *bad*," Breisach sneered with his voice rising. "Burning in Hell like that, what do you suppose he'd give for a taste of your nice, juicy cock?"

"Why don't you ask him?" said Pavel Hodicky. He fired. The bullet shattered Breisach's breastbone. The other prisoner knocked over the lamp as he flung himself against the wall. There was a cavity the size of a fist at the base of Breisach's throat. Air which had been rammed through his upper windpipe blurted out his mouth with a spray of blood. The involuntary sound was lost in the blasting report of the rifle. The dead man fell forward. His clawing right hand brushed his murderer's boot.

Sergeant Hummel slid past Del in a crouch, her weapon waist-high and ready. "What the *hell*?" she snarled as she took in the tableau.

"Victor to Blue Light," demanded the radio.

Private Hodicky walked to the set. The remaining captive scrambled away from him on the dirt floor. Hummel started to move toward the little private, but she caught herself after only a step.

The radio was one from battalion stores, perhaps one Hodicky himself had signed out one day in the past. He keyed the microphone and said, "Blue Light to Victor. We had an accidental discharge but no harm done. Over." Fresh blood and powder smoke stank in the confined shelter.

"Victor to Blue Light," said the radio. "I'll have to log this, you know. Over."

"Do anything you please," said Pavel Hodicky. "Blue Light, over and out." He set down the microphone.

The section leader touched Hodicky gently on the arm. "I'll take over," she said. "Go on out, get a breath of air while I talk to our friend here." She toed the living prisoner. He was beginning to stand up again.

Hodicky nodded and walked to the curtained doorway. Del Hoybrin moved back to let him through. Before he stepped outside, the little private turned again. In a voice of sedated calm he said, "Q isn't queer, you know. Neither of us are."

"To tell the truth," said Jo Hummel, "it hadn't occurred to me that it mattered."

Shaking her head, she began to question the wide-eyed captive.

Sergeant Mboko's boots scrunched as he ran toward the gunslit. The noise sounded louder to him than it really was. Every time his toes slammed down, his ears felt the shock of all his weight and equipment in addition to the airborne sound.

It also seemed louder because the black noncom knew exactly what would happen if any of the men in the bunker awakened. It was unlikely that even a garrison soldier could miss with a burst at a point-blank, no-deflection target.

They would rather have bypassed the bunkers. The Company had returned to Smiricky #4 looking for escape, not a battle. Though the bunkers themselves were spaced widely enough that a file could safely thread between them in the darkness, each position also housed an intrusion alarm. The sensor loops of the alarms effectively closed the interstices between the bunkers.

The plan of attack banked on a peculiarity caused by the real mission of the 522nd, which was to prevent the laborers from escaping. Both ends of the sensor loops were attached to the monitors by lead wires. If a bio-electrical field approached the charged portion of the loop, the alarm would sound. The portion of the loop which was lead wire, however, was insulated so that the outpost itself would not set off the alarms; and around the Smiricky compound, the leads were toward the outside instead of on the inward face of the enclosed area. Unless the Rubes had changed the system—and the prisoner swore they had not—the sensors were arrayed to warn of escape, not attack. Mboko should be able to get very close before the defenders realized he was there.

The edges of Mboko's knife shimmered in the starlight: very close indeed.

Hussein ben Mehdi lay on his belly, wishing the herbicide sprayed on the valley every quarter had been more effective. The growth which managed to sprout on the blasted soil was stunted and deformed even by Cecach standards. None of it was over a hand's breadth high, so it was as useful for cover or concealment as the felt on a craps table. The thorns jabbing at his sixth and seventh ribs, however, were as long and as sharp as anything he had felt on this planet— might the Stoned One devour it!

There were four White Section troopers beside the Lieutenant. They were watching dust puff around Mboko's boots as he sprinted the eighty meters to the dug-outs. The troopers were tense, ready to follow their Sergeant if he were successful.

Lieutenant Hussein ben Mehdi was with them because he was their only hope of survival if the shit hit the fan instead.

Sergeant Mboko ran in a crouch, ready for the shock of the bullets which would prove he had failed. Ben Mehdi felt a shiver and looked away from the non-com. His grenade launcher was two centimeters shorter now than issue, the amount which had been tattered by its own blasts in the tank intake. Gunner Jensen had suggested that ben Mehdi switch weapons with another of the grenadiers, but two practice rounds had proved to the Lieutenant's satisfaction that the short tube still had what it took. His hands knew the launcher's grip and fore-end. Objects may not have souls, but familiarity can give them the semblance of one.

If the guards in the bunker opened fire, somebody had to lob grenades through each of the gunslits. No one in the Company could be trusted to do that at night except Hussein ben Mehdi.

Everyone in Fasolini's Company was armed with a real weapon, even the nominal 'lieutenant' who had been signed on as a negotiating tool. Most people thought that ben Mehdi had chosen the grenade launcher over an armor-piercing squeezebore because the former was relatively light. That was not the case. The recoil of the squeeze-bore made it almost impossible to fire from a prone position, hugging the ground with the greatest surface of your vulnerable flesh. By contrast, ben Mehdi could launch gas-propelled concussion grenades all day and never have to lift himself in the face of fire.

And he had gotten very good, against the day that the Colonel might decide that his five grenadiers were superfluous to a company of tank busters and should be reëquipped. The Lieutenant had wanted to be able to prove that *his* skill, at least, was too great to be discarded.

That skill had just set him at the Windy Corner.

Sergeant Mboko reached the bunker and flattened himself against the face of it, between a pair of gun-slits. He waved back at the troopers waiting to follow if he made the run himself without tripping the alarm. Quickly but in single file, the five mercenaries scrambled to obey the summons. Further back in the darkness, the remainder of the Company lay tense but immobile until the leading team had cleared the bunker.

Lieutenant ben Mehdi was the last man in the file, but he got to his feet without hesitation. Him in a shock commando—him!

And the strangest thing of all was that, as Allah willed, the situation did not seem to be bothering him the way it should have.

The bunker was dug halfway below surface. Its roof was only a meter above ground level. Sergeant Mboko braced his left hand on the top and sprang up, directly onto the soldier sleeping there.

The Cecach soldier started up with a cry which would have been louder if much of the breath had not been driven out by the mercenary's hips. For the Sergeant, it was like stepping onto a platform that was not really there. The irregular, sand-bagged surface had hidden the guard in the darkness. Mboko had kept his face-shield up because depth perception was more important to him than light-gathering while he sprinted toward the bunker.

Now Mboko swung wildly at the cry in the same instinctive horror with which he might have brushed a spider from his eyelid. The knife jarred and twisted in his hand despite its keen edge. The human bulk beneath him kicked while its throat made clucking noises. The Sergeant had not slashed through the neck as he had intended; he had buried ten centimeters of his blade in the soldier's temple.

Mboko could hear the troopers of his section running toward the bunker. With a desperate fury, the Sergeant tugged his weapon clear. The soldier's heels were drumming on the sandbags. It seemed impossible that the guards within the bunker would not awaken at the perfect time to slaughter the five men. Mboko braced his left hand on the Cecach soldier's chest.

The soldier had been a woman. Her breasts lay like gelatine over muscles which were going rigid in death.

The knife came free. There was no sound from inside the bunker.

The first of Mboko's troopers vaulted to the top of the position as the Sergeant waved them on.

It was not a neat operation, but they were not in a business where neat bought any groceries. The six mercenaries poised at the narrow doorway. That many men would be in each other's way inside. Ben Mehdi and another trooper knelt, facing the Complex proper. Mboko counted with his raised fingers for the others. As the Sergeant dipped his hand the third time, Dubose launched himself into the bunker. He carried a knife in his right hand and a light-wand in his left. The Leading Trooper flicked on the wand, silhouetting Mboko against a background of dull yellow as the Sergeant plunged through the doorway himself. The other two of the entry team were a step and a step behind.

There were three Cecach soldiers inside. One was up on his elbow, awakened by the scuffling above him. The guard had time to shout and raise a hand before Dubose landed on his chest. The mercenary tossed the light-wand aside reflexively as he grappled, striking twice at his victim's throat. Three of the dying soldier's fingers came off as his hand convulsed on the blade it had clutched in desperation.

The light-wand was necessary for speed and safety, but its saffron glow awakened the other two guards as well. The section leader ignored them. He jumped past Dubose to the alarm monitor in a corner. Mboko put the toe of his boot through the screen. The alarm disconnected with a pop and a stench mingled of ozone and arcing components. Only then did Mboko turn to find that his men had handled their tasks with the necessary competence.

Butter Platt was cursing. He had tripped on a foot-locker and cut his own left hand badly. That had not prevented him from ripping his target all the way from belly to collarbone. He had kept the blade of his knife to the right of his victim's sternum, where the ends of the ribs are still cartilaginous in a young man. The opened body cavity gaped like a run spreading in a stocking. The point had not nicked a bowel, so the bunker filled with a smell like that of blood on turned earth. When the curly-haired mercenary looked from his own wound to the damage he had caused, he began to smile. His uniform developed a bulge where it covered his groin.

Chen did not care for knives. Because of the bunker's low ceiling, he could not swing his entrenching tool properly. Instead, he stabbed down as if the short-handled shovel were a fishing spear. Its sharpened edge bit, but the Cecach soldier somehow managed to scream until the shovel had chopped him three more times.

The light-wand had rolled under one of the cots. Sergeant Mboko picked it up. In its yellow light, the four mercenaries appeared to be smeared with a black that glistened on their skins and molded their uniforms stickily to their bodies. The section leader took a deep, shuddering breath. "OK," he said, "that's it."

The troopers began to file out. Mboko called after them, "Dubose, get a dressing on Platt's hand."

"Christ, Butter," Dubose muttered as he glanced from the cut to Platt's face, "you're a real sicko. You really like hurting people, don't you?"

"Hey," said the other trooper as he stepped into the night, "do I talk about you and your little girls?"

Mboko switched off the wand. He held it in one of the sand-bagged firing slits and flicked three pulses toward the darkness and the rest of the Company. They were keeping strict radio silence now that the ridge no longer shielded their transmission from the receivers in the Complex itself. All clear. No problems.

God, what a way to make a living.

The Sergeant stepped out of the bunker and drew another deep breath. The fresh night air flushed the abattoir reek from his lungs, but nothing could clear his mind.

There were no guards posted outside the *Katyn Forest*. The bridge scuttle was retracted and all three cargo holds were clam-shelled shut. Nothing could be done about the rent in the hull where the bomb had punched through, however. The hand-holds meant for operation in a vacuum gave access of a sort up the curve of the hull. It was not access which would have done Albrecht Waldstejn much good without Trooper Hoybrin above, hauling him up by rope to the point the cylindrical hull began to curve in again, however.

Panting, the Captain reached the hole on which they depended for entrance. Sergeant Hummel and three Black Section troopers were already there. Waldstejn, with his familiar face and uniform, had to be the first inside.

Necessarily, they had made a great deal of noise on the hull. The lights visible within the Power Room meant nothing—in that location, the glow strips were probably permanently charged. Waldstejn braced his hands on the impressed lips of the bomb puncture and let his legs dangle. Maria. If a squad of Republican guards were waiting for the first man through the hole . . . well, it would be quick.

Churchie Dwyer gave him a thumbs-up signal and a stainless steel grin. Waldstejn grimaced, then dropped to the deck with a clang.

He was facing the muzzle of a rifle. The bearded First Officer—Captain Ortschugin— watched him over the sights. His eye was as cold as that of any of the Company's gunmen.

Albrecht Waldstejn picked himself up carefully. He raised his hands, but he smiled. "Vladimir," he said to the grim-faced spacer, "we need to talk, and I'll take a drink if you've got something handy. I think we're each other's tickets home."

CHAPTER TWELVE

Thorn was running through the pre-flight check with other spacers in the stern compartments. Except for that, Ortschugin was alone on the bridge with Waldstejn. The Cecach officer felt cramped, especially after the days he had just spent without a roof over him.

"I don't mean I'm not in this," the spacer said. "These—fanatics, it is not possible for normal people to live around them. Only by staying sealed off in the ship can we survive here, and if they carry us back to Budweis, well. . . . But we have no chance, not really. Just crossing the whole compound—" he spat tobacco juice into a can—"pft!"

Waldstejn grinned. "You haven't been with these mercs," he said. "I—in garrison, there wasn't much to choose between them and the 522nd, you know? Soldiers with nothing to do but raise hell. But out

there, Vladimir, Mary and the Saints. . . ." The
Cecach officer shook his head. "Nothing's sure.
But I'm as sure as I can be that we'll get clear of
here without a problem. For the rest, well—Bittman
talked big, but their front-line tanks are going to
have more to worry about than just us. We'll have
to trust some to luck and your hull plating, sure,
but . . . if it doesn't work, they'll believe you were
hijacked at gunpoint. And for the rest of us, there's
no other chance anyway."

A mercenary with drooping moustaches and a
look of unexpected enthusiasm came clashing along
the corridor from the holds. "Captain," he said as
he burst into the bridge, "Guns says to tell you the
old girl herself's back there! And the ammo!"

"Your cannon?" Waldstejn translated uncertainly.
He glanced at Ortschugin. "What's the cannon doing
here?"

The Swobodan nodded. "All your gear," he said.
"Their gear, I mean, the mercs. Next week, when
the pylons are laid to here, we carry it back to
Budweis with ourselves and the copper—all spoils,
useless here but of value to the Return, you see."

Thorn turned from his controls. He said something to his captain which Waldstejn thought was
a report that they were ready to go.

Ortschugin confirmed that. "Whenever you
want," he said to the Cecach officer in English.
"Thorn says the board's green."

Albrecht Waldstejn stood. "I'll check with the
others," he said. "There's still three hours to dawn,
no need to lift before everything's locked down
tight." He grinned at Cooper, the mercenary who
had brought the report, then looked back at Captain Ortschugin. "Hell, Vladimir," he said, "I know

it doesn't matter a damn whether their gear's aboard or not, not for getting to Praha. But doesn't it make you think that—well, keep a crucifix handy, hey?"

The young officer was laughing as he strode off down the echoing corridor. He had changed in a very few days, thought Vladimir Ortschugin. An impressive man, now. A pity that he was going to die so young.

"Hold Three, ready," said the intercom in Sergeant Mboko's voice.

"Hold Two ready," it immediately added as Sergeant Hummel.

Sergeant-Gunner Jensen nodded to Albrecht Waldstejn across the dim interior of Hold One. "Hold One ready, sir," the blond man said.

"Waldstejn to bridge," the Cecach officer said to the intercom on the bulkhead beside him. "Raise the hatches."

When the mercenaries first filed aboard the *Katyn Forest*, there had been no copper stored in Hold One. Now the length of the hatches on both sides were lined with a waist-high breastwork of ingots shifted from the other two holds. The mercenaries who knelt along the breastworks stiffened as machinery began to squeal. The metal-to-metal seals of the six great doors broke. The Company had boarded by the narrow bridge scuttle because of the noise entailed in opening one of the holds. Now there was no choice. Gray light spread in Hold One as the top-hinged hatches swung up along the full length of both sides. All lights within the holds proper had been doused, though in One and Three there was a slight scatter from the bow and stern compartments. The noise of the hatches rising might not itself provoke a reaction from the garrison, but it would certainly awaken everyone in Smiricky #4 and focus a fair number of eyes on the starship. Ideally, they would have waited until they were under way, but the auxilliary power unit could not winch up the hatches and raise the ship simultaneously.

One after another, the hatches squealed to a halt. Their lower edges hung a meter above the hold's decking. Every member of the Company able-bodied enough to shoot now knelt behind the inner barriers of copper. The four seriously-wounded troopers were in the crew's quarters, while all the personnel of the freighter itself were at their stations.

Albrecht Waldstejn squinted into the night. His hands trembled violently on the assault rifle he had never before fired. Any time now, he thought. Any time.

The intercom crackled in Russian. A moment later, Captain Ortschugin repeated his laconic statement in English: "Lifting ship."

Its lift engines driven by the full power of the overloaded auxilliary power unit, the *Katyn Forest* began to lurch toward the lines of pylons and the havoc sure to come.

A twenty-kilo ingot of copper clanged to the deck before the drive steadied. Alone of the troopers in Hold One, Del Hoybrin did not wonder what would happen if the whole bulwark shifted in on them.

The vibration bothered Del because it kept him from aiming steadily. They were supposed to open fire as soon as anyone shot at them, though not before. The way the ship was bucking, however, Hoybrin was afraid that he would not be able to hit much. He hoped nobody would shout at him if he messed up.

The *Katyn Forest* accelerated too slowly on its lift engines for the effect to be felt. Now that static inertia had been overcome, however, the buildings of the Complex had begun to slide by at a fast walk. None of them were lighted. The vibration damped itself to an acceptable level, and Del began to study things through the holographic gunsight.

The ship was passing the truck park. The hole cut in the chain-link fencing had been sutured with a web of steel tape. A pair of soldiers in mottled fatigues leaped to their feet. As the starship passed twenty meters away, one of the guards threw his rifle to his shoulder.

Del killed both of them with a short burst. The Cecach soldiers flopped back against the fence as all the guns on the port side slammed into action. Trucks beyond the dead men lighted with pinpoint flashes as projectiles ripped along them.

The *Katyn Forest* was swinging around the west corner of the park. There was a hesitation as Captain Ortschugin attempted the unfamiliar business of locking their jury-rigged antenna onto the broadcast power system. There were more guards at the gate. It was closed now by an ore carrier parked across the ragged opening. Del fired the rest of his magazine into the men. Because of the angle, dust sprang up ten meters beyond the soldiers like a line of surf on a strand. An instant after the big trooper had squeezed off, the parked truck and the men falling beside it caught the full force of the twenty port-side gunners. Grenades burst amid gravel fountains which the high-velocity projectiles had already sprayed up.

Del Hoybrin reloaded with the perfect economy with which he did everything that had become instinctive. He was worried. He wished desperately that he could talk to Churchie beside him. There was no time now, and it was too noisy to be heard over the gunfire anyway. The troopers on the starboard side of the ship were engaging the bunkers while those on the port ripped the buildings of the Complex proper.

Del had not waited for the Rubes to shoot first. Instead, he had squeezed off reflexively just because a guard was aiming a rifle at him.

He was afraid he was in trouble again.

Rosa Brionca was as nervous as the watch officer in the communications building. The phone only burped her call sign once before her hand stabbed from the blanket roll to snatch it. "Mole One to Victor," she said, not yet awake. "Go ahead."

The Council of Deacons did not enlist women into armed formations, even into rear echelon units the way the Federals did. General Yorck had honored his agreement to enroll the 522nd, however, men and women alike. It may have been that from Yorck's strait viewpoint, the males of the turncoat battalion were already degraded to the level of females.

The Republicans had given a choice to the officers of the 522nd. They could be reduced to the rank of Private and assigned to rifle companies, or they could keep their commands as provisional officers, Ensigns, in the Lord's Host . . . under the tutelage of the Chaplain who would be assigned to direct the moral welfare of the unit. Rank hath its privileges, Captain Brionca assumed as she took the latter option and the command that went with it.

The main privilege rank brought to those who had defected to the Lord's Host was the privilege of failing while Chaplain Ladislas Bittman watched. Brionca had realized what that meant even before two platoon leaders were hanged beside Major Lichtenstein. Their units had not been transferring mercenary stores to the *Katyn Forest* with the alacrity which the Chaplain expected.

"Three of the bunkers are reporting noise from the starship," the watch officer said. Brionca could not remember who had the duty tonight, her mind was too fuzzy. "Ah, I heard it too."

"Right," the nominal commanding officer mumbled. She thrust her feet into her boots. Brionca had begun sleeping in her uniform on the floor of her office. That way, whatever happened she could at least make a show of dealing with it before Bittman arrived. The night before, two soldiers had drunk glycol coolant and gone off their heads.

Brionca had ordered them shot.

"Get on the horn," she decided abruptly. "Get their captain over here to my—no, get them *all* over to my office, fast." She hooked her equipment belt, juggling the handset between shoulder and jaw. "And—"

The gunfire outside silenced her as surely as if every round were fired through her brain. Brionca dropped the phone and stumbled for the door without bothering to slide up her boot fasteners."

"What *is* this, Ensign?" shrieked Chaplain Bitt-

man as he threw open the door of his room. It had
been the Sergeant-Major's office. *"What is this?"*

The outer office was pitch dark, but Brionca had
learned there was no safety in that. She hit the
door with her shoulder, then rolled on the ground
outside as she had not done since training exer-
cises five years before. One boot flew off. She ignored it and ignored also the *thunk*! as Bittman
too plunged through the doorway. She had gotten
out just in time to see the signals building destroyed.

The *Katyn Forest* was sliding toward them along
the pylons one hundred meters away. The belly of
the ship's dark bulk glowed with vaporized sabots
as shots gnawed through the commo building.

The balloon supporting the directional antenna
was starting to sink, but it had already served to
mark the commo center for the merc gunners. The
facade exploded inward, then the roof collapsed
under the concentrated fire. Anyone inside was as
surely dead as the electronic equipment shorting
and sputtering in the rubble.

An anti-tank rocket burst and lighted twenty
meters of the vessel's port side. Brionca tugged out
her own pistol. "The antenna on the front!" she
screamed uselessly as she aimed. "Shoot off the
power receptor!"

The *Katyn Forest* was broadside to the HQ building now, and the mercenaries' fire shifted to the
new target. The muzzle blasts were not as loud as
the crashing shock waves of the projectiles themselves as they ripped overhead. The pistol that
Brionca had meant to fire remained frozen in her
hand as she sprawled in the dirt.

The night the Company had broken out, a single
distant marksman had raked the building. This

time, the fire of twenty guns wrecked it with a vengeful thoroughness. Lime dust and sand spurted from the structure like smoke from a smudge pot, hiding the ex-captain and saving her life when she had given up on it herself.

A grenade went off with a distinct bang. Then the starship was past, dragging the pall of dust into fanciful shapes in its slip stream. There was a fire burning somehow in one of the perimeter bunkers. It winked like a distant reflection of the blaze starting where the signals building had been.

The dust was choking. Ensign Brionca stood up, stumbled, and kicked her remaining boot off into the night somewhere. Maybe the laser in Gun Pit East would stop them.

Bullshit. Maybe the ground would open and they would all fall into it.

Chaplain Bittman staggered toward her. He was hacking and wheezing so badly that he had to shake his fist to assert his fury. The slim man's uniform was limed white. His eyes stared as if inset on a skull. The sound of gunfire was a rasping background for him when he finally found his voice. "You're a traitor, whore of Satan!" Bittman wheezed. "False not to Man but to your Lord, all of you! And as the Lord shall burn you in everlasting hellfire, so shall I—"

Rosa Brionca shot him. The Chaplain looked surprised. There was a tiny, dark fleck on the front of his dusty uniform. He raised a hand as if to touch it.

Brionca's pistol had been buried in dust and grit. She thought it would jam after the first shot. To her surprise, the gun instead functioned perfectly nine more times.

*   *   *

The warhead sent a sizzling white line across the interior of Hold One. The shaped charge had penetrated the hundred millimeters of hull plating and sent the metal spurting as an ionized stream to gouge the far bulkhead. Molten steel splashed back over most of the dozen mercenaries in the compartment.

High-velocity shrapnel would have done more real damage, but the dazzling spray caused momentary havoc. "Shoot or by Christ you *will* burn!" roared Sergeant Jensen. He fired twice into the night without a specific target, just to drive home the order. A thumb-sized welt was rising on his own cheek, but he knew that the Company's only chance was to keep the garrison down by sheer volume of fire.

Jensen found his target in the fluid shimmering that characterized light enhancement. The curving berm, the lattice-strengthened tube, visible from the angle he overlooked it. He fired, his sights a useless blur beyond the intervening face-shield. When he flipped the shield out of the way, the holographic reproduction still quivered too badly from the unsteady drive effects for Jensen to make the difficult shot.

The blond man howled a curse. He was furious now that Waldstejn had not allowed him time to set up the automatic cannon. Its dampers could have kept it steady despite the vibration, accepting input only from the controls. Sure, it might have taken an hour longer to weld the outriggers to the deck since there was no dirt for the spades to bite in. But an hour would be cheap if the choice was—

Jensen fired a three-shot burst. Strong as he was, the recoil punished him. The gun barrel jumped as the stock hammered Jensen's shoulder back and down. Riflemen were firing from the bunkers toward which the ship hurtled. The mercenaries around the Sergeant-Gunner were angling forward to blast away at those active targets. The worst someone with an assault rifle could do was to kill a few of the troopers lining the holds. The laser cannon, if it were still operable when the *Katyn Forest* cleared it, would burn them to slag as surely as it had the decoying trucks four nights before.

Jensen ripped out another burst. He tried desperately to anchor the fore-end but failed because the problem was not with the barrel but with the shoulder supporting the stock. They were hissing by the gun pit, now, eighty meters away and ignored in its stillness. Jensen's gun slammed and ejected its empty clip. He might have hit the laser . . . but he was sure he had not. Bullets spanged on the hull and the copper breastworks. Mercenaries ducked, as if that mattered a damn if the laser were not destroyed.

Jensen turned. His normally-pale face was suffused with rage and frustration. His big hands were fumbling with a fresh magazine, but this shoulder-bobbing toy was not a real gun, was not *his* gun. "Lieutenant!" the Sergeant-Gunner screamed to the third man down the firing line from him, "for *God's* sake, the laser!"

Hussein ben Mehdi turned momentarily toward the cry. His face was that of a reflective balloon. A face-shield was no handicap to a man who shot by instinct and not through his sights. The Lieutenant wheeled. His right hand was on the pistol grip, his left on the barrel which he lifted with the precision of an aiming screw. The grenade launcher jumped three times. The slap of its gas discharges were inaudible against the background of high-velocity fire ringing through the hold.

The *Katyn Forest* lurched as it took the line that would speed it out the west end of the valley. Gunfire ceased abruptly. They were out of the bunkered compound, and the mercenaries' guns no longer had targets they could bear on.

Roland Jensen's hands suddenly remembered the pattern. They reloaded his gun while the big man blurted, "Did—did you hit it, sir?"

Hussein ben Mehdi raised his face-shield. He could not remember the last time a Company non-com had called him 'sir' and sounded as if he meant it. "Well, we'll know in a few seconds, won't we, Guns?" he said with a deliberate cruelty of which he was at once ashamed. His own fear was personal. Roland Jensen's fear was for his section and the Company, not for himself. "As Allah wills, Sergeant," ben Mehdi added in an apologetic voice, "but—yes, I think it pleased Him to guide my arm."

In Smiricky #4, some survivors were blasting useless rounds after the ground-hugging starship. Few of the bullets would hit as the range continued to open. None would do more than fleck the hull.

Other Cecach soldiers were tending the wounded or staring in shock at their dead. In Gun Pit West, there were moans, but no one remained to give aid. The crew, huddled behind their berm, had been saved from the carnage to the very last. Then, as the ship pulled past and heads lifted in relief, three grenades had turned the laser above them into deadly shrapnel.

The *Katyn Forest*'s bulk blotted the last visible pylon. Then the pylon reappeared and the starship vanished forever from Smiricky #4.

CHAPTER THIRTEEN

"I don't *care* whose fault it is," Colonel Kadar snarled to his Communications Officer. "I need to get through to Headquarters. If the Smiricky link isn't working, find another one!"

Except for the road, the plain had been a single giant wheatfield stretching as far as the eye could see. The wheat still remained, its stalks green and the heads just beginning to be tinged with gold. It was no longer part of a farm, though. Farms, even latifundia, are human things. There was no longer human interest in the plain as a place where food grew.

The road remained important, and it grew death and wreckage.

The vehicles of Tank Regiment Seven lay in a defensive star. The tanks and personnel carriers faced outward like the segments of a watch face while the support vehicles clustered together at the hub. There should have been twice Kadar's present total of fighting vehicles, six APCs and a pair of tanks. The second element had left Budweis only twelve hours behind the first and should have joined Kadar by now. Instead, only the support vehicles had caught up with him. All the Captain in charge of them could say was that the armor had been diverted two days earlier on secret orders.

And now, however he fiddled with the triple-braced antenna, the Communications Officer could not make the tight-beam contact with Sector Command.

Dismounted soldiers chewed on wheat stems as they waited. The swathes the vehicles had cut across the wheat were a green darker than their tawny surroundings. Kadar's eyes wandered from one blank stare to the next. The most powerful unit in the Lord's Host—except that half of it was missing and the rest was stalled while its commander tried to find out what in the *Lord's* name Headquarters was thinking of! Kadar slammed his fist against the turret of his tank.

The command frequency snarled back at him so suddenly that Kadar froze. Subconsciously he feared that the blow had set something off. The dished antenna on the commo van was finally receiving signals, routed to the huge Henschel tank by a scrambled transponder. An aircraft was replacing the balloon relay at the captured mining complex . . . but the content of General Yorck's furious message gave Kadar no time to wonder why.

The Colonel signaled an acknowledgment. The transmission snapped off as curtly as it had begun. Its message was stored in the tank's memory, available either on screen or as hard copy if the commander required it.

Kadar did not need a repetition. The orders were as simple as their accomplishment should be.

A ripple of interest was running through the troops who a moment before had been waiting in bored lethargy. They knew a signal had been received, but only Colonel Kadar knew what the message was. Exulting in the power of secret knowledge, Kadar himself swung the turret of his tank. His gunner peered up at him, as much at a loss as were the infantrymen outside.

The laser had been in ready position, zero deflection, zero elevation. Instead of aiming, Kadar kept his foot down on the traversing pedal as he squeezed the hand switch. The weapon drew a pale line across the daylight. The beam merely hissed until the turret rotated it through the nearest broadcast pylon. Steel latticework vaporized with a roar and a coruscant white glare. Larger, fluid gobbets spit from the supports and sparkled as they rained into the dust and stunted vegetation below.

The Republican soldiers were on their feet now. Heads twisted even from the commo van to watch the fireworks. The power-broadcasting antennas waved madly as their support toppled, taking them out of the circuit. Kadar continued to traverse his blade of pure energy. A pylon of the east-bound roadway collapsed as the beam slashed it also. There was now a one-kilometer gap in the Praha-Smiricky truck route. Both halves of the lines were still energized, but the receptor antenna of a vehicle could not align across the gap and leap it.

MERCENARY IDOLATORS IN CAPTURED STAR-

SHIP PROCEEDING WEST ON ROADWAY FROM SMIRICKY the message had read. WEAPONS CAPABLE OF DEFEATING LIGHT ARMOR. IMMOBILIZE AND DESTROY VESSEL BETWEEN SEVERED PYLONS.

There had been a further direction. It had struck Colonel Kadar as an unnecessary one, given the bubbling Hell into which his lasers would convert the starship after they sliced through the outer hull. Still, General Yorck was known for spelling out requirements precisely. It was to be expected that he would close with TAKE NO PRISONERS.

The truck cartwheeled off the line. It was an empty ore-carrier returning from the battle area to the temporary road-head at the Smiricky Complex. The *Katyn Forest* had swung out slightly to bring her port side to bear on the unsuspecting vehicle on the other line. A three-shot burst from the automatic cannon had ripped low through the truck, demolishing half the drive fans and letting the vehicle scrape down at its full forward speed.

The effect was spectacular. Troopers cheered. Some of them, however, and all the command group, knew that it was going to be different if and when they met real fighting vehicles.

Jensen nodded to Pavlovich. The crewmen had been in the gunner's seat for what was, after all, no more than a training exercise. "Good," the section leader said. "Damned good. I couldn't have done better myself." And if a target on a fixed course two hundred meters away was not a great test of skill, then the statement was still perfectly true, and it was made by a man whose praise counted. Pavlovich flushed with pleasure.

The *Katyn Forest* continued to plow forward at a sluggish fifty KPH. Her lift engines were designed for maneuvering at maximum loads, not for high speed transit. Still, the Company was separated from safety by something more tangible than mere distance. Since the engines acted by direct impulse, there was no air cushion to smooth irregularities in the drive. The buzz and tiny lurchings were disquieting at any time and were quite impossible to deal with when multiplied by undamped gunsights.

Albrecht Waldstejn rang a knuckle on the inner face of the hull. "How long if a laser hits it, Vladimir?" he asked soberly.

Captain Ortschugin was sitting on one of the carboys of mercury which shared Hold One with the mercenaries' stores and the automatic cannon. He shrugged and said, "Who knows?" But spacefaring was not a profession that encouraged question dodging. "Ten seconds?" the Swobodan amplified. "Perhaps fifteen, perhaps more if their guns don't hold a target perfectly. I doubt that. . . . And a few seconds more still before something vital is hit and we go like—that." He waved a morose hand sternward, where the wreckage of the shot-up truck had presumably strewed itself.

"Fine, the hull," said Sergeant Mboko, "and if we have any chance we got the doors open, right? So we can shoot back." He gestured. The hatches and breastworks were still up as they had been during the break-out. "What happens when a laser slides across that?" The black sergeant snapped his fingers with a power and a suddenness which startled even his listeners. "Not ten seconds, I tell you. Not one. I say we dismount now. We're just a target here."

"Maybe Stack's right," said Sergeant Jensen. He glanced at his cannon with sad affection. They had welded it solidly to the deck of Hold One. The barrel had a 360° traverse and a practical arc of fire of almost 90° to either broadside now. "Lasers aren't a good way to punch through armor, I don't care what they say. Not when the metal itself fogs the beam when it burns away. But sure, they'll aim first at the openings. And I can't claim that the old girl has much chance to knock out a tank from the front."

Captain Waldstejn's face had gone blank in the midst of the Gunner's assessment. Sergeant Hummel, ignoring whatever the officer might have found of interest, snapped, "If we walk, we're dead for sure, Guns. You think they're going to roll into another ambush? Look, if we ground the ship as soon as we make contact we can try and shoot out the lasers again. I know, they're going to sweep the holds and a lot of us aren't going to be lucky, but at least—"

"Vladimir, how much will the pumps that evacuate the holds handle?" Albrecht Waldstejn interrupted. He rapped one of the deck gratings with his boot.

Ortschugin shrugged again. "We can empty the holds of water three hundred meters down in a one-g equivalent," the spaceman said. "Bulk cargos, grain, we discharge that way too. There are atmospheres that dense, some places we dock, you know."

The mercenary leaders looked in confusion from Waldstejn to the bearded, passive face of the ship's officer. "I think," said Waldstejn, "that we just might have an answer."

CHAPTER FOURTEEN

The idiom of the bridge displays differed from that of normal human optic nerves. If one knew what to look for, however, the displays gave a very clear picture of the world—including the drone which had been following the *Katyn Forest* for the past ten kilometers.

Vladimir Ortschugin pointed. "See, Albrecht," he said, "just above the horizon. Your friends could shoot it down, perhaps?"

To Waldstejn, the pip coasting through the shadows of the holographic analog was whatever the space captain said it was. He shrugged. "I suppose. If they've got one, they've got others, though." The Cecach officer swallowed. "No sign of—other vehicles?"

The spacer grinned like a demon at the euphemism for 'tanks'. He gestured toward the analog display. "We can't see through rocks, after all, and we've never had ionospheric radar fitted. Who can say? In—" the calculation process was natural to him, but the figures, surface speeds and distances, gave Ortschugin a pause— "one hundred and twelve seconds, then we should have a good view of the plain beyond."

The bright, metallic echoes of the pylons stretched at spaced intervals behind them on the shadowed landscape. There was still one sharp peak ahead, before the holographic display faded off into a land unknown to its radar primaries.

"They'll be waiting," Waldstejn said with the detached certainty of a man about to become part of an air crash. "Start the pumps. I want the starting load on the broadcast grid, not the APU."

Captain Ortschugin nodded. He threw a pair of yoked switches. Then he slid another control up through the gate, into the red zone on its face. "Full power from the auxilliary," he explained. He grinned again. "Seventeen seconds," he said.

"Who'll join me in a game of twenty-one?" asked Churchie Dwyer. He riffled his cards.

"Shut the hell up!" snapped Sookie Foyle. No one else in Hold Three spoke. Some of the soldiers did not even look up from the weapons which they held in front of them like flags at a service of honor.

"Well, I only asked," Dwyer protested mildly. He wriggled his shoulders against the copper bulkhead. The corner of an ingot scratched where his fingers could not reach. He began to flip the deck over one at a time in a game of privy solitaire.

Sometimes you could get people to play when

their minds were on something else. They made
dumb bets, took cards they didn't need, and forgot
the rules in useful ways. Way deep down, the troopers in Hold Three were sure they were all going to
die.

The hatches were closed. All of Black Section sat
with the wall of copper between them and the
coming fire besides. If the starship hit the ground
hard, those same ingots were going to pulp everything human that shared the compartment.

The thing was, if you went West, it didn't hurt
you to have a pocketful of other people's money.
And if just maybe you came through . . . well, hell,
Praha was quite a town for a bright fellow with
the ready. Why stare at your gun when there wasn't
a damn thing you or it could do to change the
odds?

"Vector two-two-zero!" the intercom blared.

Churchie's cards spewed over his lap as he too
snatched up his weapon.

Their targets were four kilometers away as the
Katyn Forest bellied over the rise, and Roland Jensen could not see them yet. He sat where he
belonged, in the gunner's seat. Pavlovich and Cooper were flat on the deck, waiting to take over
when the section leader was killed—if they did not
all die together. Like Jensen, the gun crewmen
wore suits from the vessel's stores, meant for operation in corrosive atmospheres. The suits could
not deflect a direct hit from a tank laser for more
than a few microseconds.

The automatic cannon was angled forward and
to the right, at 390 mils—the sharpest angle possible that would clear the bulkhead. The ship swung

as it slid forward on the slope. Gravity was urging the *Katyn Forest* to a greater speed than the lift thrusters themselves could drive her. Jensen could see wheat through the firing slit instead of the indigenous scrub of moments before. All the landscape was cloaked in a silvery mist as the pumps rammed mercury out of the vent above the hatch.

"Three hundred!" Captain Waldstejn's voice reported, "three-fifty—"

There was a black speck in the gunsight. It sprang into a tank, distorted into a lowering blur by the spray of liquid metal. The pale beam of the laser was only a quiver as it sheared the power antenna behind the starship.

"Got her!" roared Sergeant Jensen. With one gloved hand he squeezed the lock which would keep the muzzle aligned with its present target. As his other hand squeezed the trigger, the *Katyn Forest* took off.

The starship's lift engines did not need to hug the ground the way an air cushion vehicle did. The auxilliary power unit of the *Katyn Forest* did not have enough juice to raise her to high altitude or even simultaneously to maintain forward motion and climb. By straining the APU, however, and by trading velocity for climb, Captain Ortschugin managed to slant his lurching command some ten meters in the air. Kadar's target was not where his computers had put it on the basis of data fed in at leisure. As the two Republican gunners snatched in panic at manual overrides which they had not expected to need, Jensen's projectiles sleeted in on the right-hand tank.

The mercury fog blurred the gunsight, but it had no real effect on the osmium penetrators them-

selves. The hull and turret face of Kadar's tank
rippled in a silver spray as eight rounds a second
struck them. The projectiles did not hole the armor.
Ten or a dozen hits at the same point might have
blasted a gap in the frontal slope of even one of
those Terran monsters; but the range, plus the
vibration and maneuvering of the weapons platform, spread the hose of bullets instead across the
whole bow of the tank. The laser tube disintegrated.
Dispersion and the big gun's cyclic rate accom-
plished what accuracy could not have managed
under the circumstances.

"Rotate!" screamed Gunner Jensen, but Ortschugin had never ceased to spin his vessel on her
vertical axis. The *Katyn Forest* had lost the momentum of her forward plunge and with it the capacity to stay aloft on auxilliary power. Now she settled
between the two cleared roadways in an explosion
of dust. The yellow-gray doughnut billowed up
about the ship. The remaining laser stabbed her
regardless like Polonius through the curtain.

All the tankers knew was that they had cut their
target away from the broadcast grid but that she
was still moving. The vast bulk of the starship was
a reality which overwhelmed concepts such as armor and weapons effectiveness. The preset program had gone to hell when the *Katyn Forest* lifted.
Now the tank gunner spun his sight picture across
the scarred hugeness of the vessel's plating. He
was not trying to lock on and pierce a single point,
but rather to catch and destroy the gun which had
just devoured his consort.

In Hold One, Sergeant Jensen felt a mild vertigo
which was lost among the other chaotic sensory
inputs. The section leader was trying to traverse

the automatic cannon faster than the ship itself spun so that his muzzle would be waiting when the second target slid in view. The two axes of rotation differed, and the blur in his electronic sight would have been disorienting anyway.

The laser beam was a clapper, ringing on the hull of the *Katyn Forest*. The tank weapon cut a whorl of geometric roundness through the roiling dust. The tough hull surface scaled off in sparks and vapor, even though the beam was only glancing across it while it searched for its real victim.

"Vector three-fifty!" cried the intercom, and Jensen's world exploded.

Cooper saw the gun and his section leader in relief against a glare brighter than the heart of an arc light. The beam's fusion-powered spike struck the fog of mercury droplets and scattered cataclysmically. To the tankers and the infantry still more distant in their APCs, the raging blue scintillance meant the guts of the starship had vaporized. In fact, the actinic glare was almost entirely beyond Hold One, not within it.

'Almost entirely', when power like that of the tank laser was involved, meant that the hold was a blue-lit Hell.

The beam slid down the length of the open hatchway with a roar of heavy-element ionization. The tankers had no target but the firing slit itself. They raked it as the starship continued to lurch forward, wheeling like a dying shark. Despite the scattering effect, ingots in the breastwork welded together. Sergeant-Gunner Jensen was slumping out of his seat.

Cooper's mouth was open behind his face shield.

Even he could not have said for sure whether he was screaming in the noise and stink and light. He dragged his section leader down behind the copper and took over the gun himself.

The atmosphere suit made the controls unfamiliar, and Cooper had no idea where his target might be anyway. He had been belly-down until the instant he took charge, with no more picture of the action outside than the stacked copper ingots could give him. Now the plain gaped and the tank was only a speck at four kilometers distance. The laser beam itself gave Cooper his target. It lanced back to its source from the coruscant far end of the hold.

With a calm he had never felt in training, the mercenary pedaled in right traverse. The gun mechanism performed flawlessly despite the flash of Hell-light that had taken out its gunner. The tank was a sudden blur in the funhouse mirror of the sights. Its turret was rotating to draw the beam back across the hatchway. The ionizing discharge began to encroach on a sight picture already fogged by the last of the mercury being sprayed from the vents. "Got her!" cried David Cooper. The hammering recoil of the automatic cannon drove a bass note through the snarl of the laser.

Down range, the second tank began to come apart under the osmium hail.

As before, the Henschel compound armor adequately withstood the battering. The crew within did not. The laser tube and the tank's outer surface shattered like a sand-blasted ice carving. Though the armor did not give way, it flexed and rang like the head of a tympany. The tank captain, a veteran of APCs but new to his present Terra-built command, panicked. He threw open his hatch and tried to bail out.

Projectiles from the automatic cannon did not ricochet from the armor. Their velocity was far too great for that. Instead, they splashed like meteors on stone. Each round coated and vaporized a collop of density-enhanced steel. The wave-fronts sprayed the Republican officer and ripped him apart like so many white-hot razors. His body dripped back down the hatchway through which he had jumped. Screaming with the contagion of madness, the two crewmen followed their commander up and to the same end.

When the second can of ammunition had run through the chamber, Pavlovich shook his partner. "You can stop, now, Dave," he said. "You can stop."

"Yeah, Bertinelli says it'll be a day or two before the bandages come off, but he ought to be OK," said Sergeant Mboko. "It was shock, mostly. He's wrapped in a heating blanket and that turtle of his is being as much nurse as she can with her own breaks."

The ship rocked with another short burst. In Hold One, troopers cheered as Cooper and Pavlovich took turns in the gun seat.

"Gun Section's been taking it on the chin," Lieutenant ben Mehdi remarked. He flashed a grim smile around the group crowded into the bridge. "Glad they got a chance to get a little of their own back."

The starship's visual sensors did not magnify their images, but fresh mushrooms of flame were clearly visible against the background of wheat.

The field was marked by more than a score of fires, now. Some of them had burned down to smudges of rubber and lubricants and flesh. The lighter Republican vehicles had been laagered far enough from the tanks that they would not be damaged while the starship was being destroyed. When the gun crew had time to turn to them, they were dark blotches against the grain and still easy targets. While the *Katyn Forest* crawled under auxilliary power across the gap in the pylons, the automatic cannon smashed the thin-skinned vehicles one after another. The few which still survived were stopped. Their crews had abandoned them to the projectiles which would probe inexorably for their fuel tanks in any event.

"Got it," Captain Ortschugin muttered. The starship shook herself as her lift thrusters began winding out on broadcast power again.

Sergeant Hummel was staring at the analog display with a look of glum disapproval. To the radar, an armored personnel carrier was much the same whether or not it was a burned-out wreck. The unchanging hologram suited Hummel's mood better than did the cheers echoing from Hold One. "Fine, we chew up a reserve squadron," she said. "We're twenty klicks from the new Front, still, aren't we? What's going to be waiting there?"

"Jack shit unless our luck's a lot worse than it's been so far," said Albrecht Waldstejn. The question had surprised him until he realized how little the Company knew about the general situation on Cecach. On some worlds, no doubt, the conversion of an armored battalion to scrap metal would be a minor datum on the weekly Intelligence Summaries. Here, though—

"Look," the young captain explained, "you knew those tanks were imported—but did you know there weren't fifty of them on Cecach? And that *they* were what changed the whole face of the war in the past year, year and a half? People, what you've done here and back at 4B—you may have stalled the whole Rube drive. Those were the reinforcements they needed to put them through. I don't think they'll risk more tanks, even if they could shift them into position in time. And the rest we can pretty well take, so long as we keep moving so they can't drop the heaviest high-angle stuff on us."

There was a startled silence on the bridge. "I be damned," said Jo Hummel. "You mean we've got a chance after all?"

Thirteen hours later, battered and with two more troopers dead from a well-directed anti-tank rocket, the *Katyn Forest* set down again. She was in the spaceport around which Praha had developed during its centuries of human colonization.

CHAPTER FIFTEEN

The *Katyn Forest* was reduced to scale in the closed repair dock. Even a small starship so dwarfed the norms of human habitation that the vessel had taken down cables and a few balconies during the last kilometers of its passage. Ortschugin, cursing in Russian, had let his bows overhang the escorting troop carrier when it slowed for crowds of amazed spectators. The spacer would not feel safe again until he had rung his command into stardrive once more. That was at least days in the future, even with only minimal repairs to the vessel . . . but Captain Ortschugin had no desire to add even a minute where it was unnecessary.

"Point that thing somewhere else," Sergeant Hummel said to a disembarking Federal soldier, "or I'll feed it to you." With her finger, she gestured away the assault rifle the man carried awkwardly.

Ten kilometers beyond the current Front, they had paused to load a Federal platoon. The Praha authorities had been at best confused by the reports Lieutenant Albrecht Waldstejn had been sending in clear through attempted Rube jamming. The authorities were not so confused that they would permit a Trojan Horse into the heart of their supply system, however. The platoon had verified that the starship was what her passengers had claimed ... but the *look* of the mercenaries had bothered the Cecach troops very much. It was not so much that the men and women of the Company looked murderous. It was more that they looked as if they did not *care* how many more they killed.

If there was any truth to half the stories they told, mostly to one another, the mercenaries really did not care.

Hold Three was open. A cat-walk had been run out to disembark first the indigs, then the Company. The last of the Cecach soldiers marched off in a column of fours past the platoon already drawn up within the dock. Some of them glanced back nervously.

"Waldstejn, Albrecht W E," shouted the leader of the waiting unit. His voice echoed in the enclosed dock without losing any of its sneering arrogance. "Number W-nine-three-nine-five-one—"

"That's me," said Albrecht Waldstejn. He was third in the sluggish file of mercenaries. Stepping past Hummel and Powers, the Cecach officer walked toward the speaker.

"—five-two-eight," the speaker concluded loudly. Two of the soldiers with him dropped their gun muzzles to cover the returned lieutenant. Their commander looked up from the long print-out in his hand. "Waldstejn?" he demanded. "What kind of uniform is that?"

Albrecht Waldstejn did not need the brassards or the strack uniforms to identify the unit arrayed to greet them as part of Morale Section. The chain-dogs had always frightened him, even before he was conscripted. Their brief was limited in theory to members of the armed services, but many of them shared with their Republican opponents the belief that righteousness took precedence to human distinctions.

They seemed less frightening now, to a man who in the past week had learned that death took precedence even to righteousness.

"It's what there was available," the Lieutenant said mildly. He fingered the off-planet synthetic. It was already losing its coppery tone to take on the shadows of the dock interior. "Christ knows, it looks better than the one I was blown through the bushes in."

The Morale Section officer was a colonel, though his name tag was too dim to be read. He slapped Waldstejn across the face. "Watch your tongue, soldier!" he said. "You're in enough trouble already!"

There was a pause in the shuffling of boots behind Waldstejn, a restive silence like that of a cat tensing to spring. The Cecach lieutenant turned. "*Stand easy*!" he shouted. He managed not to add the curse that would have brought another blow—

and what he was praying he could avoid. Waldstejn's cheek burned. His body trembled with the
lightness he had never thought to feel after they
reached safety, reached Praha. "Stand *easy*, I
say!"

The mercenaries' weapons were closer to use
than the crisply-uniformed chain-dogs realized.
None of the hands Waldstejn glanced across were
thumbing guns to safe again, but there was a slight
relaxation. The line began to move again.

The Colonel blinked. He had been startled by
the incident, but he did not understand it. He
glanced back at his print-out—names and ranks,
Waldstejn could see now, and enough of them to
be the entire complement of the 522nd Garrison
Battalion. "All right," the Colonel said, "all members of the Cecach garrison of Smiricky #4, front
and center! Cecach Armed Forces only!"

Pavel Hodicky was just crossing the catwalk between Troopers Hoybrin and Dwyer. Like his
lieutenant, Hodicky had been issued a uniform
from the Company stores aboard the *Katyn Forest*.
Before the Private could speak, Churchie Dwyer's
palm swung across his mouth. Albrecht Waldstejn
was saying loudly, "Sir, I was the only member of
the battalion not to turn traitor. The rest of these
troops are off-planet volunteers, under contract to
the government."

The Morale Section officer looked from Waldstejn
to the soldiers who had broken out of Smiricky #4
with him. More of the men than not had shaved
when they got the opportunity, and all the troopers wore fresh uniforms. They were still a savage,
alien presence eying the Colonel and the crisp-

looking platoon with him. "Right," the Colonel said. He found he had to clear his throat before he could add, "Who's in charge of you lot, then?"

There was a pause too brief to be called hesitation. Hussein ben Mehdi strolled forward. His left thumb was hooked in his equipment belt. It seemed natural enough that his right palm would rest on the grip of his holstered grenade launcher. "I am," he said in a drawl which emphasized disdain instead of volume. "Since the native battalion we were supposed to be supporting decided to turn coat and murder our Colonel. What seems to be the problem?"

The chain-dog commander blinked again. Ben Mehdi's moustache was its precise line again despite the thin welt of pink scar tissue angling across his face. His tone of suave superiority, coupled with the implications of the words themselves, shook an officer who was used to deference from even generals with line commands. "Ah," he said, "your men will accompany Captain Kolovrat here to the Transit Barracks for reassignment. Stack your weapons. They'll be returned to you when required."

Someone in the Company rank cursed audibly. Lieutenant ben Mehdi gave a chuckle which sounded more natural to others than it seemed to be to him. His mind was quivering with memories of the tank that howled and shuddered as he fired down its intake duct. "I'm afraid that won't be possible—" he gestured as if he could not recall Federal rank insignia and saw no reason that he should— "Captain. We'll continue to billet ourselves on the starship here. I'll be obliged if you'll make arrangements for our commissary—" he paused—"and for proper bedding, yes."

"Who in the *hell* do you think you are, soldier?" the Colonel roared.

"I think we're—" and ben Mehdi's peremptory gesture brought the three sergeants forward. Jensen's face-shield down even in the dimness of the dock—"the people whose contracts you broke, Mr. Government!"

"We didn't—" the Colonel began. Around him guns pointed at the mercenary sergeants, then wavered as Morale Section soldiers met eyes as flat as the reflective face-shield.

"Captain, you put us in a position of danger in which we were attacked by Federal troops," the Lieutenant said flatly. "By Cecach Armed Forces. That's a breach of contract, pure and simple. All deals are off until we've made a composition of damages with the hiring authority."

It was a flawless performance, thought Albrecht Waldstejn. He supposed that it would usually have been acted out in a conference room, with Colonel Fasolini there to provide the bulk and bluster. Individually the three sergeants were the faces of Death. Together, they were the Furies, and their silence had lowered over the Cecach platoon as surely as Colonel Fasolini must have done in dozens of meetings with dress uniforms.

"There are three bulk carriers in port that seem to have been converted to carry troops," said Sergeant Jensen. His lips, cracked and gummy behind the shield, caused him to enunciate with great care.

"Yeah, just how many other contract soldiers

are there right here in Praha?" rasped Sergeant Hummel. She pointed a finger at the Morale Section officer. Her slung weapon waggled also, its barrel parallel to the line of her forearm.

"And don't think the units at the Front haven't heard how Federal troops turned on us," added Sergeant Mboko somberly. "Praha wasn't the only place we talked to when we sailed through the lines."

The Cecach Colonel was opening his mouth to speak. Before he could do so, Lieutenant ben Mehdi applied the counter-stroke to the whip-saw. "Of course," he said, "we don't hold you *personally* responsible, Captain . . . but until legal responsibility is determined, I think you'll agree that matters had best be left to your superiors."

The Colonel turned abruptly. "Take that one away!" he snarled to the pair of soldiers holding Albrecht Waldstejn. As sharply, he whipped back around to ben Mehdi, but he did not meet the mercenary's eyes. "For the time being, you can remain aboard," he muttered. "Someone will see about rations and bedding."

"Some problem about Captain Waldstejn, I see?" said Hussein ben Mehdi. He thumbed idly toward the sound of boots echoing out the rear of the enclosed dock.

"*Lieutenant* Waldstejn," snapped the Morale Section officer. He was out of the quicksand and his arrogance had returned in full force. "And there's no problem, no. An internal matter which even hired killers can understand, I suppose."

Ben Mehdi raised his lip and an eyebrow instead of asking the question out loud.

"The 522nd had orders to defend its positions to the last man," said the Cecach colonel in a rising voice. "Lieutenant Waldstejn instead chose to retreat."

"Even *your* sort shoot soldiers who desert in the face of the enemy, don't you?"

CHAPTER SIXTEEN

"You understand, Mr. Mehdi, that the, ah—" Benoit paused to look around the bridge of the *Katyn Forest*, even though he knew that he, Captain Ortschugin, and the mercenary lieutenant were alone there. The plump man was factor for a dozen off-planet space lines besides Pyaneta Lines; but he was legally a Cecach citizen and thus subject to local law if the wrong person heard him imply that there were two governments on the planet— "the Republicans had no right to seize the *Katyn Forest*. That, of course, affects your claim for salvage for rescuing her."

"The Rubes poked guns in my face and told me the ship belongs to the Lord's Host," said Vladimir Ortschugin. "*You* were going to come from Praha and tell them they were wrong?" The spacer spat ringingly into the cuspidor.

"Yes, I believe the Captain has noted the salient point," ben Mehdi took up smoothly. He had stripped off his holster and bandoliers for this interview. Now he luxuriated in an absence of weight which to him was by no means primarily a physical thing. "It isn't significant for purposes of the present discussion whether the loss was due to piracy or to the act of a duly-constituted government. The fact is, the loss *did* occur—"

"The vessel was still under the control of her crew when you, ah, boarded her," the Factor interrupted.

"In the possession of her crew," said the mercenary, "but under the *control* of the cannons trained on her, wouldn't you say?"

The hull shuddered. A pair of gantries had begun to winch the damaged fusion bottle out of the Power Room. The omni-directional bracing had been cut, but the weight of the unit itself had pressure-welded the bottle to the deck during years of service.

"Not that we plan to be unreasonable, Mr Benoit," resumed Hussein ben Mehdi. He unfolded a print-out run from the *Katyn Forest*'s own manifesting computer. "In fact," the mercenary said, "we have a proposition here that will reduce the out of pocket cost to your client by twenty percent."

Forty percent, in all likelihood, ben Mehdi said within his smiling face—though he would hold out for thirty-five down to the last. But Pyaneta would take the deal.

By Allah, they would take it if the Company had to ram it down their throats with gun barrels.

*   *   *

"How they hanging, Pavel?" asked Churchie Dwyer. He did not look up from the lap board on which he was dealing cards.

"Churchie, good God, he's been condemned!" blurted the Cecach private. "One of the repair crew just told me!"

"Yeah, that's old news," said the veteran, continuing to deal. "Guess you wouldn't have heard it, not leaving the ship—" he grinned up at the deserter—"so you don't get recognized and wind up in the next cell."

"Old news?" Hodicky repeated. He squatted to bring his face nearer to that of Dwyer. "You *knew* that?"

"Yeah, we been playing poker with some of the guards at the Karloff Barracks," Churchie said. "They mentioned it a couple nights ago, didn't they, Del?"

Del Hoybrin was seated on the deck beside Churchie. He nodded happily. "Hi, Pavel," he said.

"I can't believe this!" Hodicky said. "The Lieutenant saves your butt how many times? And all you care about's how much money you can win from the guys who're going to *kill* him!"

Dwyer peeked at each of the hands he had just dealt. He sighed and slid them together into a pack again. "Win?" he said. "Not with the cards I've been getting, kid. Why, even Del here's been making out better'n I have."

"That's right, Pavel," agreed the big trooper.

"Tried everything, you know," Churchie went on while his fingers shuffled as if with their own sentience. "Been carrying over liters of industrial ethanol, cutting it with juice while we play. Hell, those hunkies still clean me out every afternoon.

And don't they crow about it!" The gangling man
dealt the cards, face down as before.

Half a dozen workmen began manhandling the
base unit of a vibratory cutter through the hatchway. The holds and the compartments aft were
theirs, twenty-four hours a day while the repairs
went on. The bridge and the cramped quarters
forward provided a little privacy but no real quiet.
Troopers had rented several rooms outside the port
with the tacit approval of Federal officials while
negotiations continued.

The Cecach private licked his lips. Anger gone,
he pleaded, "Churchie, I *know* you don't mean
that. Look, if you know people in the place he's
being held, maybe you can get through to see him.
There's got to be something we can do!"

"Churchie says he can appeal," put in Del
Hoybrin. He frowned as he generally did after he
had spoken of his own volition.

"Appeal!" Hodicky shouted. "Appeal! Sure, to
Commandant Friis. His *is* Morale Section. Mary
and the Saints, he complains that his men ought
to have the same authority everywhere that they
have within ten klicks of the Front. To shoot people without *any* trial for 'crimes against discipline'!"

"Ever been in Karloff Barracks?" Churchie asked
unperturbed. "Thought you might have trained
there or something."

The little man shook his head. He was unsure
where the question was leading. "No," he said,
"the place has just been the military prison since
before I was born." He grimaced. "They stopped
executing people there a couple years ago. Too
many complaints about the shooting right in the

center of town, since Friis really got Morale Section 'organized'."

"Well, Pavel," said the veteran judiciously, "I don't see there's much good in you getting your bowels in an uproar, then." He began to turn over the hands he had just dealt. "Feel like a game of something?"

Pavel Hodicky slumped. The anger had burned out. Now the hope was gone too. "Then that's it," he said dully. "After all he did for you, and you're just going to leave him to die."

"Umm, I don't remember that I said that," commented the veteran. He glanced over toward the dockers who were hoisting their apparatus into position. The six poker hands were now face up on the board in Dwyer's lap. The first four of the hands he had dealt so swiftly were straight flushes, king through nine in each suit. The fifth hand was four sevens and the ace of spades.

The last poker hand was a trey and two pairs—aces and eights.

Churchie Dwyer picked up the last hand, the Dead Man's Hand which Wild Bill Hickok had held when a bullet spattered his brains over the card table. "No," said the veteran, "I don't remember saying that at all."

"Hey Doc," gibed one of the troopers in the rented room, "his hang better than yours. Maybe you ought to go back to bodies."

The crewman from the *Katyn Forest* beamed over the other sewing machine. He had just enough English to catch the drift of the compliment.

Marco Bertinelli gestured angrily. "Maybe you'd like nice business suits?" he demanded.

"Hey, I don't need the shears in my eyes," said Iris Powers, though the gesture had not really been that close. She stood with her arms out, ready for the Corpsman to drape her with the swatch he was cutting to length.

Bertinelli bent to his work again. "Look," he said, "tailoring, it's an art. My old man, he'd kill me—sure. But if you make fatigues—" he nodded to the wedge of camouflage print against Trooper Powers' arm— "they've got to look like fatigues, right?"

"Goddam," said Sergeant Hummel as she tried to tug down the legs of her own new garment. "I swear this crotch seam has teeth. But yeah, you're right, Doc. We're rolling our own instead of picking them up ready made so we don't ring too many bells. Looking like the Federation Guard isn't exactly a low-profile idea."

"There's plenty of troops around in tailored uniforms," objected the trooper who had made the first comment. "Hell, Praha's so rear-echelon it's ninety percent asshole."

"Sure," agreed Marco Bertinelli. Perfect, the cuff would be a centimeter too long. "But it isn't the strack troops who get assigned to *this* kind of duty, is it?"

Pinched lips rather than words indicated agreement all around the room.

CHAPTER SEVENTEEN

"Kings full!" sang the Sergeant of the Guard as he slapped his cards on the table. "Sweet bleeding Jesus, Churchie, it was the best night of my life when I ran into you in Maisie's last week. I swear to God, you're buying the best poker education a man could want."

There was a buzz from the monitor in the glazed booth attached to the guardroom. "Sarge," called the soldier there, "it looks like the van, but it's early."

"Well, handle it," said Sergeant Bles. His fingers trembled, organizing the pile of large-denomination scrip he had just swept from the table. The other two guards in the game watched their sergeant enviously, but they had folded after the draw. One of them took the deck as Churchie Dwyer passed it with a glum expression.

"I don't understand their papers," the man actually on duty called plaintively. The guard post was a brick room built against the inner face of the wall. The booth had a view of the entrance road, from the double-barred gates to the line of barracks converted to prison blocks. A fiber-optics system gave the monitors in the booth both a close-up and a panorama of anyone who pulled up to the front of the gate.

"God *damn*, Stieshl," muttered the Sergeant as he stood up. "Does your mommie got to hold your cock when you pee?" He strode toward the booth. "They got a pass for 1430, they get in. It says 1530 like we was told, then they cool their heels in the steet for an hour, right?" He bent over his subordinate's shoulder to see the paperwork the blonde driver of the van was holding to the receiver.

Churchie Dwyer got up and stretched. He could see the monitor past the two Federal guards. "Well, Del," he said, stepping casually toward the booth himself, "I guess it's about that time."

"Now, what the hell," Sergeant Bles muttered toward the screen. He turned and saw the knife slide out of Dwyer's sleeve.

The mercenary punched him in the solar plexus as hard as his ropy muscles could drive a short blow. The Sergeant's breath whuffed out with a sound too muted to call attention to itself. The fifteen-centimeter knife blade had split all four chambers of his heart. The dead man could not really be said to have felt its passage.

Dwyer cleared his knife with a sucking sound but little blood. The guard sergeant was collapsing in the half-flinch, half-crouch to which the punch would have driven him even without steel on the

end of it. Churchie did not have to worry about the
men behind him, not with Del Hoybrin in the
room. There was a bleat from one of the card
players, then a loud crunch. The deck scattered.
Some of the cards flicked Churchie's back as he
leaned toward the man in the booth.

On the left monitor, the truck driver was saying
urgently, "Wait a minute, buddy, I've got it right—"

As the puzzled guard started to look back again
for his sergeant, Churchie's left hand gripped his
hair to position his head. He stabbed through the
base of the guard's skull. The Federal soldier
squawked. His torso began to draw itself backward into an arch. The mercenary swore. His knife
hilt was clamped against the victim's spine by the
convulsion. The blade was sunk for half its length
through bone and up into the cortex. Churchie
yanked sideways in a panic. Even the density-
enhanced blade had its structural limits. It flexed,
then snapped off in the skull. The guard's limbs
flailed, knocking over his chair and hammering
against the wall of the booth.

Dwyer reached over the body and threw the gate
switches, outer and then inner. He was breathing
very hard. "Bastard!" he panted. "Bastard!" He
flung his broken knife against the wall in a clatter.

The van pulled up outside the booth. Two men
in Federal fatigues jumped out of the closed back,
Leading Trooper Gratz and Hussein ben Mehdi
wearing sergeant's pips as the best Czech speaker
available for the guard post.

Churchie looked behind him. Del was standing
by the overturned table, more or less as he had
been when he crushed the skulls of the two card
players against one another. One of the sprawled

men was breathing stertorously. Neither of them
moved.

"—ing door!" ben Mehdi snarled as he rattled
the panel beside the booth. The van whined off
toward the euphemistically-titled Transit Block,
accelerating.

Churchie stepped to unlock the door he had
forgotten. Before he did so, he paused to pry the
wad of money from Sergeant Bles' dead hand.

"Hey Lieutenant," the young jailer called as he
led the way down the corridor, "they're here for
you early." There were a number of ways to deal
with the knowledge that most of the people with
whom you worked would be dead in a few days.
This jailer handled it by ignoring the fact and
treating his charges as if he were an enthusiastic
hotel manager.

Albrecht Waldstejn thought that brutality might
have been preferable. But then, it was hard to be
sure.

Waldstejn stepped back from the shower. The
spray continued to swirl down the cell's sole drain.
"They can damned well wait, then," he shouted to
the steel door. "Or they can carry me out like this.
God knows it doesn't matter to me."

"Get your clothes on and do it fast!" snarled
another voice through the observation gate. "I'm
not spending any time here that I don't have to.
You, get the door open!"

"Sir," the jailer objected, "there's no need—"

"Do it!" There was a click as someone laid a
magnetic key against the lock plate.

Waldstejn was not sure until the door swung
outward. A company of mercs who could not be

assigned forward till a contract dispute was settled, well. . . . But Private Pavel Hodicky was back in Federal uniform, this time with captain's insignia and a sneer on his face to match the false commission. The little deserter was the only man or woman aboard the *Katyn Forest* who could carry on an extended conversation without being branded an outlander. If Hodicky looked young for his rank, then the casualties of the past year had meant sudden promotion for more men than him.

No one spent much time in chit-chat with members of a death squad, anyway.

"Snap it up," snarled Hodicky in a voice like that of an angry lap dog. Beside him stood the jailer in a gray service uniform. He carried a shock rod, the only variety of weapon permitted within the unit. Two of the three other soldiers waiting in Federal fatigues were mercenaries whom Waldstejn knew by sight but not name. The third was Sergeant Johanna Hummel with a set of Cecach handcuffs instead of the molecular springs which Waldstejn knew the Company stocked for its own use. The condemned officer felt a fleeting surprise that he did not see Iris Powers—but Powers spoke no Czech and might have endangered them all by ignoring a chance direction.

Waldstejn slipped on his boots. As he straightened from fastening them, Pavel Hodicky seized his wrist. The deserter's fingers trembled with suppressed hysteria. "Lock them," he said to Hummel, "and let's get this over." The Sergeant obeyed with a clumsiness which could have been explained by embarrassment. The Cecach officer caught the light in her eyes, though, and he knew that she was wired for battle, fearful and exultant together.

Waldstejn's own expression of shock was real enough, *Maria*; and it was yet to be proven that death did not lie just beyond the cell, as he had assumed when they gave him word that morning that his appeal had been denied.

"Ah, Lieutenant?" the jailer said. "There's your cap and—"

"Forget it," interrupted Private Hodicky. He gave Waldstejn a push in the middle of the back. "Mary and the Saints! How long is he going to need it, anyway? Now move, sweetheart, *move!*"

The condemned man stumbled as he marched down the corridor in the middle of four soldiers as grim as any the jailer had ever seen. The man in gray shook his head sadly as he stepped back into the cell.

He had to get the room ready for the next, ah, customer.

"Hey!" said the clerk behind the counter, "*everybody* signs. Don't you know that?"

"Hey?" Hodicky snapped back. "Who the hell do you think you are, soldier?" He glared through the reinforced glass at the arms-room attendant. "All *I* know is they rotated us back for a rest and gave us *this* crap! Now, if you've got any more bloody forms, hand them through so we can get our guns and get out of this place."

The little private turned from the counter with an ostentatious flare of his nostrils. It had been easy once he had learned to think of them all as images on a computer screen. Just like nights in the lyceum office, inputting data that the system, the System, thought was true.

Of course, a mis-key here and they really would go out as garbage.

Lieutenant Waldstejn was bent over as if he were muttering a prayer to his boots. "Names . . .," Hodicky heard him whisper.

"Lichtenstein," Hodicky said, pointing at Sergeant Hummel, "you sign first." God the Savior, what would have happened if all three mercenaries had filled out the forms in non-Cecach names? Thank the Lord, thank the Lieutenant. "Then Breisach, then you, Ondru," he continued aloud. If he sounded like an obsessive-compulsive with a burr up his ass, then that was reasonably in keeping with his present persona. Three soldiers who did not know their own names were more of a problem.

The door guard was watching them instead of his screen. "Wouldn't be surprised to get a little rain," he remarked with a wave toward his monitors. There was not enough sky visible on them to make the comment more than a hope for conversation. In the alley dividing Transit Section from the next unit over stood the van they had stolen and restenciled for the purpose. Churchie Dwyer had claimed that was easy. The harder trick had been to get two more rifles and a pistol for the 'Captain', but there were too many troops quartered around the capital for even that to look like an epidemic of theft.

"All right," the clerk said. He laid the three rifles and the sidearm in the drawer and slid them through to the anteroom proper.

"You boys be careful," said the guard as he pressed the latch button. He was trying a joke since the previous ploy had been ignored. The bolts

in the outer door snicked back into their housings.
"Yes sir, this one looks real dangerous—for a no-
guts deserter!"

Nobody spoke this time either. The high-voiced
officer paused a moment before he thrust his
stooped prisoner toward the doorway. The guard
did not like the look in the Captain's eyes.

And he did not like the muttered reference to a
Delete key.

"There's a van," Lieutenant ben Mehdi called
tensely. He was hunched forward, feeling horribly
exposed in the glass booth. If he leaned back,
however, he stuck to whatever had spurted onto
the chair cushion. There were things ben Mehdi
had seen often enough, now, to know that he would
never get used to them. The interior of the guard
post was one such thing. "Allah be praised, it's
them!" He stood up, waving toward the van which
was high-balling out of the compound interior.

Another horn squealed angrily. There was a truck
outside the gate as well. It looked exactly like the
one in which the mercenaries were about to escape.

"Bloody hell," muttered Churchie Dwyer as he
peered past the Lieutenant. The close-up screen
showed clearly the gate pass the driver was holding up to it. "Fifteen minutes early. . . . Say they
got to wait, that's what Bles would've done."

The four bodies were stacked in a corner where
they could not be seen through the booth's glazing.
Ben Mehdi could have done without a reference to
the man he had replaced, however. "Are you crazy?"
he demanded. He threw a switch and the outer
gate slid back. The van pulled up to the inner one.
"You think they're just going to watch when we

all get in a truck and drive away?" The Lieutenant closed the gate behind the incoming vehicle and opened the one in front of it. The van with Trooper Powers driving and the Cecach private beside her in the cab waited. Its turbine whined on more throttle than idling required.

"Del," ordered Churchie Dwyer.

The incoming van pulled through the gate and stopped in front of the identical vehicle waiting to exit. An officer stepped out of the cab. He ignored the gate guards. Instead he shouted to Trooper Powers, "You! Soldier! What do you think you're doing in one of our trucks?"

Hussein ben Mehdi fumbled to find the door latch. It was not really a 212th Service Company truck, just one repainted to look like it, but that would not help matters. A member of the real firing squad was leaning out of the back of their enclosed van. The officer reached for Powers' door.

Allah help—

The Federal officer jerked open the door. Powers' weapon was across her lap. Its off-planet design was a dead giveaway. She thrust the muzzle into the officer's belly and blew him back into the road. The projectile itself would have left only a punch-mark on entrance and exit, but the man's flesh had to absorb also the spurt of propellant gases and the vaporized sabot. The combination eviscerated him, leaving his spine bare and his soft parts from ribs to pelvis a spray across the truck he had stepped from.

"Now, Del!" Dwyer shouted. He fired through the glass of the booth. Lieutenant ben Mehdi shrank down to the floor, bawling with pain from the blasts as Trooper Hoybrin promptly emptied his own weapon into the van in two long bursts.

The booth windows blew outward, crazed by the projectiles but showered onto the road by the muzzle blasts themselves. A Federal soldier flopped out of his van and lay howling on the pavement with no visible wound. Powers drove across him. Her back tires splashed the puddle of burning fuel that dripped from the other vehicle.

"Come on come on come on!" Churchie Dwyer was screaming as he vaulted the emptied window frame. Hoybrin followed with Gratz, who had not as yet fired a shot in the operation.

It was Hussein ben Mehdi who remembered to open both gates before he too stumbled out of the booth.

CHAPTER EIGHTEEN

"It's started," said Sookie Foyle. Her fingers trembled, but they were precise enough to throw the toggle switch which would do the rest.

The ship's radioman watched the brunette approvingly from the bridge proper. The Communications Bay of the *Katyn Forest* was little more than a one-man alcove off the bridge. With additional equipment welded to its bulkheads, even someone as short as Communicator Foyle had to watch her head as she stood up. The crewman smiled through the tangle. "Come have a drink with me, hey?" he said. "Relax."

"Are you out of your mind?" Foyle retorted. "Go on, I'm busy."

Pavlovich tapped the crewman on the shoulder. He murmured something in low-voiced Russian. The two men walked down the corridor together while the Communicator strained to listen through the welter of recorded orders and dialogues she had just set the *Katyn Forest* to broadcast.

There were demands to police and security forces, directing them to deal with riots, bombings, and commando raids in various parts of the city. There were reports from firemen and patrol vehicles of wrecks, robberies, and tenement blazes. There was even an order, tight-beam and scrambled, to Spaceport Control, that all vessels lift off at once to avoid rebel attack. All the signals were broadcast from the starship. Its transmitter hopped frequencies automatically with the abruptness of a scanning receiver. And all of the messages were recorded, because nobody aboard now was competent to carry on a live dialogue in Czech. It could not be expected that the blurted demands would be obeyed, but at worst they would increase the confusion and cause real orders to be discounted as well.

Between each flurry of signals there was a five-second pause. During these pauses, the transmitter of the *Katyn Forest* was not blanking her own receivers. It was then that Sookie Foyle strained to hear a message on the Company's emergency push.

Not, of course, that there was a great deal those remaining on the starship could do, except listen to their comrades die.

The back of the van had eight passengers for six seats, and one of the eight was Del Hoybrin. Albrecht Waldstejn was not complaining. The choice was more room and the sullen faces of a real firing party watching him. Still, when Sergeant Hummel said, "Hell, forgot the cuffs!" she poked him in the eye with the key.

The rescued officer cursed by reflex, then took the key and said in apology, "You people shouldn't have done it. I . . . I mean—"

"Yeah, well," said the non-com, "save the congratulations for about ten blocks, huh?"

The only view from the back of the van was through the small communication window into the cab and through the windshield. Dwyer and Gratz were standing bent over, trying to peer out. Trooper Hoybrin braced his partner against the jolting vehicle, while Gratz tried to grip the side panel with one hand and Dwyer with the other. A third trooper was slitting the sheet metal with his knife. His eyes would not have time to react to the blur through so small an opening, but Waldstejn could not see that it would do any harm to try.

The squeal of the brakes was no adequate warning. Deceleration slammed everyone against the back of the cab.

"Roadblock!" said Churchie Dwyer as he struggled to clear his weapon from ben Mehdi's legs.

Waldstejn could hear Private Hodicky shouting, "Out of the way, fast! We've got orders to arrest saboteurs at the Port immediately!"

"Blue berets," Gratz whispered. Sergeant Hummel had elbowed her way to the glass to look for herself. "Two trucks across the steet."

"Defense Police," the Cecach lieutenant said. He realized as he spoke that the identification was valueless at this juncture. It had been spewed out by a mind that wanted to avoid the realities of the moment by focusing on trivia.

"Sorry, sir," said a Czech speaker who did not

sound in the least sorry. "My orders say nobody, so nobody gets through. You want to take it up with my Colonel, fine."

"All right," murmured Sergeant Hummel. "Dwyer, Hoybrin, Gratz, and Diesson—out the back on three, turn right, and kill it if it breathes." She touched the door latch with her left hand. In her right she held the assault rifle which had been part of her disguise. It was better for this job anyway. "Rest of you bastards, follow me to the left. Same drill."

"I need a gun," said Albrecht Waldstejn.

Hummel looked back at him through the tangle of soldiers sorting themselves to her instructions. There was no anger in her expression, only grim appraisal. "For *God's* sake," the non-com said, "will you keep your head the hell down?"

The young officer could see himself in the veteran's glance, even after she had faced back and started the count. "One." Pasty and soft from ten days in a narrow cell. "Two." Unarmed and hopeless with a gun if there had been one available. "Three!" and Hummel took her troops onto the street like bluefish into a school of herring.

Albrecht Waldstejn followed them out anyway.

The officer in charge of the roadblock died before he could glance toward what was happening at the back of the van. Dwyer's shot snapped through both his temples and splashed the colloid of his brain in ripples from the interior of his skull. Simultaneously, Sergeant Hummel sprayed three soldiers who were still on the open back of their ground-effect truck. After that, it was a shooting gallery; but the ducks shot back.

Two air cushion trucks had been swung across the street with a platoon of Defense Police aboard.

The road behind the mercenaries had already jammed solidly, but their van was the first west-bound vehicle to have been stopped. Ten seconds earlier and they would have gotten through un-challenged. As it was, the blue-capped troops were still deploying and were more concerned with set-ting up the roadblock than with the vehicles they had begun to stop with it. The Federals wilted under the unexpected fire.

The eight mercenaries rushed the trucks. The Defense Police who had not died in the first blast flopped to cover behind their vehicles. Trooper Gratz fired through the door of one of the truck cabs, then jerked it open. The driver was hunched down on the seat. He shot Gratz in the face with his assault rifle. The mercenary stumbled back-ward to the street. Waldstejn snatched at the dead man's gun and fought his rigid muscles for it. He twisted back with the weapon to receive the shot which he knew must be coming.

The police driver was dead. Gratz' preliminary round had drilled through the Federal's body from neck to pelvis. The tiny, directionally-stable projec-tile had killed the man quite surely, but the mas-sive internal haemorrhage had not been fatal in time to prevent the victim from revenging himself.

Waldstejn jumped into the cab and locked the far door.

The truck clanged as mercenaries fired through its skirts to get at the Federals on the other side. Somebody had crawled onto the bed of the vehicle, but a burst of rifle fire had stopped or killed him. The Cecach officer dropped the weapon he had appropriated in order to drag the driver's body aside with both hands. The corpse slid out from under the wheel, and Waldstejn took its place.

The power was on. Waldstejn found it hard to see the controls while he bent over because his nose was almost on the dashboard. A Federal was tugging at the locked left-side door, shouting questions at him. Waldstejn let the turbine rev to full power for several seconds. Then he reached for the attitude control.

Someone fired an assault rifle point-blank into the door.

The light bullets disintegrated on the outer panel. They hit the inner panel as a spray of steel and glass. The portion that burned through into the cab proper flicked across the tall officer like a line of boils. He screamed. His fist slammed the control forward so abruptly that only the immense torque of the electric drive motors kept the fans from stalling. The truck lurched, then buried itself in the shop window across the sidewalk.

There was another ripping burst from an assault rifle. Waldstejn rose and twisted to look out the back window. His left arm and side were alive with cold fire. Jo Hummel was reloading her captured weapon by the cab of the second truck. When Waldstejn slid the lead truck forward, the Sergeant had the shot she had been waiting for. Her burst raked the line of Federals whose cover had just driven away from them. A dozen Defense Police sprawled on the pavement now. Trooper Powers sent the van through the gap between the trucks. She made a tire-squealing left turn as she cleared the cab of the vehicle which was still in position. Blue-bereted soldiers leaped away from her bumper.

The mercenaries stood and shot them down like driven deer.

"Come on, come on!" Powers was shouting. She reversed to clear the line of east-bound vehicles which the roadblock had stopped also. Most of them were already abandoned. One of the mercenaries began firing into them deliberately until a fuel tank blew up.

Waldstejn staggered out of the shop into which he had driven. He was dragging Gratz' weapon by the sling. His body was not working as it should have. All his mind could hold was his determination to reach the van before it drove away. He stepped blindly into Del Hoybrin and recoiled, nearly falling.

"Churchie's hit!" the big man wailed. He had just slid his comrade's form off the back of the truck. Dwyer was as limp in his arms as a grain sack. The front of his tunic was bloody from shoulder to waist.

"We'll get him back," wheezed the Cecach officer. He pointed to the van. Sergeant Hummel was poised beside the vehicle. She fired into a clot of Federal bodies where movement had suggested volition.

Trooper Hoybrin swept his left arm around Waldstejn's chest. He began trotting for the van, ignoring the weight of the two men and three weapons which he carried. Albrecht Waldstejn began to lose consciousness.

Blackness was a welcome relief from pain.

There was a check-point at Gate 2, a tunnel under the blast wall of the spaceport. The check-point was unmanned, and that was a very bad sign.

Hussein ben Mehdi got out of the van awkwardly. The two sprawled casualties made a close fit closer, though Hummel had ridden off in the cab and Gratz was not taking up any room at all.

"Well, I can drive in," the petite blonde was saying.

Sergeant Hummel stood beside her open door, peering across the boulevard. There was no traffic on it, presumably as a result of roadblocks elsewhere in the city. "Hodicky," the non-com asked, "did you ever know them not to have gate attendants here?"

The Praha native shook his head. "Let me check the Lieutenant, huh?" he said. He squeezed past Hummel as ben Mehdi walked forward.

The three-story buildings around the port were all sixty years old or less. That was the date that the fusion bottle of a freighter too large for the docking pits had failed. The first construction that had taken place afterwards was the encirclement of the whole port with a berm instead of trusting pits to deflect catastrophe from the city. An arched ramp with broadcast pylons led the largest vehicles up the vertical eight-meter outer face of the berm and down the inner slope. Radial tunnels ducked below ground level to serve lesser traffic. But there were always movement controls, especially now in wartime. And with multiple emergencies, real and imagined, crackling over the airwaves . . . the booth should not have been empty.

"Well," said Lieutenant ben Mehdi, "the attendant ran away. Big deal."

Sergeant Hummel frowned. Passers-by were nervously watching the van and the troops around it. The squad was a nexus for the crisis that worried the civilians. "Maybe," said Hummel, "and maybe they decided there wasn't any way to hold this side." She waved at the blank wall across the peripheral boulevard. It was defended only by the empty kiosk and a tipping-bar gate. "Let's you and me walk through and see what's on the other side, Lieutenant."

Ben Mehdi went cold. Trooper Powers got out of the cab on her own side. "I'll go along," she said.

"Not till you learn some Czech, Bunny," said the non-com. Her voice sounded light until it cracked. "Lieutenant, leave that—" she pointed to the grenade launcher—"and take Diesson's rifle." She looked up at the troopers around her. "How's Dwyer?" she asked.

"Be okay if he gets to Doc pretty quick," said one of the men. "The Captain's coming around, sort of."

Hummel nodded. "Okay. Diesson, you're in charge. If this one's blocked, head for the ramp— Hodicky'll know where to find it. Let's go, Lieutenant."

Ben Mehdi followed the Sergeant numbly. There was, by Allah, no question of who was in charge, not here. He supposed he should be thankful to be considered an acceptable follower at a time like this. She would not have brought him a month ago, the bitch.

The Lieutenant was getting dizzy, in part because his torso was too tight to permit him to breath. His clam-shell armor had not been among the loot in the *Katyn Forest*.

Hummel glanced into the kiosk as they walked past it. The little booth was as empty as it had appeared to be from across the street. They could flip the pole up easily if they wanted. The van would not even have to break it off as they drove into the tunnel. "Well, who knows, Lieutenant?" the non-com said as she settled her rifle where she wanted it. "You might even be right about everything being clear."

They started down.

The tunnel dipped, then rose in a single fluid curve. Like the berm itself, the tunnel was designed to redirect a blast. It was quite impossible to hope to absorb the full potential of a fusion unit. The tunnel was concrete lined and three meters high, although the vehicular height was less since roof lines cut the chord rather than following the arc. There were steps along the right wall, but the two mercenaries kept to the vehicle way. The grade lengthened ben Mehdi's strides despite his nervousness.

The tunnel was only fifty meters long. The mercenaries were halfway through, at the nadir of the curve, when six armed soldiers appeared in silhouette at the spaceport end. "All right!" one of them shouted. "State your business."

"Sir," Hussein ben Mehdi called back, too caught up in the situation to be worried about the quality of his Czech, "we were ordered to stand by at the freighter *Boudicca* and await further orders." He could not tell the sex, much less the rank, of the troops because the bright daylight was behind them. Their weapons were clear enough, though. Automatic rifles like the one he carried, deadly in trained hands as his were not ... and the squat, solid outline of a heavy grenade launcher whose capacity ben Mehdi was well able to imagine. But Allah would not permit his servant to be trapped in this hollow killing ground when—

A seventh figure strode against the background of the sky. "What's this?" the newcomer demanded. "You there, drop those guns! And—say, *I* know you!"

It was the Morale Section Colonel who had met the *Katyn Forest* when she docked.

"Run!" shouted Jo Hummel as she sprayed the Federal soldiers. Ben Mehdi ran, because there was nothing else to do.

The Colonel and two of his squad flopped face down on the concrete. The others sprang away as if flung by the muzzle blasts. The angle protected them from the second burst which Hummel sent up the tunnel as she herself turned. The opening behind her danced with motes of concrete settling upon the bodies.

"Tell—" the Lieutenant heard her shout. Then the grenade went off.

There was no reality in the tunnel but that of the blast. The Federal grenadier had lobbed the round in without exposing himself to rifle fire. That showed a competence the Lieutenant could appreciate, even as the shock wave pitched him forward. The grenade detonated on the tunnel roof. The curve protected even Sergeant Hummel from the shrapnel that rusticated the smooth concrete from which it ricochetted. Ben Mehdi glanced back as he rose. The Sergeant was sprawled in a fog of white lime and smoke from the bursting charge. She did not move, the bitch, the *bitch*, and the Lieutenant scrambled back to her side.

The shadows against the dust-smeared daylight were more than bodies and blast residues now. Federal troops were peering into the tunnel to see whether the grenade had cleared it. Ben Mehdi swung his rifle toward them. The unfamiliar weapon would not fire. Perhaps the safety was still on or he had not charged the rifle properly. He threw it down and began dragging Hummel by the arms.

A rifle bullet winked on the tunnel wall and spattered both mercenaries with bits of itself. "Hold it there, you swine!" one of the oncoming figures shouted. The Federal's instincts were those of a policeman, not a combat soldier. At the moment, ben Mehdi was as defenseless as any deserter dragged out of an attic.

"Get down!" somebody cried in English.

The Lieutenant threw himself flat. Trooper Iris Powers squatted on the steps, halfway down the slope. She held her weapon low. The first armor-piercing projectile would bring a storm of automatic fire which would sweep all three of them into—

The little blonde emptied her magazine in a single twenty-round burst that was almost a directed explosion. Not even Del Hoybrin could have stood up to that recoil and kept the muzzle down. Powers managed by butting the weapon against a step and letting the concrete instead of her shoulder receive the jack-hammer blows. Precise aim was as impossible as it was unnecessary. The osmium projectiles ricocheted instead of shattering like bullets from the assault rifles. Buzzing projectiles and chunks of concrete ripped through the dusty tunnel like a round of canister.

Lieutenant ben Mehdi rose to his hands and knees again. His fingertips were bleeding from the way he had unconsciously tried to dig himself into the pavement. It hurt his hands too much to drag

Hummel. He threw one of the non-com's arms over his shoulder and began to stagger up the slope with her in a packstrap carry.

Iris Powers did not help him with the burden. She reloaded and backed out behind the others with her weapon to her shoulder. Twice she fired into the reeking fog. The mercenaries were well clear before there was return fire from the inner mouth of the tunnel.

The truck and the troops with it waited as the trio stumbled back across the boulevard. There were sirens converging on them from three directions. To their rear, the wall around the port was as bleak as the one against which the condemned are stood.

She caught the signal just as another dummy message began to cycle through the transmitter. Foyle's hand flashed out and killed the transmitter's power in time for her to catch his tag, "—in Allah's name, Big Brother!"

Sookie Foyle slapped in the patch which fed all the intercoms into the main unit. "Big Brother has you," she said, hearing echoes of her voice from the bridge speakers and each compartment sternward in a reflected-mirror pattern. "Hold one for—"

Before the Communicator could get the word out, Sergeant Mboko's voice boomed "White One to Sister, tell us what you need."

Foyle listened with her eyes open as she always did. If her duties had required her to find a switch or dial instantly, her body would have responded. Her mind was in the world of visualized sounds crackling out of the speaker.

"Sister to White One," hissed the voice of Hussein ben Mehdi, "we made it to the wall but we can't get through and we can't get back. They got us bottled in a building across—" there was a blast of white noise which was not atmospherically generated. Something had exploded close enough to the commo helmet to overload its filters. The Lieutenant's voice resumed, "Save what you can, Stack. This was a good try but it—" an automatic weapon overprinted his signal— "Over."

Sergeant Mboko was on the bridge. Captain Ortschugin stood at the lip of the Commo Bay, listening to the speaker as intently as Foyle did.

"Sister, hold what you got!" Mboko said. "You're at the entry point? Over."

"See you in Paradise, White One. Over and out."

Sookie Foyle stared at Ortschugin as the Captain turned away. "I'll prepare to lift ship," she heard him say to Sergeant Mboko.

The roof of the adjacent building was afire. That meant there would not be another attempt to rush them from it. Six Federal soldiers had died before one had fired his grenade launcher as he fell back through the trap door. That had ended the rush, but it had not helped the trooper sprawled beside Albrecht Waldstejn with a bulged skull and a hole between his eyes.

Automatic rifles yammered across the boulevard. Waldstejn cursed and fired back. He cursed again. The recoil had hurt him, as usual, and he had, as usual, missed. There was one body crumpled on the inner slope of the blast wall, but Del Hoybrin had nailed it there. Now Federals within the spaceport slid only far enough up the berm to fire in the general direction of the roof overlooking them across the boulevard. They would probably duck back even if Waldstejn did not respond ... but the next time they might pause long enough to aim, and that could be all she wrote for the two men still alive on the roof.

There were wrecked emergency vehicles in either direction along the boulevard. A truck and several police cars were burning. Water still leaked from the riot control vehicle which a garbled message had sent to the scene with its water cannon. Surprise and confusion had made cold meat of the first waves who did not realize they were being dropped straight into a war. But killing Federal troops was not going to do any long-term good for Albrecht Waldstejn and the team which had tried to rescue him.

Nothing was.

Del Hoybrin fired across the radial street. He was too late. The *shoop* from a window there became the shattering detonation of an anti-tank rocket. It demolished much of the second floor of the building in which the mercenaries were holed up. The van in which they had arrived burned in the street. Its smoke was at least an edge of cover for the rest of the team on the ground floor with the wounded.

The Cecach officer had stumbled up the stairs, pushed by the big trooper since there was not enough room to be carried. Churchie Dwyer had been alive when they left him, and Jo Hummel was breathing though unconscious with streaks of dried blood beneath her nose and ears. Enforced motion and the pain of his cracked ribs had ridden Waldstejn out of the state of shock into which he had begun to slip. Now he was becoming increas-

ingly dizzy. The building seemed to tremble even
after the warhead's racket had died away. The
blast wall across the boulevard was expanding as
his eyes tried to focus on it.

The blast wall was not moving. A starship was
sliding toward it, broadside, at a measured pace.

The rest of the Company were coming for them,
and they were bringing the *Katyn Forest*.

"Clear the area!" blatted the starship's external
speakers in bad Czech. "This area is about to be
destroyed! Clear the area!"

Cooper tensed as the volleys ripped out from
Holds Two and Three. "Get *down*," croaked Gunner Jensen. The skin of his face was red, and it
would be weeks before he had eyelashes again; but
he was master of his gun and his section, by Saint
Ultruda!

The inner face of the berm was turf. It absorbed
the hail of projectiles with no sign of their passage.
The score of Federal troops there had been concerned only with the building on the other side of
the blast wall. They leaped and died against the
turf, scythed down by the shots from behind them.
There was no target worthy of the automatic cannon as yet, and Jensen did not want his three
crewmen endangered by rising to fire their shoulder weapons when the infantry sections had the
business well in hand.

Herzenberg tried to smile at her section leader.
The effect was grim, but the thought brought her
an equally-awful rictus from Jensen in reply.
Herzenberg had insisted on being in Hold One
with the rest of Gun Section, though she could not
have been of much practical use even if she were

better trained. The polymer splints on her right arm and leg permitted her to move without restriction. Nothing could change the blinding pain such movement caused, however, except enough drugs to knock her flat anyway.

The *Katyn Forest* was steadier under her own power than she had been when she drew from the broadcast grid, but she still bucked as she started to lift. The sloping berm dropped below as they approached it. Someone stood on the nearest of the buildings, waving a gun butt-upward.

The brick and stone facades of other buildings began to powder as the troopers in Holds Two and Three opened fire. They were leaning over their copper breastworks to shoot down at an angle. The cannon could not be depressed in its present mounting. A target had to be in the same plane for the gun to bear. The speakers continued to call their warning, but it was doubtful whether words could be heard over the muzzle blasts. Still, it was the most chance that Mboko could give noncombatants under the circumstances.

The *Katyn Forest* began to settle as if to land on the peripheral boulevard. With her belly ten meters in the air, the vessel paused. The intercom boomed in Ortschugin's gruff English, "Bridge to Guns—here we go." With a gentleness that belied the Swobodan's looks, the starship managed the incredibly difficult job of rolling two degrees on its axis. Jensen's sights swung down across building fronts, then over the Cecach soldiers and vehicles huddled along the structures where the angle protected them from the trapped mercenaries. The Federal troops were blazing away furiously at the *Katyn Forest*, though bodies and cratered facades showed the damage the Company's infantry was wreaking.

Sergeant Jensen started a block in front of the starship's bow and traversed left on Continuous Fire.

The big osmium slugs took buildings down in a row like a demonstration of controlled demolition. The lighter weapons had blown gaps in the facing walls. The cannon's slow traverse sawed through the massive but brittle structures, including the load-bearing firewalls separating adjacent buildings. Bricks and blocks and humans, most of them civilians huddled in their rooms, cascaded into the boulevard. Federal soldiers flattened to the pavement while Jensen's fire ripped overhead. The debris avalanched over them.

The shattering fire paused momentarily while Pavlovich slid a fresh drum into the ammunition feed. Then Jensen dumped the full hundred rounds down the street by which the rescue commando had approached the port. The gun raked buildings on both sides with the exception of the one on the left corner from which Albrecht Waldstejn had waved as the starship loomed over the blast wall. Secondary explosions blew geysers of brick and stone from the stately cascades that filled the street.

"Set her down, Control!" Jensen called as Cooper this time reloaded the automatic cannon. The *Katyn Forest* rocked level and settled onto the boulevard. The ship had hovered less than a full minute to give the big gun a chance before the locals were ready to react to the situation.

When the cannon opened up, the infantry had shifted its fire to concentrate on the buildings to the left of the one in which their comrades were trapped. The Federals in that stretch too had already been silenced. But as familiar figures staggered from the corner building, the Gunner opened fire again. In part, it was for safety's sake, demolishing everything in sight that faced the boulevard. That way no one could crawl to a window and shoot a trooper on the edge of safety.

There was more to it than good technique, however. Roland Jensen was a veteran who knew that killing was a matter of business, not emotion. But there were two figures fewer than there should have been running toward the ship, and three of those he did see were being dragged or carried by others.

It gave Gunner Jensen a certain pleasure to see Cecach buildings collapsing with a roar as he drew his sights through them.

CHAPTER NINETEEN

"Are you all right, Captain?" asked Roland Jensen. He spoke with the calm born of experience with wounds.

"I'll live," said Albrecht Waldstejn. He touched the tape over his ribs. Hold Two was a babel of enthusiasm and minor casualties, but it was big enough for that and the cargo of metal as well. The Cecach officer looked from the general confusion to the men who had joined him in the corner where he sat staring at his hands. Jensen, Mboko, ben Mehdi . . . even Vladimir Ortschugin. "You got me off-planet with my life," Waldstejn continued. "I guess we're off-planet? I was getting these—" he touched the tape again— "done . . .?"

"We entered the envelope six minutes ago," Ortschugin said with satisfaction. "Six minutes and . . . thirty-nine seconds."

"Yeah, well," said Waldstejn. He looked from his hands to the other men again. "Hey, I don't want you to think I don't appreciate it. They were going to kill me, I know. Only . . . only . . ." He breathed as deeply as the tape would allow. "Look," he went on, "you won't be able to understand this, I know, but—that was home. I'm alive, and I don't have a home or a, hell . . . don't have a future." The young man grinned bitterly. "You need an engine-wiper, Vladimir? Or maybe the Company could use a trooper who's proved he can't hit a damned thing with a gun?"

"I can teach anybody to shoot," said Sergeant Mboko. "I can't teach them to think better than I do."

"We want you for our Captain, Mr. Waldstejn," said Roland Jensen. "Call yourself Colonel like the Old Man did, if you like."

Waldstejn straightened. His eyes searched for the member of the command group who was missing.

Lieutenant ben Mehdi understood the look. "Worried about Hummel?" he said. "Don't be. Bertinelli's still working her over, but it was her idea to begin with." The Lieutenant's mouth quirked into something with less humor than a smile. "That was before we crashed back into Smiricky—while some of us didn't see much use in planning for the future."

"I'm going back to the bridge," said Captain Ortschugin. He thrust out his hand to be shaken. "But look—you saved my ship, which is nothing, I am no Excellency to pull strings . . . but also you saved a ship of the Pyaneta Lines. It could be that something other than engine-wiper could be found for you." The spacer strode off, spitting tobacco juice at random into the jumbled ingots.

"Can I have a little while to think about it?" Albrecht Waldstejn asked his hands.

The two non-coms exchanged looks of surprise. "Ah, I don't know if you realize what this means when we're *not* on service," Sergeant Mboko said. "That's three full shares of what's usually a damned big pie."

"I appreciate that, Sergeant," Waldstejn said with raised eyes and a sharper tone. "If you need my decision now, however—"

Hussein ben Mehdi stepped between the two men. He gave Waldstejn a salesman's broad grin. "Hey," he said, "it's three days before we dock on Novaya Swoboda. No hurry, sir, *no* hurry." He put his hands on the shoulders of the two big non-coms. "Come on, boys," he added, "we need to settle bunk arrangements now that the crew's quarters are the sick bay."

The three men walked forward. Albrecht Waldstejn was staring at his hands again.

Churchie Dwyer cried out sharply and awakened. Del Hoybrin held his comrade's hands firmly until he was sure that Churchie would not strike himself in the face the way he had an hour before. "Are you all right, Churchie?" the big man asked.

"Jesus, Del, Jesus," the wounded man whispered. The drugs left him without physical pain, only patterns of weights and pressures which trapped his body. That made it hard to tell reality from dream . . . but Del Hoybrin was here, and in his dreams—

"Jesus!" the veteran repeated. He tried to focus

on the concerned face of his friend. Bertinelli glanced over, then went back to the trooper whose grazed scalp needed a fresh dressing.

Churchie licked his lips. "Del," he whispered, "how many people have I killed, do you suppose? The ones that I could see, I mean."

The bigger soldier wrinkled his brow in concentration. "Gee, Churchie," he said, "I don't know. A lot, I guess?"

"Every damned one of them deserved it, sweetheart," the wounded man said. He closed his eyes. "Nobody alive don't deserve it, and it don't bother me a bit to handle things. . . . You know that?"

"Yes, Churchie," Del said. "But why don't you go back to sleep now?"

The Doc had told him it was best for Churchie to sleep for the next twenty-four hours or so. Del really did not like it when his friend was asleep, though. Churchie kept moaning all the time.

"Hey, Lieutenant," called someone as Hussein ben Mehdi walked through Hold One on his way to the bridge.

He paused, looking for the speaker. Trooper Powers waved. She sat on the end of a cot; but it was Sergeant Hummel, supine on the same cot, who had spoken. Hummel raised herself to one elbow and beckoned him over.

Ben Mehdi obeyed with a blank face. "Didn't expect to see you here, Sergeant," he said neutrally.

"Had them shift me out as soon as I woke up," the non-com grumbled. "If I'm going to feel like hell, I may as well have some elbow room while I do it." She paused. Her eyes and the cold blue eyes of Iris Powers were on the Lieutenant. He shifted his weight, preparing to leave. The Sergeant stopped him by adding, "Bunny tells me we owe you one."

Ben Mehdi looked at the seated woman, then the reclining one. "Yeah, well," he said. "I'm just as glad it was you being carried, not me."

Sergeant Hummel nodded, then grimaced at the pain. "I'm not worth a *damn*," she muttered to no one in particular. Then she focused on ben Mehdi again. "Yeah," she said as the officer fidgeted, "but we got three days of this, they tell me." She looked at her blonde friend and asked, "Bunny, how long's it been since we really partied?"

Trooper Powers' mouth spread in a wide, slow grin. "Podele's World, wasn't it?" she said. "Sure, Podele's World. The bartender."

Hummel looked back at ben Mehdi. "I'll tell you what, Lieutenant," she said. "We'll get a room in a good hotel when we dock in. And we'll lay on enough booze and food for—" she pursed her lips as she examined the officer—"four days, let's say. And then we'll party."

Ben Mehdi's eyes widened. He stared at the older woman, then the younger one. Both of them were smiling wickedly. "Allah!" he said. He started to point but caught himself. "You mean *both* of you?"

"Hey, Lieutenant," said Iris Powers. The smile was in her voice as well as on her lips. "Don't knock it till you've tried it." She chuckled aloud. "And I don't remember *any*body knocking it then."

After a further moment of gaping, Hussein ben Mehdi began to grin also.

CHAPTER TWENTY

"Hi, Lieutenant," said a voice. Its language and familiarity broke into Albrecht Waldstejn's black revery better than a shout could have.

"Hi, Pavel," said the ex-officer, ex-Cecach citizen. He gestured toward the jumble of ingots on which he sat. It occurred to him that he would need to borrow some kit for at least the next three days. "Make yourself at home."

"Thank you, sir," Hodicky said shyly. "I suppose I ought to call you Captain now." When Waldstejn looked at him with an odd expression, the smaller man added, "They've signed me on, sir—into Black Section with Churchie and Del. I'll be under you again. Ah, if you join."

Waldstejn managed to smile. He put out his hand. "Congratulations, Trooper Hodicky," he said. He shook with his beaming former subordinate.

Then the smile faded. He added with the bitterness which had until then been internal, "It's not quite what you were raised for, though, is it?"

"Oh, you mean supply?" the new Trooper said in surprise. "Oh, that was just the army. But Lieutenant Mehdi says if I want, I'll get trained on really hot electronics, the sort of thing I'd never see back on Cecach. Not just computers, but commo and sensors like you wouldn't believe!"

"I suppose I meant the killing, soldier," the ex-officer said flatly. "That's the bottom line, isn't it? For a job as a 'contract soldier'."

Hodicky's face changed, but he did not edge back from the man beside him. "Yes sir," he said, "I suppose it is. I guess I can handle that, sure." He paused. "And I guess I'd rather do it for other people. Leave *them* with the hate that eats them up every night. I don't like to feel that way myself."

Waldstejn blinked at the younger man. "Sorry, Pavel," he said, "I don't—"

"Don't understand what it's like to be so small that anybody on the block can beat the crap out of you?" Hodicky said. "And smart enough, smart-*ass* enough, that most of them want to try?" He took a deep breath and swallowed. With less passion he continued, "I guess your family had enough money that it wasn't a problem anyway. I'm glad for you, sir. . . . But the first person I ever met who needed me and wanted *me* around was Q. And him and you were the only two who ever tried to stand up for me, ever. Well, I've got a family now, sir. It's not screaming kids and an old man who beats me with a chair leg whenever he's sober enough to move. I'm in the family business. And I'm going to be good at it, all of it."

The anger that had welled up out of the little man's past suddenly evaporated in a smile. He reached out to Waldstejn again, touching the older man on the wrist. "But Mother of God, sir, I won't be as good as you. You talk about killing? You *saved* the life of everybody in this ship!" He waved at the hold and beyond it, the troopers beginning to settle in for another night in a freighter. "And that's why they saved you. We saved you."

Albrecht Waldstejn turned his arm to link his hand again with that of the younger man. "Pavel," he said, "you don't have anything to justify. Certainly not to me."

Hodicky squeezed the hand, then released it as he stood up. "Look, sir," he said. He had lost both the shyness and the anger of previous moments. "I'm not a priest. Maybe Q's burning in Hell, even though he died to save me. But I don't think so. And I don't think God gave us talents we weren't supposed to use. You've got a hell of a talent for leading troops, sir." Smiling again, the little man gave a finger-to-brow Federal salute before he strode away.

I envy you your belief, thought Albrecht Waldstejn. His lips passed only a smile.

The tall, young man looked at his hands. This time he really saw them, the flesh and the crucifix ring, instead of shadows from the past and future. Most of the scrapes and cuts had healed, though there was still a pucker where the head of a deep-driven thorn was working back to the surface.

Waldstejn had not killed anyone, not directly. He was fairly sure of that, as clumsy as he had proven to be with a gun. But the flesh would have looked the same if every shot he fired had snuffed out a life.

And his soul?

It was a big universe, even the human part of it. Perhaps Hodicky was wrong, perhaps there was no God who granted talents ... but at one level or another, Waldstejn, too, felt that doing a job well was good, a Good, and that doing a job in the mutual respect of one's companions was a Good as well.

Even if the job were slaughter.

The air whispered with a nearby presence. Waldstejn looked up. Sookie Foyle stood as Hodicky had, with a trace of nervous shyness on her plump face. When she caught the tall man's eye, she smiled into sudden beauty. "I just wanted to, to say I'm glad you made it, sir," she said. "And that I'm glad you're with us."

Instead of gesturing the Communicator to a seat, Albrecht Waldstejn took her by the hand. As he guided her gently down beside him, he said, "You know, Sookie, I've pretty well decided that I'm glad too."

THE END